Also by Ray Robertson:

Home Movies (1997)
Heroes (2000)
Moody Food (2002)
Mental Hygiene: Essays on Writers and Writing (2003)
Gently Down the Stream (2005)
What Happened Later (2007)
David (2009)
Why Not? Fifteen Reasons to Live (2011)
I Was There the Night He Died (2014)
Lives of the Poets (with Guitars) (2016)

1979

Ray Robertson

BIBLIOASIS
WINDSOR, ONTARIO

FIRST EDITION

Library and Archives Canada Cataloguing in Publication

Robertson, Ray, 1966-, author
    1979 / Ray Robertson.

Issued in print and electronic formats.
ISBN 978-1-77196-096-0 (softcover).--ISBN 978-1-77196-097-7 (ebook)

    I. Title. II. Title: Nineteen seventy-nine.

PS8585.O3219A62 2018   C813'.54   C2017-906991-8

                                                    C2017-906992-

Edited by Daniel Wells
Typeset and designed by Chris Andrechek

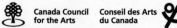

Published with the generous assistance of the Canada Council for the Arts, which last year invested $153 million to bring the arts to Canadians throughout the country, and the financial support of the Government of Canada. Biblioasis also acknowledges the support of the Ontario Arts Council (OAC), an agency of the Government of Ontario, which last year funded 1,709 individual artists and 1,078 organizations in 204 communities across Ontario, for a total of $52.1 million, and the contribution of the Government of Ontario through the Ontario Book Publishing Tax Credit and the Ontario Media Development Corporation.

The author acknowledges the support of the Canada Council for the Arts, the Ontario Arts Council, and the Toronto Arts Council.

PRINTED AND BOUND IN CANADA

Naming these things is the love-act and its pledge
—Patrick Kavanagh, "The Hospital"

Chapter One

I was the paperboy, so there wasn't much I didn't see or hear. A thirteen-year-old paperboy is just *there*, like the weather or today's date or your own life. And if anyone did happen to notice me, everyone knew that I was the Buzby boy, the boy who came back from the dead. People tended to tell me things they wouldn't tell anyone else, let me see things no one else was allowed to see. When you've been dead and then you're alive again, people like to believe you know something no one else does. But I was just a kid—who was I to tell them any different?

My father wasn't always the tattoo guy. Before he opened his shop on William Street down by the train tracks, next door to the old man who sold old bottles, he worked at Libby's, he worked at a junkyard, he worked at Bidell Tires, he even worked at Ontario Steel for awhile, where some of my friends' fathers worked. But that was before I can remember. For almost as long as I could recall, my dad was the tattoo guy. I could still sort of smell it when he worked at Ontario Steel— fingernail grease and underarm sweat and the grilled cheese sandwich and bowl of steaming Campbell's tomato soup my Mom would make for him when he came home for his eight p.m. lunch break when he worked the four-to-midnight shift—but that was so long before, that was when they were still married. For as long as I was me, Dad was the tattoo guy and Mom was the woman who used to be a stripper who married Bill Buzby and then got religious and divorced him because he was a sinner.

"Your father is proud," she said when I was seven and I asked her between sobs why she wasn't going to live with Dad and my sister and me anymore. "The Lord has offered to forgive him for all of his sins and to give him eternal life, but he's too proud to accept His unconditional love."

Later that night, after all of her lotions and nail polish and perfumes weren't on the bathroom counter anymore where they were supposed to be, I asked my older sister Julie, who was sitting cross-legged on her bed doing her homework through the camouflage of her long brown hair, what Mom had meant, because pride was something I'd always thought was a good thing, like when Mrs. Jackson, my homeroom teacher, would say that neat handwriting was something every student should be proud of. Julie looked up from the black binder open in front of her like I'd just asked her the stupidest question anyone had ever come up with. It was a look I was used to.

"She's lost it," she said.

"What do you mean? What did she lose?" Whatever it was, maybe that was why she talked so funny lately and why she was at that church downtown all of the time, the one where the pet store used to be.

Julie fingered her parted hair into two equal strands behind her ears, her signal that she was about to give me her full attention, so I'd better listen up because this was a limited time offer. I made sure that the toes of my white stocking feet weren't touching the blue carpet of her bedroom floor. One morning at breakfast, a few years before she'd announced that since she was now eleven everyone needed to start respecting her privacy as someone who was practically almost a teenager, and that in the future no one was allowed to enter her room without her permission. As Dad wasn't there when she'd made her declaration and Mom still made her bed and did her laundry and put it away, the new rule seemed to apply exclusively to me.

"Mom's a Jesus freak," she said.

That was something else that didn't make sense. Although we never went to church—and still didn't, because Dad wouldn't allow Mom to take Julie and me with her to the Cornerstone, one of the main things they argued about until she moved out—everybody knew that Jesus was a good thing, just like a freak was a bad thing, like the way Tommy Ecclestone at school was a freak when he would catch flies at lunchtime and get everyone to dare him to eat them.

"Does she love Jesus more than she loves us now?" I said.

I didn't know I was crying until Julie told me to come in her room and sopped up the tears from my face with the baggy sleeve of one of Dad's blue plaid flannel shirts which she'd taken to wearing.

"Sit at my desk," she said, getting up and going to her combination record player/eight-track tape/ AM-FM Sears Candle stereo. "You can sit there while I do my homework. But you have to be quiet. And do *not* touch anything. I'm serious, Tom." She selected an album from the red plastic Sealtest milk crate that Dad had gotten her and carefully slid the LP from its sleeve, put the album cover on top of the crate, and placed the black platter on the turntable. The only record that I could call mine, that I actually owned, was the I'd-Like-to-Teach-the-World-to-Sing-in-Perfect-Harmony 45 that Mom had sent away for when I was five years old. It was also the only song I knew all the words to. All you had to do to get a free copy was write to the Coca-Cola company and ask because they wanted everybody to sing in perfect harmony while they drank their Cokes. Coke was the real thing.

Although I was always pestering Julie to play her albums—if entering her room without her consent was forbidden, listening to her records when she wasn't there was unfathomable—I didn't feel like hearing music right now. I missed Mom and wanted to keep talking about her, even if talking about her made me miss her that much more.

But the Beatles, the one Julie knew I liked best, the one with the song about the girl named Lucy and the one about the pepper band and the other one with the rooster and the horse and the dog sounds in it and the whole thing a great big ball of bright happy colours, even when the songs were slow and made you feel sort of sad for no good reason. When both sides were finished, Julie shut her binder and got up but didn't take the album off the record player.

Looking down at the still-spinning disc, "You know how records, when they're over, they make the arm of the record player lift up?" she said.

I didn't, but, "Yeah," I said.

"This one is never over, the Beatles made it that way. If you didn't take it off yourself, it would just keep playing forever."

"Wow," I said. I didn't know what *forever* was either, but "Wow," I said, again.

"Emotionally Deserted" Husband Asks Wife to Move Out of House
"I Had to Do It for the Children"

SHE'S GONE. *GONE.* But, then, there wasn't much of her left to leave anyway.

Ghost limbs that look and feel like flesh but which disappear when touched and don't desire back. Mute reproof where there used to be a cheering voice. Absent—when not avoiding—eyes. And impossible to file a missing person report because, that's right, officer, Tracy Buzby (nee Lawton) is still here, it's just that I don't know where the hell my wife went.

Not that it was ever perfect—what is? But a better marriage than most, that much was obvious, even to the two of them. The first time he saw her she was swaying for pay at The Rankin. Strip clubs he could take or leave, but it was Stan Jackson's birthday and all of the guys from Bidell's had headed over after work one Friday—and, yes, initially all he'd felt was what he was supposed to: a stirring everything, a messy mind movie, a bulge. But when he returned alone two nights later and talked to her—first, during and after a three minute lap dance; later, over coffee at the Satellite Restaurant down the street—her dancing blue eyes and vigorous laughter and head-bobbing enthusiasm were what moved him most. And she listened. When he told her that what he really wanted to do was open his own tattoo parlour, she said he had to do it, he absolutely had to do it, that everyone needs a dream and if that was his dream he shouldn't let anything stop him. Or at least stop him from trying. When he asked her what her dream was she said she wanted to be normal. "I want all of the normal things I never thought I'd ever want," she said. He didn't ask her what she had wanted before. Eight months later, they were married.

For a long time, normal was enough. Saving up for the shop; a daughter and later a son; and finally, by the fall of 1971, William Street Tattoos, which demanded most of his time, admittedly, but which was worth it, obviously, was his business and no one else's—and hers, too, he'd remind her when she'd feel lonely and claustrophobic stuck at home with just the kids. It was their dream come true, don't forget. Without her support, it would have never been more than a pipe dream, remember that. And normal doesn't happen all by itself—takes a lot of hard work to get it and keep it that way—and it's difficult to cry for no good reason when there are diapers to change and laundry to do and meals to make.

Going to extremes to avoid going too far quite often works until it doesn't. The first time he noticed something wrong was seven years after they were married, during the Canada-Soviet Summit Series, the entire country TV-tethered and O Canada O.D.ing, granted, but she wasn't sleeping at night, every Soviet victory a hair-shirt nightgown, every Canadian win a twitchy reason to talk and talk and talk in bed until Hon, seriously, we've got to get some sleep, I can't go to work a wreck and the kids will be up in a couple of hours. And she'd never even liked hockey. Once they were dating she'd admitted to him that when she was young and stupid and growing up in Windsor she'd briefly gone through a Benzedrine thing, but swore she hadn't touched any drugs, not even aspirin—even when she was stripping, even though most of the other girls were all on something—since she'd turned twenty, and he believed her. But when she came home one day after setting out for Pet World to buy goldfish food but returned with a handful of blotchily mimeographed material that stank of fresh ink and which kindly informed humanity of, among other things, the imminent end of the world and the necessity of accepting Jesus Christ as your personal savior, he wished that she was on drugs. At least there are professionals you can talk to and treatment you can receive when you're a drug addict. Who do you call and what do you do when your wife has discovered the hallowed truth and found everlasting peace?

The newly converted conversion rate: in direct proportion to how much her every day is made that much more miraculous by the euphoria-inducing power of directly experiencing His perfect love, the more despondent he becomes because she seems to care less and less about him and the kids every day—the insistent offer of eternal life not nearly as satisfactory as an hour on the couch at the end of another long day with a couple of gin and Winks while watching All in the Family, a ten minute homily on the blood of Christ not nearly as nutritious as two school lunches you don't forget to pack for your kids for school. (But what the hell, who was he to tell her what to believe? Who knows what someone else needs to make them whole? And nothing lasts forever, especially not unbounded happiness, so

if he just kept quiet and had a little more patience…)
But if only faintly condescending at first in the way
she wished that he and the children (never "the kids"
anymore, always "the children") could only feel what
she felt, only know what she knew, better, anyway, than
the eventual smug silence that echoed throughout the
house by the time the Cornerstone became not just an
indulged Sunday excursion but her all-but-literal real
home, Pastor Bob eventually interchangeable with Jesus
as the most important man in her life.

Pastor Bob: he couldn't lie, he couldn't help but
wonder if it wasn't just his wife's soul to which the
Pastor was so assiduously tending. But the only time
he capitulated to his wife's pleas to visit the church (not
to feed his soul, but to satisfy his curiosity), the bare
tubes of florescent light and the smell of long-gone
guinea pigs and rabbits still stuck in the carpets convinced him, at least on that score, that he had nothing
to worry about. When you spoke to him, Pastor Bob
used your name in every other sentence and his eyes
never wavered from your own, like there was nothing
he'd rather be doing than talking and listening to you,
but why he never stopped smiling was the real miracle.
Nine parishioners, a front window with a long crack in
it, and a church that stank like dead pets: these were not
the credentials of the kind of man with which his wife
would cheat on him.

Except that she did, although he didn't know it until
after she'd moved out of the house. He'd been willing to
wait out everything—the pea-brained theology lectures
at home; the evangelizing to strangers on the street;
her refusal to sleep with him until he was born-again
clean—but when he discovered Tom crouched and

crying in his bedroom closet and coaxed him out and asked him what was wrong and discovered that she'd told their son that unless he and his sister could convince their father to let them go with her to church, they would go to hell where their eyes would boil in their sockets and their skin would melt like candle wax and their mother, who was going to heaven, would never see them again, he gave her twenty-four hours to pack up and get out. She was gone by supper. Pastor Bob's station wagon idling in the driveway, she told him she felt sorry for him, she really did. "That makes two of us," he said, and shut the door.

I climbed into the hole because that's where my ball was. It was a Super Ball—small and clear but flecked with blue specks and silver sparkles and extraordinarily bouncy—and was really only good for banging off the blacktop at school to see how high it would go. To bounce it like an ordinary ball was asking for trouble.

It was just after my mother had left home and we still lived on Vanderpark Drive. August afternoons usually meant a street full of suburban bedlam, summer-holiday-sprung children of every age running and screaming and racing around on bicycles or tricycles or roller skates or else sitting on the curb in dejected packs being preternaturally bored. That day, there was no one else around. It was hot—Southwestern Ontario August hot—breathing meaning swallowing air so humid it felt thick travelling down your throat, body sweat in places you wouldn't have suspected could perspire—but only a few houses had air conditioning, so that couldn't have been where everyone was and why I was alone. And if I hadn't been alone I wouldn't have climbed down the sewer hole, someone would have told me it was a bad idea, that the ball cost forty-nine cents at Woolworth's and wasn't worth it and to forget it and anyway I think I hear the Dickie Dee coming.

But no one was around. Why wasn't there anyone else around? If I wasn't supposed to go down there and get lost and then be found, why had I ended up in the sewer?

Later, I remembered how easy it was pulling the partially displaced manhole cover free the rest of the way and climbing down the metal ladder, which had felt surprisingly cold at first but good on my overheated fingers, even if slimy and dirty and slippery in places. I remembered how much quieter it became as I lowered my self down, an entirely different kind of silence from the hazy stillness of the empty street above. I remembered hearing the sound of my running shoe dip into the water, and realizing I had a choice: to put my foot back on the rung and climb toward the light, or to get my feet wet and find the Super Ball in the semi-dark, which, I figured, had to be floating nearby.

The water only came up to my ankles. It would have been too cold and rotten-egg smelly, the tunnel too dark and frightening, if I hadn't been so focused on finding my ball. My mom had bought it for me and she didn't live with us anymore and I wanted my ball. I thought I saw it more than once, but it was always something else: a rotting clump of leaves, an ice-cream wrapper, an orange hockey ball. There wasn't enough light to see that it was orange, but I knew it was a hockey ball by its size and smoothness. You got them from Canadian Tire; that was where my dad had bought me mine.

The thought of my dad and my own orange hockey ball in the garage alongside my sticks and net suddenly made me feel lonely and then, for the first time, scared. It was when I decided to give up and go back that I realized I was lost. From that point on I can't recall much. Yelling as loud as I could for help, somebody help me, I'm down here, down in the sewer, somebody help. Looking for a light above that could be around every corner but never was. Hearing something—hearing someone else!—then realizing it was only myself, softly sobbing. Noticing I had the hockey ball clamped tight in one of my hands and it being very important that I not let go. I nearly tripped on a cement block and decided to sit down and lean against the cold, slimy wall, staying in one place for a moment maybe a better way to get my bearings. I'd been down there for probably no more than a couple of hours, but it felt as if I'd been walking through the dark forever.

I didn't decide to pray. I'd never prayed before in my life. I didn't put my hands together or kneel or bow my head or clear my mind of anything except God or whatever else you were supposed to do when you prayed. After sloshing through the water a few feet that way and getting scared and coming back to my cement block, then walking a few feet the other way and getting scared and coming back to my cement block, I started to cry—not gentle sobbing this time, but full-on tears and a snotty, runny nose—and I heard myself talking to God. It was easier than I thought it would be. It was like speaking on the phone to a friend who didn't answer back but who you knew was listening.

"Dear God. I'm sorry I came down here. I know I shouldn't have. I wanted my ball that Mom gave me but I know I shouldn't have come down here, I know.

I'm sorry. I'm *so* sorry. Please, God, help me get back. I'll never come down here again. I promise I'll never go anywhere I know I'm not supposed to go anymore. *I promise.* Please help me find my way back even though I know I don't deserve it, God. I just want things to be like they were before. I know I don't deserve it, but please let things be like they were before."

Maybe I said more, maybe it was less, I might have said it differently, but that's what I said when I spoke to God. The next thing I remember was being found.

Mother of Two Is Saved, Didn't Walk Away from Her Children
"I Walked Toward the Light"

TREES CAN BE dead and still stand for years. Trees don't realize it when they're dead, though. Lucky trees. People have been blessed with consciousness, so know when they're alive as well as when they're not. Unlucky people.

She was born there, her parents were them, she grew up wanting to be, and none of it counted for much because her real life began when she was returning from the grocery store with two screaming children in the back seat of the station wagon and she wondered if she'd remembered to buy ketchup and mustard—they'd been on her list for weeks now, but every time she went shopping she somehow managed to forget them—and realized that if, when they got home, she hadn't, she'd burn down the house with all of them in it.

She put the groceries away (she'd remembered the ketchup and mustard after all), made the children lunch, let them watch TV even though it was a warm, cloudless day and ordinarily she would have sent them outside to play and went into the bathroom and locked the door and sat on the edge of the tub and, first, screamed, then cried into a towel. Why now? All she knew was that it was suddenly very clear that her entire life she'd been jaywalking in rush hour with the sun in her eyes. She did the lunch dishes and put a load of laundry in the wash and sat at the kitchen table and wrote out a new, non-grocery store list. Among other things, she needed to pick up food for Julie's goldfish.

Why Cornerstone? Why Pastor Bob? Because. Because because because. Better than a brain rush of good uncut speed, better than a toe-cramping orgasm, to everything—finally—there is an answer. The Answer. She felt as if the world and her place in it finally made sense. She felt as if for the first time in her life she could breathe.

But even the blessed are bothered; they don't call this world a vale of tears for nothing. How could she not want her husband and her children—her children!—to be saved as well? What kind of mother would she be if she didn't do everything in her power to open their eyes and their hearts and their souls? Isn't an eternity of bliss worth a little understandable confusion and a few tears now?

Apparently not—at least according to their father. Their biological father. As Pastor Bob said, "No amount of praying and preaching can soften a hardened heart intent upon denying what it wants and needs." The best she could do was keep the children in her own heart and her prayers and know that there's a reason for everything. Everything. Because.

When the firemen rescued me—a policeman in the search party finally spotted the opened manhole cover—I'd been underground the rest of that day and most of the night, the sewer gas eventually rendering me unconscious. The rotten-egg smell, the firemen told my dad, was hydrogen sulfide gas, which is produced by the breakdown of waste materials. Even though they said there was a high enough concentration of gas in the section of the sewer where I ended up to be fatal—high enough that it *should* have been fatal—there I was, lying on a stretcher and breathing pure oxygen through a mask yet undoubtedly alive. My eyes were itchy and I felt dizzy and sick to my stomach and there was concern about respiratory damage, but other than a few nightmares and a cough that lasted several weeks, I was fine. The firemen, the ambulance attendants, the front-page newspaper story, the reports on the radio—everybody—said it was miracle. Said that, since I was supposed to be dead, I must have come back to life. It didn't feel like a miracle to me, but that didn't matter, that's what everyone else decided it was.

When the firemen brought me to the surface it was nighttime, but the flashing coloured lights of the fire engine and the ambulance and the police cars were like liquid firecrackers exploding across the dark sky. I remember being put on a stretcher and my father holding my hand while the medics wheeled me to the ambulance. Along the way, somewhere on our crowded front yard—half the neighbourhod seemed to be there, along with a reporter from the *Chatham Daily News* and someone from the local radio station—I heard the voice of my mother say several times in a loud voice that it was a miracle, praise the Lord, God had mercifully given me back, I was blessed.

"Stupid bitch," my father said, quietly enough that I wasn't supposed to hear it, but loud enough that I did.

I knew right then that I'd never tell him I had prayed. Or that I'd gotten what I asked for.

Chapter Two

When it was time for me to have my own stereo—until then, making do with the dial on my white plastic handheld transistor radio faithfully glued to AM 800, CKLW out of Windsor—of course I got Julie's hand-me-down. She was five years older so I was always getting stuck with her stuff that was either out of date or didn't work properly anymore. I'd even been forced to wear a pair of her discarded tights when I was too young to know that boys didn't wear tights. Only years later, when I noticed a picture in the family photo album of three-year-old me happily romping around the living-room floor in my T-shirt and inherited red tights, did I feel the indignation to which I believed I was entitled.

But I was thirteen now and too old to be fooled into wearing girl's clothes and I needed my own music. Julie was eighteen and in grade twelve and not even a chin-dripping face full of tears would have allowed me access to her room and her record collection. We were fellow guests in the same two-star hotel who vied for the shared bathroom and who didn't feel obliged to make small talk if we happened to run into one another in the hallway.

"Julie got her own stereo when she was my age."

My father didn't look up from the arm he was working on, the tattooing needle in his right hand making slow but steady progress burning flesh and leaving behind ink. We lived above the tattoo parlor now and it was a rule that I had to check in after school, even before I went upstairs and dropped off my red Adidas bag full of fusty gym clothes and the occasional book. My mother had moved to Toronto with Pastor Bob after the Cornerstone closed down just like the pet store before it, so it was just Dad and Julie and me. In lieu of an extra set of parental eyes, Dad had rules.

"You've already got a stereo," he said, eyes never leaving his work. My father and the man sitting in the chair with his extended bare arm looked alike—both had beards and shoulder-length hair pulled back into tight ponytails and with ink covering most of their exposed skin—but unlike his short and scrawny customer, Dad was tall and still muscular, with only the beginning of a potbelly, and whereas most of the little man's tattoos were just words spelt out in thin, shaky lines of pale blue ink, my father's were like the end of the cardboard kaleidoscope tube I used to have, every colour imaginable and all of them swooping and soaring in and out of each other with perfect symmetrical sense.

"My *own* stereo. Not that old piece of junk. Sometimes an eight-track won't even play right and you can only get it to sound normal by sticking a butter knife in there."

Instead of immediately recognizing the severity of his son's audio equipment quandary, my dad bore down even more intensely with his needle. The little man in the chair continued to stare at the wall. I waited for my father to say something—even *No* would have been preferable to being ignored—before picking up my Adidas bag.

"There are muffins on the counter," my dad said. "They just came out of the oven so the pan might still be hot. Be careful." At this, the man snuck a peek at my father as if to confirm that the muffin-baking man completing his tattoo was the same one who'd started it.

There was a door beside the tiny bathroom that opened on a dark stairwell to our apartment, but my father only allowed it to be used when there weren't any customers in the shop. Another of Dad's rules: you could talk like they weren't there, but you had to pretend you didn't live in a crappy little second- and third-floor downtown apartment on top of a tattoo parlor. I hoisted my bag over my shoulder and went to leave the same way I came in.

"You should get yourself a paper route," a voice, not my father's, said. The only reason I didn't just keep going was because you couldn't be rude to a customer. "Young buck like you, you could buy yourself whatever you wanted in no time at all. I bet your dad here had a folding-money job when he was your age."

My father had grown up as an only child in the country; liked to say he never saw cement until he came to Chatham to go to high-school. His mother had died long before either Julie or I was born, while his father was just a misty memory of silver hair and the smell of cherry pipe tobacco. When she was still living with us and I asked Mom why we never saw our grandparents on her side of the family or any aunts or uncles or cousins, she said that her parents had kicked her out of the house when she was a teenager and she swore she'd never talk to anyone in her family again. When I asked her why they'd kicked her out, she said it was a long time ago, she couldn't remember.

"Sure," I heard him answer the man.

"Okay," I said. "See you."

Hitting the snow-dusted sidewalk, *Yeah, right*, I thought. *A paper route. What a jerk. What a spaz.* When I got home, I couldn't find the phonebook with the number of the *Chatham Daily News*, Dad must have left it downstairs.

The day my mother came home and declared she'd been saved was the same week my sister called a family meeting to announce that henceforth she was to be referred to as *Cher*. Mom's was obviously the more significant news, but since at the time I had a much clearer idea of who Cher was than Jesus, Julie's announcement made the bigger impression. I'd never attended a family meeting before—had only seen one on the Brady Bunch, where I suspected my sister got the idea—and it was exciting, like we weren't just the Buzbys anymore, but a real family, like on TV.

These days, Julie's idea of a feminist role model had shifted from a wise-cracking variety-show co-host and occasional AM radio rebel ("Half-Breed," Cher's top-of-the-charts condemnation of hypocrisy and racism, the soundtrack to Julie's PRIVATE! KEEP OUT! closed bedroom door the fall of 1973) to girls I had never heard of—that no one had ever heard of except Julie and her new best friend, Angie, who'd moved to Chatham from Toronto with her parents the summer before the start of her and Julie's grade twelve year. And it turned out that her new heroes weren't *girls*, either. Julie made sure I understood at least that much.

A Buzby sit-down breakfast for three, Julie's fat biology textbook and a copy of Patti Smith's *Easter* album occupying the empty chair at the table. Julie was at the kitchen counter topping up her cup from the busily brewing Mr. Coffee Maker—eighteen now, she could ingest as much caffeine as she wanted and could even write her own absentee notes for school—and I leaned over and picked up the album with the hand not being utilized to munch a piece of strawberry-jam-laden toast.

Spinning around, "What do you think you're doing?" she shouted.

"Let's take it down a notch, okay?" Dad said, blasted from the sanctity of his sports page.

Before I was on the second sneering syllable of "Nothing" Julie had snatched the record from my hand. "What's your problem?" I said.

"My problem is people touching things that aren't theirs without asking." She studied the album front and back, as if expecting to find cigarette burns or obscene graffiti. Dad vanished again behind his newspaper.

I took another bite of toast and looked at the album cover while Julie continued to scrutinize the back. "Gross," I said. Because neither my sister nor my father asked me to elaborate, "That girl is gross."

"You wouldn't call a hockey player a boy, would you? Would you?"

"I don't know."

"No, you wouldn't."

"I might. You don't know."

"No, you wouldn't. This is a *woman*," Julie said, pointing at the cover photo of Patti Smith, bare arms raised to reveal her *au natural* underarms. "When you call a woman a girl you denigrate her. You equate her mind to that of a child's."

"You're just saying that because Angie talks like that." The first time Julie brought Angie over to our house she'd been wearing a T-shirt that read A WOMAN WITHOUT A MAN IS LIKE A FISH WITHOUT A BICYCLE. The shirt was made of thin yellow cotton and I could see the straps of her blue bra underneath. All my sister's bras were white.

"I'm out of here," Julie said, grabbing her book and record.

Without either speaking or ceasing to peruse the sports section, Dad extended an arm in the direction of the breakfast mess that was the kitchen counter. I set the table and did the dinner dishes; Julie was in charge of cleaning up after breakfast, mornings dubbed her domestic domain by our father mainly because he said the coffee she made tasted better than his. Mom had been the family coffee maker before the Lord's call had beckoned her away to distant kitchens.

"I'm going to be late," she said. "And I've got a test."

"You should have thought of that before you decided to argue with your brother."

"I wasn't arguing—I was trying to educate him. Obviously somebody around here has to."

Eyes on his newspaper, Dad replied by lifting his arm again.

"Whatever," she said, slamming both the book and the record on the countertop even though the latter belonged to Angie, toward whose frequently borrowed music and books she was usually so fastidious. "I can't wait until I'm *really* out of here." Julie was one year away from having to worry about university applications, but, being a straight-A student, her first choice, the University of Toronto, seemed a foregone conclusion to everyone but her.

Dad kept reading. I picked up my spoon and scooped and slurped my Cheerios. Julie got on with the job at hand as noisily as possible. I wondered what it was that made a woman a woman and a girl a girl. It couldn't just be underarm hair. There had to be more to it than that.

For the first few years after she left for Toronto, Mom and the Reverend Bob would come back to Chatham so she could visit Julie and me, the Reverend Bob dropping her off and waiting at Tim Horton's. She'd call ahead so we'd know she was coming and Julie and I would meet her at the door so that Dad wouldn't have to see her. We'd usually head to the Satellite Restaurant where Julie would sit on one side of the booth and Mom and I on the other. She didn't call me her "Little Miracle Boy" anymore and she didn't talk about God quite as much. He still came up, but He wasn't something she needed to prove to anybody now, especially herself, because He was as real as the courier business, *Silver Wings*, that she and the Reverend Bob had started when he discovered it was just as difficult finding a full flock of true believers in Toronto as in Chatham. Sitting with Mom at the Satellite, sometimes *I* wondered about God. After all, the single time I prayed and asked for help, I'd gotten it. But I didn't tell her that. And when she'd return to Toronto my theological curiosity tended to hit the road too. Street hockey games, math tests, monster movies on TV: there always seemed to be something more important to think about.

Mom would ask us about school, if we had any new friends, if we were saying our prayers at night, and we'd answer *Okay, No, Yes*. I don't think she really believed we got down on our knees and talked to Jesus, I think she just believed it was important for us to know that she thought we should. Julie was older and would fidget on her side of the table and act irritated with the conversational stop-and-start, but I was happy to just sit beside my mom, to have her hold my hand while we looked over the menu together, to smell her mom smell of *Charlie* perfume and hairspray.

Then one year she was hospitalized with a shattered knee after she'd slipped on some ice and couldn't come to Chatham for Julie's birthday, although she made sure to telephone and send a card. Then she was in physical therapy and couldn't come to visit at Christmas either, and then it was difficult and dangerous for her to get around in the snow and ice with her big brace and cane, and then it became normal for her not to come to Chatham to visit us at all anymore; it became normal for her to telephone on all the important dates and to stick an inflation-resistant five-dollar bill in a Hallmark card. Everything is odd until it isn't.

Of course, if I really wanted more Mom time, I could have phoned her whenever I wanted. Dad might have made a face about the cost of the long-distance call, but he wouldn't have said I shouldn't have. That she was three hours away and content to stay there was good enough for him. Besides, if I did talk to her on the telephone and he happened to be hanging around the kitchen, he always seemed pleased to see the mix of boredom, disappointment, and sadness on my face when I hung up. Boredom, because who knew that the ups and downs of a struggling courier business could be almost as boring as the steps it takes to get into heaven? Disappointment, because I'd look forward to her birthday or Christmas calls and two minutes in I'd be bored. ("So you're another year older." "Yeah." "And you're a teenager now." "Yeah." "Are you excited?" "I guess.") Sadness, because boredom and disappointment weren't what I wanted to feel about my mother. She'd—Julie's words—"flipped her lid," gone away, stayed away, and everyone had gotten used to it, more or less, had moved on, more or less, but she was still my mother.

When she first started attending the Cornerstone and Dad was still waiting it out, hoping she'd get her fill of God and gradually drift back to us, she hung a cheaply framed picture of Jesus on my bedroom wall. I'm sure Dad didn't like it, but there it hung over my mirrored dresser drawers. I didn't mind—I only knew Jesus from the morning Bible scriptures that were read over the intercom by the principal, Mr. Park, before classes started, after the playing of the national anthem and before he read the school announcements. Jesus had long hair, for a man, and wore sandals and his clothes sort of billowed around him, but he looked all right, kind of like some of the musicians on Julie's album covers. Plus, she was my mom—if she put the picture there, it must have belonged there, she wouldn't have done something that was bad for me.

A week or so after she hung it, it was hot and my window curtain was pulled to the side to allow a breeze, even a warm breeze, and I woke up to the moonlight illuminating the picture. It looked as if Jesus was staring at me. I screamed—I didn't mean to, I was surprised when I heard my own voice—and Mom and Dad ran into my room and turned on the light and rushed to my bed and asked me what was wrong. Julie stood in my doorway rubbing her eyes and asked what was going on, why was everybody awake. I pointed at the picture.

"He scared me," I said.

I was sitting up now and my mother sat down on the bed and passed her hand through my sweaty hair, rubbed my cheek. "That's your saviour, Tom. That's Sweet Baby

Jesus. He's only here to protect you and love you. He could never hurt you."

"Oh, man," Julie said, turning around and going back to her room.

"You see?" Dad yelled. "You see?"

Still stroking my face, "Why are you shouting?" Mom said.

"I'm not shouting," Dad shouted. He picked me up like he would sometimes do when we were horsing around in the backyard, but this time no one was laughing. "C'mon, buddy," he said. "You're going to sleep in our room tonight."

Mom stood up and moved to turn off the light when Dad said to her, "You can sleep in here with Sweet Baby Jesus. You two can keep each other company."

"Collecting!"

Monday through Friday after school was for delivering the newspaper; Saturday was for distributing the week's final *Chatham Daily News* and for punching holes in collection cards. Whatever day it was, the first thing you noticed when you cut the binding on a fresh batch of newspapers was the headline on page one, big black type shouting out what was oh-so-important today. It rarely was, though. Election results and earthquakes overseas and federal inquiries into improper spending on Parliament Hill didn't stay in your head once you'd turned the page. And tomorrow they were just yesterday's headlines.

Saturday was also for getting paid, and getting paid was good—was the whole point—but getting paid sometimes meant being invited inside to wait while someone got their purse or their wallet or their cheque book and having to listen to whatever they said because they were nice enough to invite you in off the sleety porch, after all, and they were the customer and therefore always right, even if not always interesting.

"Mrs. Gibson and I would have been married forty-two years this April."

I nodded. "That's great."

Mr. Gibson continued to rummage through his late wife's purse without actually looking inside. I continued to stand on the rubber mat in the front hallway, the cuffs of my favourite pair of Levis frozen solid. Mrs. Gibson had died of cancer a few months earlier. She'd been the one who always paid me.

"That's—how old are you?"

"Thirteen. I'm thirteen."

"That's over twenty-eight years longer than you've been alive that Mrs. Gibson and I were married."

I didn't know what else I was supposed to say. "That's great," I repeated.

His hand now motionless inside the purse as if it was stuck there, Mr. Gibson looked like he either had more to say but wasn't sure what it was or he knew but was hesitant to say it.

"Mrs. Gibson kept her change in the front part, I think," I said. "There's a pouch inside at the front that—"

Mr. Gibson handed me his dead wife's purse. "Take however much it is I owe you," he said. "I know I can trust you." Shuffling out of sight in his slippers into the kitchen, leaving me alone in the hallway, "I know you know what it means to be lost, too," he said. "What happened to each of us, it's not the same, but I know that you know what it's like." It had been several years since I was lost then found, but people still remembered. Especially people who seemed like they needed to.

I didn't say anything. I counted out the money he owed me and put the purse on the table by the door and let myself out. It was snowing just as hard as it had been before.

Recent Widow—"Happily Married" for 41 Years—Feels Renewed Sexual Longing
"It's Not Something I Wanted or Even Expected"

IF YOU MEAN it—if you really, really mean it—a marriage vow is like joining the mafia: betray that oath, and you're as good as dead (inside where it matters, if not in corporeal fact). He never did and she never did and only in death (hers) did they part. He got used to living alone (their daughter worked in Vancouver as a speech therapist and came home when she could, but she had a family of her own now and was busy building a career) and at 64 he still went into the office five days a week at the Royal Bank and there were model tall ships to assemble in the evening and a cup of hot cocoa before bed and the days have a way of adding up to weeks. Still strange at times—occasionally surprised she wasn't there when he got home from work; wishing he could talk to her about how odd it felt not to have her there to talk to; bad thought days that can't be outthought, only endured—but a good end to a good life fouled only by an innocuous-looking little lump in her right breast, the banal beginning to her agonizing, then merciful, end.

Now this. But why this now? He thought he'd outlived his genitals. But young women on the city bus that his wife used to be. Young women at the bank who didn't need to be beautiful to be desirable, only young. Pushing a shopping cart with a sticky front right wheel up and down the aisles of Dominion, ripe cantaloupes and perfect pears and bright red cherries superiorly aphrodisiacal to pages 83-84 of *Penthouse* (no matter how well lit or tastefully photographed), the lonely latter only a slick centerfold squirt and sigh. Godamnit, he hadn't felt like this while she was alive—not for years and years, anyway—so why now? Why?

He'd watched the box slide into the furnace after the funeral. Dust to dust—that part of the minister's blah blah blah did make sense. And now her in a vase on the bedroom bureau where he kept his underwear and T-shirts and socks and him a schoolboy again. To every thing there is a season, they say. They're godamn liars.

Some sagacious words, someone, please.

———————

Mr. Gibson's sidewalk was always shovelled clean within an hour of any snow fall, his eavestroughs always empty of congesting leaves and twigs. The red brick exterior of his house looked bright and warm on sunny winter days, no matter how cold, and the blue-striped cloth awnings that hung over every window cast invitingly cool shadows on the spongy green grass of his lawn throughout the summer.

Not that everyone's house on my route was as nice as Mr. Gibson's. I also delivered to King Street businesses and their cramped upstairs tenants and to the houses on the tree-lined streets clustered around Tecumseh Park and a little further south. Most of my friends at school lived either in the suburbs or in the country; the houses on my route tended to be like the people who occupied them: older and more interesting.

There were Mr. and Mrs. Jones, both of whom had taught for decades at CCI—the nearby high-school that Julie went to—and who didn't have any children but who did have two blue-eyed Siberian huskies, Karl and Marx, who used to go barking berserk whenever I approached the house until Mr. Jones gave me a bag of dog treats to feed to them every time I came by. Within a week they were whimpering with expectation as soon as they saw me and my grey paper bag coming down the street. There was Mrs. Henderson, a widow whose husband had been the *Henderson* in Henderson, Lowell, and James, the law firm that occupied the vine-covered stone building near the Cenotaph downtown, and who had a library with two ladders on rollers in the front room where you'd normally see a couch and a coffee table and a big TV. There was Dr. McKay and his blond family who lived across the street from the old court house, both of the sons doctors now too, the two younger sisters, twins, still at home and biding their time being dauntingly beautiful as well as CCI's best athletes and smartest students. The entire family looked like a benign argument for the wisdom of eugenics.

Past the high school all the way to the end of Murray Street and over the Colborne Street bridge was where I completed my route, would start back home by about five p.m. with an empty bag slung over my shoulder and with thoughts of what Dad was making for dinner and what record I was going to buy that Saturday at Sam the Record Man and how little homework I could get away with doing before slouching in front of the TV with a bag of potato chips and a tub of French onion dip and a bottle of Pop Shoppe black cherry cola. The houses on this side of the bridge were as old as those on the other side and with just as many architectural idiosyncrasies (gables, wrap-around porches, screened sun rooms), but with peeling paint and weather-buckled shingles and the occasional broken window pane replaced by a garbage bag taped in place. Whites and blacks tended to cluster together according to colour (the Royal Tavern was where black people drank; the Merrill Tavern was where white people got drunk), but front car seats with stuffing poking through in place of porch swings were a home furnishing preference of both races, and the anger and suspicion and weariness in people's eyes was skin pigment neutral.

There was Mrs. Davis, whose several children ranged from my age to older than my sister. One of them, Jackie, had a baby of her own that I never saw her taking care of; it was always Mrs. Davis doing the bottle-feeding and rattle-shaking. Mrs. Davis took care of all of them. "Mr. Davis" was just a name I heard. One of the sons, who was around my age, was called Sammy. I wondered if he was named after Sammy Davis Jr. I wondered if wondering it made me prejudiced. Mrs. Davis' oldest daughter worked at the hospital. I never saw her at Mrs. Davis' house, never saw her visiting her mother or brothers and sisters.

There were the Scanlons—no one called them by their individual names, they were always just the Scanlons—four virtually identical skinny, jug-eared, buzz-cut white boys with acne-smeared faces who went around all summer without their shirts on, and their equally emaciated mother and father, cold pizza and a plastic pitcher of orange Freshie on the dinner table when I'd come by to collect—sometimes it was just cereal—and accusatory stares through the screen door like somehow it was my fault.

There was Mr. Lupien, an old man with more bushy white hair sprouting out of his ears than on his head and a French accent that made him hard to understand, who'd outlived not only his wife but two of his three children. His oldest son, he told me, lived in a nursing home in Sarnia. He visited him whenever he could.

There were more, there were a lot more, and I delivered to all of them.

Funny how sometimes it's sunniest outside when it's coldest. Mr. Bennett's science class, the period after lunch, the snow that covered the blacktop a frozen mirror reflecting lasers of sparkling sunlight into my blinking, slightly watering eyes. Eyes that should have been on the blackboard defaced by Mr. Bennett's near-incomprehensible handwriting, but which were looking out the window watching Mr. Dunlop, the school custodian, pour salt from a plastic bag over the sidewalk. Mr. Dunlop did all of his outdoor jobs with a cigarette stuck in the corner of his mouth, but on bitter days like this, frozen breath escaping his lips whenever cigarette smoke wasn't, he looked like a salt-pouring machine with a mouth for a muffler.

Science was my second-least-favourite subject, a close number two to math. Math was a crossword puzzle, but with numbers instead of words. Get just one number wrong and the entire thing was spoiled. People who were good at math, like Adam Stephenson and Kirsten McDonald, weren't like the people who always got As in English or history or social studies. Getting their relentlessly red-check-marked tests back from the obviously pleased teacher, more than being simply happy with their gaudy grades, they seemed smug, like they'd figured out how a little piece of the universe worked. *It's not life, it's just math*, I sometimes wanted to say. Because I rarely got more than a C+, though, I knew what it would sound like if I did.

Science was slightly better than math because at least you could see the things you were supposed to know. Even invisible ideas like gravity had an eventual physical payoff, Newton's head-bopping apple or the piece of chalk Mr. Bennett dropped into his palm. Today Mr. Bennett was talking about the solar system. He said that we were always discovering new things about the universe, like how until relatively recently people believed that the sun rotated around the earth. A few of the smart kids snickered, someone in the back of the class sneezed, I tried to look like I'd known it all along. Not that it mattered. Either way, Mr. Dunlop would still be outside smoking his cigarette and emptying his blue plastic bag of salt over the sidewalk so that people wouldn't slip and fall.

Then Mr. Bennett talked about the sun. It was 4.5 billion years old, he said, and about a hundred times larger than the earth. I wrote that down in my notebook. Those were the kinds of details that end up on a test. The sun, he continued, was a star like any other star you see at night in the sky, except that our star was still alive and burning brightly, making life possible on earth.

Colin McManus raised his hand. "You mean that stars can die?" Colin was always putting his hand up, even when he obviously knew the answer to his question. He thought it made him look smart. His father was a dentist, and every year Colin got permission to leave early the week of March Break because his family went to Florida.

"They all die," Mr. Bennett said, "but they're so far away, it can take four hundred years for their light to reach the earth. Your entire life, you can believe you're looking at a star that's alive when what you're really looking at is a dead star whose light went out centuries ago." You knew Mr. Bennett was enjoying himself because he wasn't standing up in front of the class as usual, but was sitting on his desk swinging his short legs back and forth. Mr. Bennett had a fat wart on his right cheek and a few of us were already taller than he was.

"But…" I said.

"Yes? But what, Tom?" I hadn't raised my hand, but Mr. Bennett didn't appear to care, was having too much fun introducing us to the universe.

"But—" I wasn't sure what I wanted to ask, but I knew I needed to know the answer "—what happens to the earth when the sun dies?" We'd already studied photosynthesis in the fall term, so I knew that plants couldn't grow without sunlight.

"Well," Mr. Bennett said, legs really swinging now, "about five billion years from now the sun will grow even larger and hotter and will either get so big that it'll swallow the earth up whole like an enormous ball of fire consuming a tiny piece of paper or it will just burn everything up beyond recognition and boil all of the oceans and lakes and rivers until they evaporate."

Just was a but-not-so-bad word. But there wasn't anything not so bad about the earth, people, animals—everything—disappearing forever. Mr. Bennett slapped his thighs through his polyester brown slacks and slid down from the edge of the desk. "But that won't be for a long, long time, and we've got more important things to think about right now. I want everyone to get their textbooks out and turn to chapter three, page 79."

I hadn't done my homework, hadn't read chapter three, but whatever was in it, I knew it couldn't have been more important than what I'd just found out.

I could have switched schools when we moved from the house on Vanderpark Drive to the apartment downtown, but I think Dad believed we'd been through enough change already, so I stayed an Indian Creek Road Public School Sun Devil and my best friend stayed Dale Sutcliffe. Dale and I weren't on any teams and didn't have girlfriends, both of which were okay because we collected Monty Python records and memorized Steve Martin stand-up skits and compared notes on our favourite horror movies and kept a notebook of all of the nicknames we had for the teachers we didn't like and all the dumb things that people would say and even the things we thought were pretty damn smart, just as long as they were also pretty damn funny. Julie was already at CCI by then, so the move downtown made getting to school and back easier for her, but now I needed to travel from one end of the city to the other for nine a.m. five days a week. Luckily, there was Mr. Brown.

Mr. Brown was not only Indian Creek's history and geography teacher, he'd also worked with my dad at Ontario Steel for a couple of summers filling in for vacationing full-timers. He lived in the east end like us, in an apartment over top of the Satellite Restaurant. He always wore a corduroy jacket the same colour as his name and round wire-rimmed glasses like John Lennon's. I'd show up in his homeroom after classes were over and we'd walk to his mustard-coloured Chevy Vega and talk away the ten minute ride home. Mr. Brown wasn't like most adults in that he asked questions about what you were up to and were interested in and seemed to actually want to hear your answers, but recently he was doing most of the talking, mostly about the plan to demolish Harrison Hall—what everyone called "Old City Hall," which had been at the corner of Fifth and Wellington since the late-1800s—to accommodate the construction of the new mall. Technically, the space wasn't even going to be part of the mall; it was eight proposed parking spaces.

"You know, this isn't just something we talk about in class, Tom. It's very important for the entire community that we do our best to preserve our oldest and most unique buildings. They're part of who we are."

If it had been any other teacher I would have just nodded and attempted to look my most eagerly acquiescent, but because it was Mr. Brown, "My dad says new jobs are more important than a bunch of old rocks."

The soon-to-be new mall—over 60,000 square feet of shiny new shops, an eight-restaurant food court, and a full-service Sears—was supposed to save Chatham's sinking downtown commercial core by stealing back the shoppers who'd abandoned it for Zellers and K-Mart and the big Woolco mall out on Highway 40. Before they could construct it, though, they needed to tear down the century-old buildings standing where it was supposed to go, most of which had been happily sold by their owners to the City at above-market cost. Harrison Hall should have been the easiest building to erase—the City already owned it, after all—but a small but vocal group of local residents, Mr. Brown among them, was attempting to change the City's mind, to get them to force the mall's developers to modify their plans and keep Old City Hall from becoming simply the old city hall.

"Your father is a business man," Mr. Brown said, clicking the Vega's turn signal and looking carefully both ways before pulling onto Queen Street. "It's understandable that he's concerned about jobs. We *all* are. No one is saying that the mall isn't a good idea. People can't eat architecture." Passing by Kentucky Fried Chicken, I thought how funny it would be if, instead of just destroying the restaurant, Godzilla plucked up the enormous spinning bucket out front and popped it into his fire-breathing mouth.

"But people need something else too," he said, "or else they won't be happy, no matter how much money their job pays them or how well—or how much—they eat." A car swerved into our lane and Mr. Brown leaned on his horn. "C'mon, buddy, pick a lane already." I liked it that Mr. Brown wasn't afraid of getting mad in front of me. Most adults pretended like they had all the answers and were always in control.

"You mean they need to know history and stuff," I said.

Mr. Brown audibly exhaled through his nostrils, though whether because of the guy who'd cut him off or because of my question I couldn't tell.

"History isn't only dates and names in books and pictures of people who aren't around any more," he said. "It means feeling a connection to the place you live, to the people that lived there before you. Otherwise, life is just…"

We'd stopped in front of the tattoo shop now, but I didn't say thanks and jump out like I ordinarily did; I waited in my seat for Mr. Brown to finish what he was saying. He looked at me. "I think you know what I mean, Tom," he said. "Or at least you know it better than most other kids your age."

I didn't, but I didn't want to let him down, so I just nodded.

"See you tomorrow, Tom," Mr. Brown said.

High School Teacher Has it "Up to Here" with Local Yahoos
"If I Can Understand Their Point of View, Why Is It So Hard for Them to Understand Someone Else's?"

HE COULD SEE their point. He wasn't some artsy shit from Toronto, after all—he was from here, just like them. Born and raised and, except for four years of university in Windsor and another twelve months at teacher's college, right back where he'd started, doing exactly what he always wanted to do: instructing, molding, maybe—hopefully—even inspiring.

The son of a factory worker at Ontario Steel and a cook's assistant in the cafeteria at Libby's, he'd been saved from a life of the same by parents who made sure he got the education they never did and by the few good teachers he'd been lucky enough to encounter along the way, men and women who considered their occupation as more than good pay with no heavy lifting and two months off in the summer and a fat pension to grow old and fat on. There had been Mrs. Johnson, grade eight, who'd instilled in him a love of reading—not necessarily to acquire information; not to keep up with what everyone was talking about; not as a way to kill time when there's no one else around to talk to or nothing on TV; but because without its inimitable spiritual shake-and-bake, how else were you going to find out what you believed, what you wanted, who you were? There was

Mr. Moritz, grade eleven, who showed him that there was a world outside of Chatham outside of Ontario outside of Canada outside of North America outside of planet earth outside of our solar system outside… There'd been Professor Evans, Eng 2041: Introduction to the English Romantics, who'd revealed yet another world to him—the real one—where seeing what's actually there entails sealing your eyes and callusing your senses to the sights and sounds, the poking and prodding, that passes for what's important if you're going to end up with the biggest or the most or be one of the insufferably respected.

He was thankful, in other words; he wanted to give thanks. And the only way to give thanks that matters is by giving back some of what you yourself have been given. He wanted to teach; he wanted to call himself a teacher. And he did, and he did.

But he could also see their point. The poetry of William Blake sounds better and makes more sense when you're warm in the winter and cool in the summer and there are two weeks' worth of groceries in the cupboard and a few extra bucks in the bank when you need braces for your twelve-year-old daughter or you have to buy a new roof when the rain doesn't care that the old leaky one isn't really that old and shouldn't need fixing. Money may be the root of all evil, but it's also pretty damn close to the source of all that's good, too. Noble thoughts and fine feelings are a lot more likely to occur when your stomach is full and your roof doesn't have a hole in it.

But a gut can only be so gorged. There are only so many times you can renovate the downstairs bathroom. And too long looking exclusively for what is necessary will eventually blind you to what is important.

I mean, Jesus H. Christ, folks, it's only one build-ing. One structurally beautiful, historically significant building that helps ensure that the town we live in is more than just a place where a bunch of different peo-ple work and sleep and procreate and eat and shit and die. Just move the frigging mall a few hundred feet the other way, people. It's only a bunch of bricks and steel.

Julie was busy waging her own campaign, and it had nothing to do with preserving Harrison Hall. Julie had saved up enough money from her two-evenings-a-week job at Dairy Queen to go with Angie to Toronto for a few days during March Break. What she didn't have was our father's permission. Not yet, anyway.

"Where do you plan on staying?" They were drink-ing coffee after dinner while I cleared the table and got started on the dishes. I had math homework to do before *M.A.S.H.* came on at nine o'clock. *M.A.S.H.* was probably my favourite TV show, and Hawkeye Pierce was probably why. He wasn't a rock star or a superstar athlete, but he was still pretty cool, came up with the funniest lines and had his very own booze still and wore a cowboy hat with a smoking jacket. But he was also the hospital's best surgeon and the one everybody turned to when they were worried about something important. Hawkeye made it seem like it might not be too bad to be a grown up.

"With one of Angie's aunts," Julie said.

"I don't suppose Angie would mind if I talked to her aunt."

"Why would you want to do that?"

Everybody has to die, but some people actually manage to live first.

Until she met Angie, it was as if she were the only one who felt like this. People who thought like you and acted like you wished you did in books and movies and songs are good to know, but you can't call up Janis Joplin or Catherine Deneuve or Simone de Beauvoir on the telephone when you want to study for your history test but you're getting your period and are cranky and feel like crying and eating barbeque potato chips and watching something you know is totally stupid on TV like the *The Love Boat* instead, and how unfair is it that guys can study as hard as they want whenever they want just because their bodies don't turn on them? The first time she noticed the new girl, Angie, was during lunchtime in the girls' section of the cafeteria, when the subject somehow came around to having kids and someone asked Angie, who'd said she didn't want any, "Aren't you afraid no one will remember you if you don't have children?" and Angie answered, "If no one remembers me for myself, I suppose I don't deserve to be remembered." It was then that she noticed Angie didn't feather her hair or wear Daniel Hechter sweatshirts or earrings or even lipstick, only a little purple (purple!) eyeshadow that made her brown eyes even darker and more difficult to decipher.

It wasn't long before they were spending so much time together—why, at a party in somebody's parents' basement, for example, stupid loud music and stupider loud people, would they talk to anyone else when they had such a good time talking to each other?—that people started to whisper (she never heard it, but she could hear it) that they were lezbos, which was why they sat alone laughing so loudly at lunch and never went out on dates and even went to the movies together on Saturday night. She didn't care. Might've cared before she'd met Angie, but she didn't care now.

Round one went to Dad, but I knew Julie would be back to fight another day. She had a way of making what she wanted happen, even when she was a child. When she was ten and had a crush on one of the characters in *Adventures in Rainbow Country*, Billy Maxwell's Ojibwa friend Pete, she managed to get the mailing address of the show and send him a Valentine's Day card she bought at Woolworth's with her own money. (On the front, a picture of an Indian in head feathers with a raised right hand and a caption that read *HOW!* and on the inside of the card the words *Would You Like to be My Valentine?*) She even got a signed photograph back in the mail, but immediately lost interest when the actor signed his own name. When she was in grade nine or ten and decided it was time she had a boyfriend but that all of the boys at school were immature, she came home from the Jaycee Fair with a guy who ran one of the rides and who had to be at least eighteen. My dad didn't know what else to do so he invited him in to wash the grease off his hands and have dinner with us. After supper he and Julie sat on the back step and ate ice-cream cones while my father kept an eye on them through the screen door. She never saw him again, but she'd had her first date.

I finished the dishes and went upstairs to my room. My math textbook and notebook lay open on my desk where I'd left them before dinner, but I didn't sit down and get to it like I'd promised myself I would. I had my own milk carton of records now, including a new double album, Pink Floyd's *The Wall*, that I'd bought less than a week before. I'd also just that day checked out of the library at school the latest issue of *Sports Illustrated*, which sat on my nightstand beside my portable radio. I knew if I clicked it on and turned it to WJR the Red Wing game would be playing. And *M.A.S.H.* was on TV in a little more than half an hour. I could hear Julie in her bedroom across the hall talking in a fervent mumble on the extension to Angie, most likely about their proposed trip. It all seemed like such a big hassle. If they just stayed in Chatham they could do whatever they wanted and no one would have any reason to bother them. After all, anything anybody could want was already here. Why did people have to make everything so complicated?

Chapter Three

A first-rate Friday; but, then, what else could Friday be?

Not only was there no school the next day, there was no school the day after *that*. Saturday got all of the songs written about it and had more things going on—adults visited other adults, teenagers went on dates or got into trouble, *Hockey Night in Canada* was on—but after the excitement of Saturday there was always inevitable Sunday, and no matter how much fun you'd had the night before, the morning after meant school or work the following day, and no matter how satisfyingly sunny Sunday was, it was always compromised by the cloud cover that was knowing—*feeling*—Monday a.m.'s melancholic imminence.

Fridays the year I was in grade seven were even better because not only did I have gym last class, so the school day felt fifty minutes shorter, but one entire period was given over to a classroom library visit. As long as you brought back the books you'd borrowed the week before, you were allowed to take out two new ones, providing they weren't on the same subject. I usually checked out a sports book or magazine and used loan number two for something about music or Bigfoot or UFOs or the Loch Ness Monster. Most of the other boys' borrowing habits were similar, while the girls favoured novels about other girls or books on animals and something called *Are You There God? It's Me, Margaret*. There was a waiting list for this one, something that had never happened before, and when you'd ask a girl what it was about, why the book was so popular, she'd smirk and say *Why don't you read it for yourself?* Scott Cassidy eventually took one for Team Testosterone and endured the girls' giggles and the furrowed brow of Mrs. Wilson, the librarian, and added his name to the bottom of the waiting list. It took so long for it to be his turn, though, that once it was, the mystery had ebbed, other unknowns now weighed more heavily upon our minds. (One day in math class, for instance, we were stunned to learn that what was once *miles per hour* was now *kilometres per hour* and that growing up to be six-foot tall really meant you were a strapping 182.88 centimetres.) When his name finally came up on Mrs. Wilson's list and Scott casually declared that he didn't want the book anymore, like it was her idea in the first place, Mrs. Wilson made him take it anyway, to teach him something about responsibility. Scott shrugged, took it, then promptly lost it (meaning no one else got to read it either), only to find it again on the last day of classes when we cleaned out our lockers (which essentially meant dumping everything into one of several steel garbage cans that the janitor placed down the middle of the halls). If he hadn't found it, Scott's parents would have had to pay for a new copy. "Check it out," he said, pulling it free from the pile at the bottom his locker. "That stupid book. Man, is that lucky or what?"

Friday: school done for the week; newspapers delivered for the day; wet boots taken off at the door; Dad sitting in a kitchen chair pulled up in front of the glowing oven watching the roast beef sweat its way to cooked completion, him still smelling like the medical-grade Green Soap he used to clean his clients' skin before and after he applied their tattoo. Friday night roast beef (with cooked-in potatoes, carrots, and onions) was a Mom tradition, the week's one big family meal with leftovers for sandwiches on Monday. Dad's roast beef was good, but it wasn't Mom's—was tender, but not fall-off-your-fork tender; was moist, but not melt-in-your-mouth moist. Dad inherited the tradition, but not the recipe. Nevertheless, "How was school?" "Okay." "Where are you going?" "My room." "Dinner in half an hour." "Okay." "If you see your sister, let her know." "All right." It smelled good all the way upstairs, all the way behind my closed bedroom door. It smelled like home.

After dinner, back in my room, I'd write down everything I'd eaten in a pocket-sized red coiled notebook I called my Journal of Consumption. In the short time since I started my newspaper route it felt as if I'd had more contact with more people than I'd had in my entire life up to that point. People who knew me as the boy who came back from the dead. Dad and Julie didn't count—they weren't people, they were my family. The newspaper and the radio might have called me a miracle, but you're never a miracle to those who know you. But when Mr. Gibson or Mr. Brown or somebody else talked to me like I was supposed to know the answer to something when I didn't even understand the question, I felt guilty, I felt phony, I felt like a fraud. We weren't Catholic and I wasn't entirely sure what Lent was, but I decided that, instead of fasting, I'd eat and drink what I ordinarily did, but would record everything in my journal for forty days. It was inconvenient, it was boring, it felt like a chore: it was ideal.

After writing down what I'd eaten for dinner, I'd listen to records and read and think about girls I was too afraid to talk to, although mostly I'd wait for it to get dark. Dad didn't really acknowledge weekends, went to bed at eleven o'clock every night, and I'd descend on our small living room (TV, coffee table, couch, Dad's easy chair) just before ten, right after *The Rockford Files*. That, and *Colombo*, were the only shows he made a point to watch. I'd sprawl on the couch and pretend to care about the *ABC Friday Night Movie* or *Dallas* until his patience was worn down by the stupidity on the screen and my determined silence, and he'd say, "Well, that's it for me. Twelve o'clock and the idiot box goes off, okay, Tom?" After that, all I had to do was get through the news at eleven before *Benny Hill* came on at 11:30.

Benny Hill wasn't actually funny, but humour wasn't why I watched it. I watched it because of the garter-belted, spiked-heeled, half-naked women, particularly the ones at the sped-up end of the show who alternatively chased/ were chased around and around, jiggling and wiggling but always just out of reach. The bra section in the Sears catalogue was okay, but the women on *Benny Hill* always wore sleek black stockings along with their crammed black bras and towering black heels. Besides, they actually *moved*, just like real women. Not that my own experience of real women extended much beyond one anxious-but-exhilarating afternoon of sweaty hand-holding with Jennifer Gordon at the roller rink (Phil Brown told her I liked her and she held out her hand to me as she sailed past) and the embarrassing-but-blissful single instance when, in Mrs. Newbury's art class, I turned my head at the exact, gloriously fortuitous moment she was leaning over my shoulder to get a better look at my macaroni-and-glitter-and-white-glue collage. Shockingly soft; comfortingly large; surprisingly warm: her right breast pressed against my unsuspecting cheek was an earthy epiphany, a two-second—tops—lesson in the universal language of flesh pressed to flesh.

Not as good as the actual fleshy thing but better, at least, than the laugh-track-goosed peepshow that was *Benny Hill*, were the women in the movies that came on after midnight on TFO, the French public television station. Because I was supposed to be in bed by the time they came on, I'd turn off the sound, which wasn't much of a sacrifice because I couldn't understand what most of the actors were saying anyway. These films were different from the movies you saw at the Capitol Theatre downtown or on the Movie of the Week on regular TV. There weren't car chases or explosions or murders to be solved or monsters to be defeated, the actors mostly simply hanging around looking either sad or nervous and talking—always talking, talking, talking. Sometimes you had to sit through half an hour or more of people doing nothing other than having conversations before you got what you stayed up for: a conversation that led to a kiss, a kiss that took a man and a woman into a bedroom, a bedroom where clothes would fall to the floor and the couple into bed, and, at last, a five- or ten-second vision of a bare breast or buttocks (hopefully a woman's). You'd be tired on Saturday morning, you'd tell yourself it wasn't worth it, but you'd do it again the following Friday night anyhow, just like you knew you would.

Saturday, collection day, Mrs. Wakowski's house was always my last stop. Mrs. Wakowski was an Auschwitz survivor, had a blue tattoo on her left forearm that was just a bunch of numbers with a letter *B* before them. She was only about ten years older than my mom, but looked like she could have been her mother. Her hair was black and streaked with silver, as if her head had been grazed on both sides by lightning, while her eyes were always red, as if she'd just been crying. Sometimes she'd be talking to you normally in her thick accent, and then, if she got too excited, would rub her hands together and start talking in Polish. Even if you did happen to speak Polish it would have been almost impossible to understand her, her tongue moving as quickly as her hands. Her husband, who'd survived the war in the Polish resistance and was a brick layer, had died a long, painful death from cerebral arteriosclerosis, and Mrs. Wakowski worked as a cook at a nursing home after she came to Canada until she slipped on some grease at work and one of her legs had to be amputated. Now she stayed at home and worried about her four teenaged daughters.

Born a year apart, the Wakowski girls were all tall with long legs and long straight brown hair except for the youngest, who was a redhead, and they were always laughing together or screaming at each other or riding away from home on their ten speeds with their rear ends raised in the air. They never spoke Polish and they rolled their eyes when their mother warned them in her heavy accent about wearing their jean shorts too short or going out with boys in cars or how during the war people didn't pay attention to who their friends were and look what happened to some of them. Mrs. Wakowski was the one who'd been in a Nazi death camp and who had only one leg and who'd sometimes get so agitated when she was speaking that spit would fly from her mouth, but it was her daughters who made me feel uncomfortable.

"Ah, it is Thomas," Mrs. Wakowski said as she let me in. No one, not even my mother or a teacher, ever called me Thomas.

"Collecting, Mrs. Wakowski."

"Yes, yes, you are coming for your money, yes. But first you sit down and we talk to each other a bit first, yes?"

Mrs. Wakowski was my last collection, so spending ten minutes talking to her wasn't so bad. Besides, as soon as I sat down at the plastic-covered kitchen table she would warm up a couple of cabbage rolls, and spread two pieces of dark brown bread with a thick layer of real butter for me. We ate Wonder Bread and Imperial margarine at home, but rye bread and butter were good too, especially for sopping up the rich tomato sauce from the cabbage rolls. Mrs. Wakowski would talk to me with her back turned while she hobbled around the kitchen on her single crutch to make up my plate.

"I hope everyone paid their debts to you today as they were supposed to do."

I'd told Mrs. Wakowski about the man who refused to pay me $5.58. He lived alone in a small shabby house he'd inherited from his mother and didn't go to work and always had a stubby brown beer bottle stuck in his hand and, depending on how early in the day he'd started drinking, was either aggressively friendly (badgering me about how many girlfriends I had or who my favourite Toronto Maple Leaf was even though I told him I was a Red Wing fan) or sneeringly silent, even when I explained to him that I couldn't punch a hole in my collection card unless he paid me for not just that week's delivery but the two weeks before that. When he still didn't say anything, just kept standing there on his rickety front porch slugging from his bottle of beer and looking like he was waiting for me to confess something, and I decided to pull the same silent treatment, he finally said, "Fuck off." I heard him, but I didn't understand. "You're not getting any of my fucking money you little piece of shit, so get the fuck off my fucking porch before I fucking throw you off." I hadn't told Mrs. Wakowski about all the *fucks*.

"I collected from everybody. I've just got you left and then I'm done."

"Ah hah! Always the business man," she said, putting my plate on the table before me. "You would like some milk too, yes?"

"No thanks, I'm not really thirsty." Even if I had been, milk was for staying healthy, not for slaking thirst; Hawaiian Punch or Freshie or, my new favourite, C Plus, was for when you wanted something cold and quick.

Mrs. Wakowksi poured me a large glass of milk anyway and placed it beside my plate before sitting down across the table. I ate and drank while she watched me. Mrs. Wakowski seemed to be always either cooking or reheating something or setting the table or doing the dishes or preserving vegetables like rhubarb from her garden, but I don't remember her ever eating anything herself. She said that when she was "in the camp" all they ever had was water and bread and turnips. You'd think that after that you'd want to eat everything, and a lot of it, but cup after cup of black tea was all I ever saw her put in her mouth.

I knew it wasn't good table manners, but I set down my fork and pulled my coiled notebook and pen out of my shirt pocket; I'd discovered that if I didn't immediately write down what I ate, I'd sometimes forget and then feel guilty for not remembering. Then I'd feel mad because making up what I ate wasn't the point.

"Now what is this you are doing?" Mrs. Wakowski said.

"I'm keeping a record of everything I eat."

"This is for school or something like?"

"No. I'm just doing it."

"And what is the reason for this?"

I put the notebook and pen back in my pocket and picked up my fork again, carved off a big piece of cabbage roll. Food, I'd discovered, tasted better once I'd recorded it. "I don't know," I lied. "Maybe just to see if I can do it."

This seemed to satisfy Mrs. Wakowski. She pursed her lips and nodded slowly as she continued to watch me eat. Mrs. Wakowski was a Catholic, the only one I knew—at school, some of the kids called them "Catlickers"—and even the walls of her kitchen were covered with crucifixes and framed pictures of the last supper and Jesus on the cross and a portrait of the Pope. "Do you mind if I ask you something?" I said. Being around Mrs. Wakowski, like being around Mom, made me think about God.

"How should I know until you ask me?"

"I mean, I don't know if you'd want to tell me. It'd be okay if you didn't."

"You ask me, I let you know if I want to tell you, yes?"

I'd finished the cabbage rolls and used what was left of the bread to soak up the leftover sauce, which also gave me a good reason not to look at Mrs. Wakowski while I asked her what I wanted to know. "We studied the Nazis in history class so I know what they did to the people they didn't like, like the Jews."

"Not just the Jews," she said, back straightening and fingers tightening around the handle on her crutch.

I didn't want Mrs. Wakowski to start shooting spit and talking in loud Polish, so, "Right, right, not just the Jews," I said. "All sorts of people, I know, they hated all sorts of people." She loosened the grip on her crutch but still sat erect, as if she were strapped to the back of the chair.

"What I wanted to ask," I said, my bread all gone now and my plate wiped clean, "was how do you still believe in God and everything"—I motioned to the walls around us—"when such bad things happened to you and everybody else?"

Even though I'd prayed when I was lost and my prayer had been answered and I was saved and everyone said it was a miracle, I still didn't know if I believed in God. Not really. That time in the sewer had been my one and only prayer session. Why would you pray if you didn't need something?

Mrs. Wakowski relaxed her posture, rested her thin arms on the Formica table. I couldn't help but stare at the blue line of numbers on her forearm. "Do *you* believe in God, Thomas?"

"My mother does," I said.

"This is good for your mother, but I ask about you."

"I wasn't brought up religious."

"Who said anything about religion? I ask you about God."

I looked up from Mrs. Wakowski's concentration camp number to the picture of Jesus wilting on the wooden cross, blood dripping from the nails in the middle of his hands and feet. "I asked you first," I said.

Mrs. Wakowski patted my hand resting on the kitchen table; used the edge of the table to push herself up without her crutch; winked at me. "We both know the bad things that happen to us, don't we, Thomas? You such a little boy and lost in the dark underneath the ground.

Yes, I remember that. And yet here we both are. You and I, we are survivors. We understand what this means, don't we? We keep going and we keep what was ours still ours. That is what we do. Yes?"

"I guess."

"Yes."

I drank the glass of milk I didn't ask for.

Polish Immigrant and Auschwitz Survivor Loves Canada—with Reservations

"People Are Very Nice, but Is Wrong They Don't Know How Fortunate They Are, Yes?"

DR. MENGELE POINTS left and the family portrait goes missing...

The Germans, understandably. Expertly functioning, very efficient machines that kill—that is what a German is. And not just kill—who enjoy killing. Not enough to extinguish mothers, fathers, children—entire families—the enemy had to be humiliated on the way to extinction, the final affront a mass grave for those deemed not human enough to deserve the dignity of their own hole in the earth. Leading up to that all-but-inevitable day, beatings for daring to not follow a command in German, a language you didn't understand; four-hour roll calls in snowstorms or cold rain or blazing heat, the prisoners malnourished and attired in little more than rags and wounding wooden shoes; beer-breathing creeping rapists in the barracks after midnight, pick your own lobster from the tank and gorge on the sweetest, freshest meat and throw away the empty shell when you're done.

But worse were certain Poles—the indigenous, German-appointed Kapos—who thought they'd be saved if they aided their Nazi masters, who ordered around their own and spied on their own and gleefully battered their own. For just the rumour of reprieve or an extra piece of bread or another few ounces of soup or—most shamefully—the opportunity to be a feared and venerated figure among their fellow prisoners, grateful slaves, eager traitors, honoured Judases. To suffer but to know that we are us and they are them was still to suffer, but when the orders and insults arrived in your own tongue, the suffering was worse. First the body, then the soul: the ancient order. Then the communal hole.

But not for Eva Wakowski. She was fortunate to be young and strong when she'd arrived at Auschwitz in the spring of '44 and was lucky enough to work in the kitchen and so could sometimes steal food, and because her Kapo would usually rather rape her than beat her, was still alive—if only barely—when the camp was liberated. Thank merciful God. Some lost their faith because of the Nazis. Both of Eva's parents, two grandmothers, and three of her four siblings were erased from her life. God was not going to be one more thing the Germans would take from her.

Liberation and slow normalization not so slowly followed by socialization, Soviet style, the Russians different from the Germans in being less methodical in their attempt to crush the Polish people, but equally determined. The history of Poland: waking up to foreigners in heavy boots standing on your throat telling you you're welcome. After years of her husband and her planning and saving and bribing and hoping,

Canada, at last, in 1967 of all years, a baby country's first-century birthday. Chatham, Ontario, wasn't much like Vancouver or Montreal or Toronto, the cities Eva and her husband had read about and looked at pictures of and talked about late into the night, but it was Canada, the true north strong and free, and not just in the anthem either. Work, school, religion, politics: do what you want just as long as you pay your taxes and don't bother anyone else. Freedom in fact and not just in slogan.

And, yes, after twelve years, truly her home and native land. Except why do people who have the right to vote not use it? People die for this right. Except why do people who are able to work not work? Hard work can bring a better life. Except why do young people who are given the chance to educate themselves and improve themselves and have a happier life than their parents not do so? Wisdom should not be wasted. Except why, if you wake up in the morning and there is food in the refrigerator and your children are healthy and there is a job for you to go to and a home to come back to and your own bed to sleep in at night and no one to tell you what to think or do the next day or the day after that, are people sad or slothful or drunkards or feel as if they somehow deserve more, that someone or something owes them happiness?

Who is this someone? What is this thing?

There was homework and then there was homework, and Julie and Angie at the kitchen table with their notebooks and textbooks and pens and pencils and calculators and empty cans of Coke implied the more onerous latter. Sometimes when they were studying in Julie's bedroom it was just so that Julie could close the door and warn me not to be loud and to keep anyone from bothering them. They might have been studying, but the music on the record player and the occasional eruption of laughter were obviously pedagogical priority number one. Physics, apparently, wasn't a subject to be tackled while Siouxsie and the Banshees screamed from the stereo speakers. A large, flat, shared work area and uninterrupted silence were what was necessary when attempting to crack the quantifiable rules of the universe, or at least prepare for tomorrow's test.

Except that I needed to get to the fridge. And for reasons not entirely clear, whenever Angie looked at me I felt like checking to see if my fly was up. It wasn't as if I thought she was hot. How could I? For one thing, she dressed weird—tonight, for instance, in aqua-green tights and a black leather mini-skirt and purple eyeliner and actual safety pins for earrings—for another, she was taller than a girl was supposed to be and didn't look anything like the Farrah Fawcett poster on my bedroom wall. She wasn't even as good-looking as Charlie's least attractive angel, Kate Jackson, who didn't have her own poster. Plus, she sometimes punctuated her sentences with a drawn out *Gawd* whenever she found a subject particularly distasteful. Ever since Mom left, God words were tacitly taboo.

I kept close to the kitchen wall, following as direct a route to the refrigerator as possible, Julie's impatience with my presence whenever any of her friends were around justification enough to become invisible. She looked up from her calculator and I knew she was tired;

she only tied her hair up when she wanted to disguise how dirty it was.

"Don't worry," I said, "I'll be in and out."

"Sounds like a guy I used to know," Angie said. She and Julie laughed. I didn't understand the joke, but I knew it was at my expense, so I gave back an all-purpose scrunched face and got my can of C Plus from the rear of the fridge where they were coldest. C Plus was my new favourite drink because it contained something called Sunkist Juice and I wanted to try out for the junior football team when I went to high school and I'd decided that I should start thinking about getting as strong as possible. It wasn't clear what exactly "Sunkist Juice" was, but it was copyrighted right on the can so I figured it had to be pretty special.

"Are you any good at science?" Angie said, pushing back from the table. She crossed one leg over the other, the toes of her raised right foot wiggling beneath the footing of her aqua green tights.

"He's in public school, Ang," Julie said, back being busy with her calculator. "And your problem with physics isn't with the help you're getting."

"*My* problem with physics is I don't give a shit about the magnitudes of the north and east components of the velocity of a plane flying at 300 miles per hour heading 30 degrees north of east," Angie said, standing up and stretching as she yawned, her raised arms pulling the bottom of her shirt just over her belly button. It was only a flash, and I could have been wrong, but it looked like it was pierced. My mouth felt dry. I popped the top of my C Plus and took a swig.

"No one does," Julie said. "Giving a shit doesn't have anything to do with it. Getting the right answer is all we've got to worry about."

Feigning an exaggerated pout, Angie sat back down like an admonished child. "Does she keep you in line all the time too?"

"She tries," I said. Although she actually didn't—not much, anyway.

Angie smiled. Because of what I'd said. I had made her smile.

"What grade are you in?" she said.

"Seven. I'm going to CCI in a year and half."

"Where your big sis will be top dog next year before she's off to U of T."

Without looking up from her calculator, "Not if she doesn't pass physics, she won't," Julie interjected. "Hint, hint."

"What about you?" I said to Angie.

"What about me?" she said, smiling again, but a different kind of smile this time. Her mouth wasn't any different—it was something about her eyes that made it another kind of smile altogether.

"Are you going to U of T too?" I liked saying "U of T" instead of the University of Toronto, the same way I liked saying "D-back' instead of "defensive back." When we played pick-up football at school and talked about what positions we wanted to play in high school, I'd say "D-back" and it sounded like I really knew what I was talking about.

"Uh, *yeah*," she said, rolling her eyes, the question so silly it barely warranted a reply. "I've been counting the days until I can leave Shat-ham, Ontario, since the moment I got here." I didn't like it that she called Chatham "Shat-ham"—she wasn't from here; only people who were born and raised in Chatham should have been allowed to say it sucked—but I took a sip of C Plus and nodded a couple of times anyway. I felt like I did that time in grade six when I pretended I wasn't Timmy Grainger's friend anymore because Jeff Hartman said Timmy's dad had left his mom for another guy. I didn't care about what his dad had or hadn't done—Timmy was a good ball-hockey goalie and he always traded sandwiches with me whenever he had peanut butter and jam and I had ham—but I avoided him like everybody else. He moved to Sarnia with his mom and two sisters the next year.

"I'm going to the bathroom," Julie said, standing up from the kitchen table. "When I get back, you decide if you want to study or if you want to talk to my brother all night."

When we heard the bathroom door close, "Busted," Angie said, leaning back in her chair, her hands clasped behind her head.

"Busted," I said, and we both laughed.

Young Woman Finds Ontological Comfort in New Pair of Pants

"When I Look at Them, They Remind Me of Who I Am"

EVERYWHERE SHE WENT her new pants went with her.

Impossible to buy them anywhere in Chatham the way she wanted them—tapered and tight at the bottom, no leftover hippie flares for her, thank you, New Wave the new age all the way—her mother used the picture she'd provided of Elvis Costello to fashion a pretty good knock-off. If not by geography, then at least by the circumference of her pant cuffs, was she an au courant Torontonian again. Well, Etobicokian, anyway. Not that anyone here needed to know that. As far as her classmates were concerned, she was as Toronto as Maple Leaf Gardens and the CN Tower, places they'd seen, if not in person, then at least on TV.

Her new pants—black and sleek and sharp—went with her on the ride to school, her father dropping her off on his way to work at Rockwell's head office, his transfer there the reason they'd had to move. Her father didn't know how long he'd be needed to "sort things out down there," so they hadn't sold their house in Etobicoke, which was a solace. She missed knowing that the Royal York subway station that could transport her downtown was a four-minute walk away. She missed her big room with the big window overlooking the big, thickly treed backyard. She missed their swimming pool. Her favorite aquatic occupation wasn't swimming, but lying out on the hot, pleasantly gritty cement near the deep end reading a paperback and getting a good sweat and an incidental tan and knowing that if she wanted to be in the water, she could, the water was always there. They didn't have a pool in Chatham.

Her new pants went with her while she drifted dulled through her classes—smart enough to not have to try too hard and nothing ever interesting enough to make her attempt to be smarter. But that was all right. She'd get to where she wanted to go and do what she wanted to do, eighty percent average and Ontario Scholar or not. People like her always found a way. People like Julie, her best and only friend here, have to make themselves up, which is hard work and oftentimes makes you sad a lot before you're made even a little bit happy and sometimes doesn't even work. Her new pants reminded her that she already was who she was supposed to be; that all she needed was closer proximity to where she didn't have to try so much.

Inside your head is no place to figure things out. An old building in an old city; Patti Smith's latest album; a new pair of pants: look, listen, feel. *Know.*

Feb. 18:

1 (one) bowl of Cheerios (with two tablespoons of sugar)
2 (two) glasses of Tang

1 (one) tuna sandwich (with lettuce and tomato and mayonnaise and onion in tuna)
1 (one) apple (ate only half)
3 (three) Dad's Oatmeal Cookies (with raisins)

2 (two) servings of Hamburger Helper
2 (two) pieces of bread and margarine
2 (two) glasses of milk
3 (three) green beans
1 (one) bowl of Neapolitan ice-cream (mostly chocolate) with most of a can of pineapple chunks on top

Also: 3 (three) cans of C Plus, 1 (one) Oh Henry chocolate bar, 1 (one) bag of barbequed Fritos, 1 (one) glass of water before bed

Chapter Four

Paul Lynde was our Oscar Wilde, *Hollywood Squares* our Algonquin round table. Because I didn't live near the school anymore, Dale and I didn't live down the street from each other anymore either or watch our favourite shows at one or the other's house. The morning after whatever we'd watched on TV the night before, however, standing around on the blacktop at school with our hands in our coat pockets waiting for the bell to ring and to be let inside, we'd run down what had made the grade and what hadn't. Our tastes were catholic yet discriminating.

First up on the critical agenda, *WKRP in Cincinnati*:

"It was all right," Dale said.

"It was okay."

We waited for the bell and watched our breath. When we were younger and it was cold outside, sometimes we'd goof around with Popeye cigarettes and pretend we were smoking. Now we were old enough to know people who brought the real thing to school, Scott Corson flashing a stolen pack of his mother's *Player's Lights* at the rear of the schoolyard, way back by the soccer field and the big trees and away from the teacher on yard duty.

"Did you see Bailey wearing those boots though?" he said.

"Oh, man."

"I know."

"Oh, man, those brown leather boots. They were, like, up to her knees almost."

"I know."

"Oh, man."

Even though Dale's dad was a lawyer who had an office downtown with his name stencilled across its frosted glass door and his family had an in-ground swimming pool and a two-car garage and got the *TV Guide* delivered right to their house, Dale didn't make you feel funny when you were around him like, say, Paul Hopkins whose dad was an executive at Ontario Hydro and who didn't sip beer at home like my dad but who made his drinks in a blender with fruit and bottles of clear liquor and ice cubes that came from an ice-making machine built right into the fridge. Paul always wore brightly coloured shirts with alligator insignias and the collars turned up, and although he never teased you for having North Star running shoes purchased from K-Mart instead of leather Nikes, when you passed him in the hallway he never seemed to notice you, and if he was smiling, it was because it looked like he knew something that you didn't and never would.

"Bailey totally blows Loni Anderson away," Dale said.

"I know. Totally."

Loni Anderson had big blonde hair and bigger breasts and everybody thought she was so hot, but Dale and I liked tall, skinny, brown-haired Bailey better. Loni Anderson just sat there covered in make-up waiting for someone to make a joke about her tits. Bailey was smarter than everybody else on the show except maybe her boss,

Andy, and dressed in men's suit jackets and jeans, which made what was underneath even sexier because you couldn't see everything that was there. It was like the best horror movies: when you didn't see the monster until the end, your mind made up its own monster. And nothing anyone could come up with was ever as scary as what was in your head.

"Did you watch *The White Shadow*?" I said.

Dale shook his head, kicked a hockey-puck-sized piece of ice across the frozen pavement. *The White Shadow* came on at 9:30 and Dale's TV time was limited on school nights and his bedtime non-negotiable. His father wasn't just a lawyer—a couple of other kids' dads wore suits to work and could get you out of a traffic ticket or would happily sue somebody on a commision basis because somebody said they'd do something for you but ended up not doing it—but, in spite of having MS and recently being relegated to a wheelchair, Dale's dad was who Chatham-Kent's member of parliament called when he claimed to have been libelled by the New Democrat candidate during his recent re-election, and who Pritchard Industries kept on retainer because they were always in trouble for allegedly polluting the Thames River. Dale didn't talk about his dad's disease, but I knew he thought about it. How couldn't he? When Mom left us, Julie and Dad and I didn't say much about it to one another. But no one didn't think about it. How could we not?

Dale's mother was almost as busy as his father, heading up one local charity or another, and his sister was a senior at CCI and the All-Ontario 1500 meter champion who was going to Cornell University next year on a track-and-field scholarship. Dale and his sister were honour students and neither one of them was allowed to be just like everybody else. Even though we weren't even in high school, his mother typed up all of Dale's projects for school. I knew he liked *The White Shadow* as much as I did—there wasn't any teacher at our school as cool as Coach Reeves, just like there weren't any students as funny as the Sweathogs on *Welcome Back, Kotter*—so I didn't want him to feel too bad about missing out.

"It was all right," I said, shrugging.

"What happened?" Dale kicked another piece of ice, but this time it broke in two, skittered this way and that.

"The coach booted Gomez off the team because his grades were crappy, so then he started hanging around with his old street gang again."

"Oh yeah?"

"Yeah."

Dale was looking at his boots. "Then what?"

"Oh, you know: the coach goes off and finds him and talks him into coming back and then everything's the same again." I'd tried to make it sound as boring as possible, but it was actually a pretty good episode. Maybe CCI would be like the high school on *The White Shadow*. There was still time for life to be like TV.

The bell rang, recess was over.

"Math," I said.

"Yeah," Dale said.

Some kids back by the soccer field were still throwing snowballs at each other. The teacher on yard duty blew her whistle; put her hands on her hips and blew the whistle again, louder.

"Five minutes to Mr. Mole," I said. Mr Cole, our math teacher, did look a little like a mole—was short with shaggy brown hair and a slight overbite—but we called him Mr. Mole mainly because it rhymed with his real name. Mrs. Rankin, the art teacher, definitely didn't resemble plankton. We stomped the slush off our boots on the large black rubber mat just inside the doors like we'd been told.

"Would anyone care to venture an educated guess?" I said in my best Mr. Mole voice. It was what Mr. Cole said when he wanted someone to answer a math question he'd written on the board.

Dale laughed. It wasn't new, but it was still a good one.

I did it again—"Would anyone care to venture an educated guess?"—but this time with eyes stretched open as wide as I could, just like Mr. Cole did when he surveyed the classroom for a volunteer.

"Oh, man," Dale said, laughing harder now.

We went to our lockers to take off our coats and get our books. Once class started, it wasn't so easy to laugh.

Dale's family was okay, but the best part about staying over the occasional Saturday night was that they weren't around much. His dad sometimes didn't come home from his office until nine or ten o'clock at night—even on weekends—and his mother was out a lot, too, at meetings or fundraisers or charity auctions. Even his sister was always either going for a run or cocooned in her room studying. Dale's house had central air-conditioning, the first house I'd ever been in that did, and during the hottest days of summer the house was so cold everyone would wear sweaters. When you stepped back outside it felt as if the seasons had changed.

It wasn't as if Dale was neglected—there was usually somebody home, at least for awhile, and there was always a meal waiting for him at dinnertime, even if it had to be reheated in the oven—but usually we got to eat in front of the television in their den and walk to the variety store after dinner if we felt like it and make prank phone calls without fear of anyone overhearing. We'd pick a name at random from the phonebook and have it all planned out—after they'd answer, one of us would say in our best Steve Martin voice, "Well, excuuuuse me!"—but we'd always chicken out and hang up when we heard the other person's voice. We'd still laugh, though, just as much as if we'd actually gone through with it. If we hadn't, it would have meant we weren't having fun.

There wasn't much I missed once we moved downtown after Mom moved out. I couldn't walk to school anymore and there weren't as many kids to play with, but the one thing I really missed was something I didn't even know existed until it was gone. I was staying over at Dale's house one Saturday night, and it was springtime and we were walking home from a ball-hockey game a few streets over. We were tired and not talking much and Dale was dragging his stick behind him, something you weren't supposed to do because it wore down the blade. It wasn't dark yet, but the street lights were starting to flicker and I could smell every front yard and backyard in the subdivision along with the cooling evening earth underneath and it was more than just the smell of grass and dirt. It smelled like… life. I wanted to say something to Dale, to ask him if he smelled it too, but I knew he wouldn't know what I was talking about, would probably just think I was weird. He lived there—how could he know what he was missing? You had to go away to know where you'd been.

Sleepovers at Dale's house aside, my only connection to the neighbourhood that had once been home was through the eight-foot-high metal fence that surrounded the schoolyard. Sometimes at recess, when the weather was nice, if there wasn't a ball-hockey game going on or no one felt like playing hotbox, I'd stand there at the fence at the rear of the schoolyard and look at the rows of identical houses with their fluorescent-green lawns—corners as sharp and square as the jaw of Sgt. Rock, the freedom-fighting hero of my favourite comic book, the suburban perfume of freshly cut grass making my nose twitch like the rabbits at the pet store downtown before it became the Cornerstone Church.

Our house had been one subdivision over from the school, so the people, if not the houses, were different from the ones I'd known. But I recognized them all anyway. There was the hunched-over old woman working in her front garden, her equally elderly, wheelchair-sentenced husband helping out as best he could, passing her the hand shovel when she needed it, both of them equally expert at pretending that it somehow really mattered. There were the men who did shift work and so were home during the day, passing the time until it was the hour to change into their work clothes again, washing their cars in their driveways or weed-whacking the manicured edges of their lawns. There were the women raising the only flag they knew to salute, hanging the family's flapping laundry on the backyard clothesline. There were the dogs on chains barking at passing cars going by too slow or too fast. There were abandoned bicycles and oversized plastic baseball bats and purple hula hoops. There were the kids walking home from school for lunch, the local radio station the only clock they needed: sitting down to their fish sticks halfway though the local and then the world news (12:07); soaking up what was left of the ketchup on their plates with the last french fries by the end of the sports (12:12); two scoops of ice cream or a jiggling helping of green Jell-O while the farm report wrapped up (12:20); and with just enough time left over to get your coat back on and get out the door as the first funereal strains of the organ that announced "In Memoriam" floated through the kitchen.

Once, when we were waiting for my dad to pick me up from Dale's—his parents had two cars plus a special van for his father's wheelchair, but they always seemed to be busy so my dad had to come and get me on Sunday morning if I stayed over—we were tossing a football on the street in front of his house and I threw a duck that flew over his head. *Whatever.* I was going to play defensive back, not quarterback, when I got to high school. Dale's dad had played football at Queen's University, and Dale used to say how he was going to have an advantage when he tried out for wide receiver because his dad had taught him what slant and hook and fly routes were when they played catch. *Used* to play catch.

The ball rolled to a stop alongside a sewer grate. Dale picked it up and tossed it back.

"What was it like when you were down there?" he said.

"Where?" I knew what he wanted to know, but I'd learned that part of the game was to act surprised.

"When you got lost when you were a kid," he said. "Down there." He caught my pass—not too hard, not too soft, right between the numbers.

"How did you know about it?" I said.

Dale would have been too young to read about it in the newspaper or pay attention to the radio when it happened, but he wouldn't have had to since someone, at some point, would have told him. He shrugged and turned the ball around in his passing hand so that his fingers wouldn't be on the laces when he threw it, a sure-fire recipe for a wobbler. He tossed the ball. I caught it.

My hands were bigger than Dale's, so I could hold the football more easily, and I never had to look where the laces were, my fingers found their grip on their own, but I looked at the ball and pretended to be thinking. It was important that I appear to be having a hard time saying what I wanted to say. Eventually, "You know how sometimes something happens that you didn't know was going to happen—because there was no way anybody could ever know it was going to happen—and then it happens anyway?" I knew that Dale would think about his dad getting sick. I threw the ball so that he wouldn't be able to say more than *Yeah*.

"Yeah," he said, tossing the football back.

I caught the ball and studied it. A passing car gave him time to look at me looking at the ball.

"At first it was like it was a mistake, like it can't be right." I threw another perfect spiral. "Then I was pissed off like you wouldn't believe."

"At who?"

"I don't know. I don't remember. I just remember being pissed off." I caught the ball and tossed it back. Just as it reached Dale, "Not long after that," I said—"a bit, but not too long after—it was… it was just what it was."

Dale nodded like he knew what I was talking about, held onto the ball.

"I mean," I said, "it didn't make any more sense than it did before. But there wasn't anybody I could yell at, and it looked like no one was going to come along and make it all alright, so…"

Dale was staring at the ball in his hands, tossing it up and down a couple of inches in the air. Without looking up, "So... so what?" he said.

"So I started really looking for a way out," I said. "I mean, who wants to be stuck in the dark?"

Former Star Athlete and Well-Known Chatham Lawyer Diagnosed with Multiple Sclerosis

"This Isn't What I Wanted; This Shouldn't Have Happened to Me"

HE'D DONE WHAT he was supposed to do. More than that—he'd done everything right. Righter than right: parent-pleasing report cards, a harvest of A+s every June; the captain of nearly every team he excelled on; every teacher and friend's father or mother happy to know that their son or daughter was a friend of his; and later, law school and a beautiful wife and two beautiful children and a very successful hometown practice and one of those fortunate people who knows that they're fortunate, is happy to assist as a Rotarian and a Big Brother those unluckily less so.

Then one day, when he was thirty-four years old, he woke up and his fingers felt funny. Didn't hurt, exactly—tingly more than truly painful, more like they'd fallen asleep—and it wasn't even all over, was only in the fingertips, but still... Funny, he thought, slowly opening, closing, both fists. That's funny, he thought.

But tremors and difficulty staying upright without a cane and chronic fatigue and slurred speech and a failing memory and difficulty concentrating and blurry sight in one eye couldn't be called funny. When he'd had trouble holding a pen one morning while writing a cheque for his daughter's piano lessons, he'd attributed it to one too many Jamesons the evening before or perhaps something he hadn't noticed he'd done golfing, but his wife had insisted he go see the doctor, so he went and saw him—was tested and waited and worried and tested and waited and worried some more—and was eventually told that he was suffering from an inflammatory disease called encephalomyelitis edisseminata or, as it's commonly known, multiple sclerosis, which damages the insulating covers of nerve cells in the brain and spinal cord.

"You're telling me I have MS?" he said.

"I'm afraid so," the doctor said.

You're afraid, he thought.

The doctor monologued on about how, like approximately one hundred thousand other Canadians, he wasn't alone, that there were very active support groups in place throughout Kent County, and that there had been significant progress made in recent years with new kinds of treatment and medication to help stem the effects of the disease—if not cure it; there is no cure as of yet—and that it's very important to remember that multiple sclerosis is not a death sentence, that the average sufferer lives only approximately ten years fewer than non-sufferers.

So I can look forward to a long, unhealthy life, he wanted to say. Didn't, of course. His parents had taught him, and he had impressed upon his own children, the obligation we all have to be cheerful—civilized society's primary social lubricant. And if certain situations don't allow for cheerfulness—and if he ever deserved a mulligan, this was one of those situations—then at least one could attempt not to make things worse, both for oneself and for others. He thanked the doctor and shook his hand and even remembered to make a follow-up appointment with his secretary on the way out.

Tremors and difficulty staying upright without a cane and chronic fatigue and slurred speech and a failing memory and difficulty concentrating and blurry sight in one eye battered his body, but almost—almost—as bad was the fact that at least once a day, though often more, he was assaulted by the same stabbing thought: I don't deserve this. What did I do to deserve this? Why is this happening to *me*? This isn't me. This isn't who I am.

He lived for many more years. He tried to be cheerful.

William Street wasn't made for playing catch or road hockey—William Street was for downtown Chatham traffic, such as it was—so when we'd moved from the suburbs after Mom left us, Tecumseh Park or the playground at nearby Victoria Park Elementary School was where you went to throw or bounce or shoot or kick (in spite of the cranky old man who lived next door to the latter and who called the police on us not once but twice, and who was almost as cranky as he was as a *Chatham Daily News* subscriber). It was an adjustment—grass was usually better than cement, and not having to scream "Car!" at any moment was a nice change, although having your own asphalt playground at the end of your driveway rivalled either of those advantages—but it wasn't long before the best possible place to get a game of hotbox going wasn't priority number one. Sports wasn't a bunch of kids making up a game of something out of nothing on an endless August afternoon anymore; sports were what were going to happen when I got to high school, CCI green and white and Friday night's game in Saturday's *Chatham Daily News* and *ra ra siss boom ba* cheerleaders, just like on TV. It was like how one day you begged your mom to buy you the "Hang In There, Baby" poster, the one with the kitten hanging onto a tree branch, and then another day you ripped it down from your bedroom wall and crumpled it up and jammed it into the wastebasket underneath the kitchen sink because how lame is it to have a poster of a kitten on your wall? *Poof* and who you were isn't who you are anymore, now you see you, now you don't.

Now what I liked to do best was lock my bedroom door and put on a record and lie on my bed and eat black licorice and read Allen Spragget's *Worlds of the Unexplained* books, where you got the real story on ESP and Atlantis and people who could talk to the dead. I'd taken his *The Case for Immortality* out of the library too, but had stopped reading it about a quarter of the way through because it sounded too much like the la-dee-da-heaven-and-angels-and-celestial-rainbows stuff that Mom used to talk about when she'd first joined the Cornerstone. I didn't know if God existed or not, but I was pretty sure that if He did, you didn't find out by being blithely reassured that everything is going to work out fine because that's just the kind of guy God is. Whoever or whatever God was or wasn't, there had to be more to it than that.

Licorice was the kind of food it was easy to forget to write down. Breakfast, lunch, and dinner were all instant reminders to get everything recorded on the page, to not exclude a single piece of bread, an extra glass of milk, the second pork chop that technically belonged to Julie but which she forfeited by taking Angie's phone call during dinner and not coming back until we were eating dessert. A few pieces of candy in the evening, however, or a can of pop on the way home from delivering the newspaper, were harder to remember, and, to be honest, a pain to record sometimes even when I didn't forget, when all I wanted to do was just enjoy my Oh Henry! bar or can of C Plus. Sometimes I just wanted to do something without having to say that I'd done it.

But if I ate or drank and delayed logging in whatever it was, I wouldn't feel right, could ignore the feeling that I'd done something wrong—or, rather, hadn't done what I was supposed to do—for only so long before my throat felt tight and my forehead felt hot and I couldn't help but think about all of the rivers and oceans and lakes bubbling to a boil when the sun exploded one day, just like Mr. Bennett said, and of all of the poor seals and dolphins and whales and everything else that wouldn't know why the only world they'd ever known was suddenly a seething hell. I'd write down what I was supposed to write down and shut my notebook and feel okay again.

Forty days was coming up, Lent would soon be over, but I didn't feel like stopping. I made a mental note to buy another notebook. Maybe more than one.

Man Grows Old and Cranky
"I Knew it Happened to Everyone, but Somehow I Thought in My Case There Might Be an Exception"

HE ALWAYS SEEMED to be falling down. And it wasn't as if he wasn't watching where he was going.

Every time you step outside your front door a catastrophe creeping to happen. Your belly goes soft, your arteries grow hard, you wonder where the hell you put your reading glasses because without them you can't even decipher the heating instructions on a TV dinner. An afternoon at the dentist as inescapable as a pit in an unpitted olive. Watery eyes a certainty whenever it's windy outside. Somebody on television says "torpedo" and you think they said "tuxedo" and you feel like a fool. If the weather is cold and damp, struggling with the plastic cap on a bottle of aspirin to get relief from crooked arthritic fingers that have such difficulty with, oh, for instance, unscrewing the cap off a bottle of aspirin.

And the enlightenment you waited and waited for—stupid youth's long, empty sputter—finally comes, and comes down to this: eating, shitting, sleeping, fucking, repeat, all of which any barnyard animal could tell you if unlucky enough to know how to talk. Because besides bodily wastes, that's the other thing human beings are good at making: words, words, words. And nine times out of ten, more often than not, just about as meaningful as a coiled pile of steaming crap. Words, words, words; turds, turds, turds. The gentle wisdom of the golden years thus.

Here's another geriatric gift for you: you miss every third word, the light's bleeding out of your eyes, you rarely leave the house anymore, and yet everything and everyone somehow manages to aggravate you all of the godamn time anyway. The kids playing road hockey outside your bedroom window solely existing to scream you awake from your afternoon nap. Downtown, no one has any manners anymore, it's always you who has to be the one to move out of the way on the too narrow sidewalk, never anyone else, everyone just rude, there's no other word for it. At the grocery store or Canadian Tire, people won't wait their turn in line, are always trying to butt ahead, as if two more minutes added to their empty lives will make them any fuller. Even other old people are an annoyance—your brother on the phone long distance, your neighbour down the street raking his leaves, the woman who works the cash at the pharmacy—all of them with *their* aches, *their* complaints, *their* diseases and minor surgeries and daily bodily discontents. Wailing infants to go with your afternoon tea and cruller at Tim Horton's; sirening mothers and fathers eager to share their sage parental counsel with the world ("Don't slurp that, Gordon!" "Put that back where you found it, Elizabeth!" "Don't put that in your mouth, Jimmy!"); human husks wheezing, shuffling, complaining: from crawling until falling, all of the colours of the rich human rainbow.

Before—before he was old—he'd always had a dog. Now he carried a Ziploc baggie of dog treats in his coat pocket wherever he went. He liked to feed dogs tied up outside of stores while their masters shopped inside. He'd always let the dog smell his hand first, then give them a treat or two. "It's okay," he'd say. "They'll be back soon. Don't worry, no one has forgotten about you."

"Lawyers," Dad said, resting the newspaper on his lap. He said it like the word tasted bad, like something sour. He liked to ease back in his recliner in the living room after dinner and read the paper with the evening news on the

TV. It felt kind of cool to see him doing something that I had had something to do with, no matter how small.

He lifted the paper. "Any chance to make a problem where there isn't one and make a buck off it, there they are, like flies on…" When he was home Dad rarely wore anything other than a white T-shirt underneath his black leather vest, and once he'd moved from the dinner table to the recliner with that day's *Chatham Daily News*, he put the elastic band from his pony tail in his pocket and looked most like the biker guy he wasn't. Sometimes I wished he didn't just look like a tough guy.

He flicked that day's front-page headline—ONTARIO HERITAGE FOUNDATION OFFERS $150,000 TO HELP SAVE HARRISON HALL—with his finger. It made a surprisingly loud popping sound, louder than you'd imagine a finger and a piece of newspaper would make. "Get a life," he said.

"Who?" I said. "Who should get a life?"

"These Save-Old-City-Hall idiots. None of them has anything better to do than stick their noses in other people's business. Probably think they're real big shots because they get their names in the newspaper."

I knew that Mr. Brown was part of the committee that had convinced the Ontario Heritage Foundation to come up with the money to incorporate Harrison Hall into the downtown development, but I also knew that he wasn't trying to do anything but keep Harrison Hall from being bulldozed. I didn't mention Mr. Brown or Harrison Hall to Dad. I knew that what he cared most about was the new mall bringing more shoppers downtown and, hopefully, more customers into his shop. He did okay—we weren't poor, weren't like some of the people on my paper route who collected welfare and bought their furniture at the Salvation Army—but everything we owned was either old or didn't work the way it was supposed to or both, like our television, the same one with lousy sound we'd had since Mom lived with us. When you wanted to change the channel on Dale's TV you just pushed a button on the changer; at our house, somebody had to get up and do it for themselves. It wasn't just inconvenient. It was starting to become embarrassing.

The news anchor said something about gorilla warfare and I looked at the TV screen expecting images of battling apes, but it just ended up being a story about civil war in some country in Central America. I didn't know why anyone watched the news—they never showed anything really interesting, like war-mad monkeys or killer sharks or the Bermuda Triangle. Dad must have been thinking the same thing, because he picked his newspaper back up and rattled the pages and began reading again, this time the classifieds. He wasn't ready to hire a real estate agent yet, but until he could put together enough money for a down payment on his own place he'd peruse the paper for buildings for sale. Saving up for the down payment was going slower than expected—right-now necessities had a way of getting in the way of one-day accumulation—but he said that once the new mall was built he'd double, maybe triple his income, and that it wouldn't be long until he owned not just his own business, but his own property as well.

Now the newscaster was talking about Iran and the revolution going on there and how university students were among the Ayatollah's most fanatical, violent supporters. We both looked at the TV and saw cars burning in the streets and piles of burning books and crowds of men with long black beards dressed in long white robes pumping their fists in the air and loudly chanting *Death to the USA!* I knew that wherever Julie ended up going to university, it wouldn't be like that, but I was still glad I only was entering grade eight next year. The news ended with a group of men screaming and stamping their feet standing around a burning American flag. They looked like hometown football fans enraged with the referee for blowing the call that cost their team the game.

"What do they want?" I said.

I could tell Dad was thinking because he kept running his fingers through his handlebar moustache while he watched a commercial for pantyhose, the ones that came in a plastic container that looked like an egg. They were the same kind that Mom used to buy. She used to give me the containers when she was done with them. Put enough of them together and you had a pretty good blockade for your G.I. Joe army.

"They're jealous of what we've got over here," he said. "And if they can't have what we have, they don't want anyone else to have it either."

"What are they jealous of?" I said. Other than having to wear white dresses and identical beards, they looked okay to me. At least they weren't starving like those poor skinny kids with flies on them in Africa that you'd see on UNICEF commercials on late night TV. Dad looked at me like I'd just sworn.

"Freedom," he barked. "Freedom to think what you want and do what you want and go where you want and with whoever you want to go there with."

Like Mom, I thought, but didn't say it. Instead, I nodded like I knew what he'd meant all along, like I just wanted to hear him say it aloud. Satisfied that I'd finally understood the meaning of freedom, he turned his attention back to the television. Big Boy restaurant was having a special on hamburgers: buy one of their world famous Big Boy Burgers and get a second delicious, world famous Big Boy Burger for half price. What a rip off, I thought. Chatham didn't have a Big Boy Restaurant. As usual, the US had all of the good stuff. You never knew for sure, though. Maybe we'd get our own Big Boy one day when the mall opened up. It never hurt to hope.

Chapter Five

February was the short one, the month that got to the next one the quickest, which worked out well because March Break was in the middle which meant it was only a few weeks away from nine straight days without school. Kids whose parents had lots of money talked about their condos in Florida or how they were going to visit the Science Centre or the zoo in Toronto. I liked to think about how for nearly a week and a half I'd be able to sleep in and stay up late and my evenings would be homework-free and whatever I wanted them to be. All I had to do was deliver my newspapers and collect on Saturdays and my time was mine.

What Julie did with her week off depended on Dad saying yes to her and Angie's planned trip to Toronto. Which was weird because he'd already said no. Said it so often, he didn't even bother to say it anymore, would just stare at his newspaper or clear his throat or walk out of the room anytime she brought it up. She brought it up a lot. Especially now that it would soon be March.

"So just don't tell him."

"Angie, I can't just… *go*. It's not like he wouldn't notice."

"Fine. Tell him you're staying with my brother and his girlfriend."

"I already tried, you know that."

"Tell him something else then. *Gawd*. Whatever."

I wasn't trying to listen. I was in my bedroom with the door closed, and Julie and Angie were in her bedroom with the door closed, but the record they'd been playing had finished and no one had flipped it over or put on another one. I couldn't help hearing what I wasn't supposed to. Sometimes knowing things was like that.

Neither of them said anything, and there wasn't any music. Ordinarily Julie and Angie were either talking or laughing or playing one of Angie's weird records, so it sounded strange. It sounded loud. Eventually, in a small voice, "You should probably just start making plans to go without me," Julie said.

"I don't want to go without you. One of the reasons I want to go is to show you some of the places I told you about. Like Larry's Hideaway and The Turning Point and the Record Peddler and all the bookstores on Queen Street. And have you meet Tim and his crazy brother and Candace and all the rest of those guys." I could tell Angie wasn't just saying she wanted Julie to go to Toronto to be polite because she never usually said things like "those guys."

"Well," Julie said "they'll all still be there when I'm at UofT. *If* I get in."

Like the rest of us, Angie knew she was expected at times like these to assure Julie that of course she'd be accepted into UofT, but, instead, "That's not until a year from this September."

"I know when it is."

"But I don't want to wait that long," Angie said.

"Neither do I, but even if I could get permission, it's still…"

"Still what?"

96

"You know. I don't want it to seem it to seem like… "

"Like what?"

"Like, I don't know, that I'm being set up just so…"

Angie laughed. "That's *exactly* what's happening."

"I know, but…" Then Julie laughed and Angie laughed too.

"Look, I told you," Angie said. "It'll just be a bunch of very cool people hanging out having a good time—we're going to see some amazing bands, you're going to *love* The Diodes—and then, you know, boys will be boys and girls will be girls."

It was quiet again until Angie said, "What? What is it?"

"I just wish…"

"You weren't a virgin. I know. And if I'd grown up here like you had, I'd still be one too. Between the hay-seeds and the mouth-breathers, I'd probably be wearing a frigging chastity belt." They both laughed. "But by the time we're back home-sweet-home in Shat-ham, you won't be a virgin anymore and it won't be anything you have to think about ever again. Or that we'll have to talk about ever again."

Julie was going to Toronto to *do it*. If she went to Toronto without Dad's permission, he'd be furious. If he knew why she was going, he'd be… I didn't know what came after *furious*, and I didn't want to find out.

I could hear someone taking the record off the turn-table and putting it back in its sleeve. Then music, then I couldn't hear any more talking.

Julie in trouble, or in danger of being in trouble, wasn't necessarily a bad thing. I wouldn't have wanted anything *too* serious to happen to her—getting picked up by the police, say, or being expelled from school—but a little drama around the house was worth a degree of hassle on her end. It was exciting when bad things happened to other people. When Scott Bolland and Jim Tate slunk into art class puffy-eyed and all-over shaky after being sent to Vice Principal French's office for fighting during recess, everyone, including Mrs. Newbury, pretended her talk about the Group of Seven was more interesting than the strapping they'd both received. They both kept their hands hidden underneath their desks for the rest of the class, but we all knew they'd been tanned red from Mr. French's strap and we couldn't help being secretly thrilled, the mystery of playground horseplay stigmata.

My newspaper bag was almost empty, all I had left was the part of the job I liked the least. The final stops on my route were dead-ended by the railroad crossing near the cemetery, five small tar-paper-covered homes that weren't much bigger than the shed in Dale's parents' backyard. As long as it wasn't snowing or raining, the surprisingly large number of people who lived inside always seemed to be sitting outside on their wooden front porch or in torn lawn chairs in their front yards, not saying or doing much, or else doing things like taking turns giving each other haircuts or letting a pet rabbit run around the lawn on a ball-of-string leash. Chatham's east end was about half white people, half black people, but the dead end of Stanley Street was all white, and although the different families had different last names you couldn't help but wonder whether they were all related somehow, had settled together near the cemetery as part of some strange new, or really, really old religion.

It was snowing and cold, and thankfully there was no one around, so I didn't have to pretend not to look at a porch overflowing with faces looking back at me as I walked up to the house with the newspaper. One, two, three, four, and one more house to go and I was done and then home and warm socks and dinner and *Charlie's Angels* at nine o'clock after writing down what I ate and maybe doing my English homework. The last house on my route, the one right next to the train tracks, wasn't only not much bigger than a shed, it *was* a shed, albeit with a couple of greasy windows and a smokestack for the wood stove inside. Its sole occupant was a fat woman named Bertha who pulled a handmade wooden cart with two bicycle tires for wheels behind an old bike and scavenged other people's garbage for the leaky garden hoses and old Styrofoam coolers and chipped jam jars that filled her yard. The property was large enough that she not only had enough room for all of her garbage-day collectibles, but also a chicken coop at its rear. If she'd had any other neighbours someone would have probably forced her to get rid of it, but because it was Bertha who sold everyone on Stanley Street their eggs, no one ever did.

I stuffed Bertha's newspaper inside her front door— none of the houses on the street had mailboxes—and was officially done for the day, except I couldn't ignore the sound of a clucking chicken that wouldn't shut up. Apart from eating them, I didn't have much experience with chickens, but this one sounded like a cartoon chicken, its non-stop *Bawk! Bawk! Bawk! Bawk!* sounding funny— Bugs Bunny, Saturday-morning-cartoon funny. I looked to make sure Bertha wasn't around and saw that her bicycle and cart were gone and walked to the rear of her property where the sound was coming from.

A dead chicken was lying on the frozen ground in front of the old wood-and-wire coop. Beside it hopped the hysterical chicken I'd heard making so much noise. I could see a few other chickens inside the coop, apparently content to stay warm and peck at their food or stare through the wire mesh at the overcast afternoon nothing, the *Bawk! Bawk! Bawk! Bawk!* chicken the only one who seemed to care about their fallen friend. The snow was slowly covering the dead chicken in a thin white blanket, but there was nothing the other chicken could do about it except hop up and down and cluck and cry.

If Julie ran off to Toronto with Angie, I didn't know how bad it would be for her when she came back, but it would be bad. Dad didn't enjoy getting mad at us—he wasn't like Mr. Laidlaw, the shop teacher with the big red nose who seemed like he wanted someone to do or say something wrong just so he'd have a reason to yell and slam his fist down on his desk—but he had no problem grounding us or taking away our TV time if he felt he had reason to. If Julie did what I'd overheard Angie and her talking about, it wouldn't mean she had to clean the house Sunday afternoon instead of going to the movies or that she wouldn't be able to watch *Saturday Night Live*. I didn't know what it *would* mean, but I knew I wouldn't want to be there when she found out what it did.

Old Woman, Known Only as 'Bertha' to Neighbours, Dies

"You Don't Remember Her? The Old Lady with the Bicycle and the Cart? The One Who Fed All the Stray Cats?"

SHE SMELLED. *BAD*. Let's start with that. Like overripe cheese; like long-expired meat; like a stomach-churning sulphur leak infiltrating every pore from somewhere, somehow, as plain as the pinched-nostrils nose on your face. You wanted to be polite, you didn't want to make anybody feel bad, but godamnit, the woman stank.

And no wonder why. Some people have sunburns, their exposed necks scorched ring-around-the-collar red; she bore a deep tan of imbedded dirt summer and winter both. She was squat and plump, but her fingers were long and thick and filthy: grime-crammed fingernails, scabby knuckles, nicotine-stained skin. Her fingers looked like diseased sausages. A paperboy accepting her money, for instance, would jam her payment deep into his pants pocket and hope that it would lose its awful ickiness by mixing with the good clean money already collected. He'd want to be polite, he wouldn't want to make anybody feel bad, but godamnit...

Her clothes—rough corduroy skirts, saggy brown nylons, polyester-cheap, too-large men's sweaters; white running shoes no longer white, knee-high rubber boots when the weather turned cold or wet—were neither new nor secondhand because she'd always wore them and never replaced them. In the evenings, when she'd sit on her small porch and no one would stop in to talk, she smoked a pipe as old as the rocking chair she always occupied, both items likely having belonged to a long-dead relative or a still-missed lover or perhaps no one she'd known at all.

How she paid her way in the world was impossible to tell—selling a few dozen fresh eggs to her neighbours every week wasn't enough, that much was for sure—but she got by by getting by: a tin-roofed shack without hydro or running water to shut out the rain and snow; a wood stove to help keep her warm in winter; a vegetable

101

garden to supply her with what food her many chickens didn't; pop bottles and scrap metals and whatever else salvaged with her bicycle and cart from other people's trash and turned into dimes and quarters and sometimes even whole dollars. Anyway, she got by.

Her world was Stanley Street, and Stanley Street knew her and accepted her, always had a "Hi ya, Bertha" or a "How you doin', Bertha?" for her as she pedalled her way past her neighbours and through their shared secret days. But no one but the stray cats that she fed every evening after supper came to visit, no one came to see if she needed wood for her stove or a new roof for her outhouse or whether she'd managed to avoid that nasty flu bug that'd been going around town.

Then she died; she just died. An ambulance without flashing lights quietly took her away and there was no need to find out when or where she was born or what her last name was because there wasn't any tombstone, and the only ones who really missed her were the cats who kept coming around for their evening meal long after she was gone, until they, too, forgot all about her.

When the city cleaned out her house, there was a tin box full of old postcards. "Penny postcards," they used to call them, covered with scenes and sayings that used to be called "funny." —MY WIFE SAID SHE WANTED ME TO TAKE HER SOMEWHERE SHE'D NEVER BEEN. —SO WHAT DID YOU DO? —I SHOWED HER WHERE THE KITCHEN IS! Some were addressed to "Dearest Mother," others to "My Own Isabel," others to simply "Father." They ended up at the dump with the rest of her garbage.

"If you don't want me to stay with Angie's brother, maybe I'll call Mom then," Julie said.

Julie placed her coffee cup on the kitchen counter and crossed her arms. I rested my spoon in my bowl of post-dinner cereal. Dad lowered his newspaper, didn't respond. One second left in the game and backed all the way up to her one-yard line and needing a touchdown to pull out the win, this, apparently, was Julie's last-play strategy to get Dad's okay to go to Toronto: take the snap, shut her eyes, and hurl a Hail Mary that the old girl would guide with spirally grace to waiting, paydirt-hungry hands, Godspeed, my fleet-of-foot friend, and run, run, run.

We didn't talk about Mom much, especially not around Dad. What was there to talk about? To Julie and me, she was a slightly eccentric aunt who moved away when we were kids and to whom we intermittently talked to on the telephone at holidays, on birthdays, and even more infrequently in person when she came to visit. To Dad, she was... someone we weren't encouraged to talk about. Dad knew we occasionally spoke to her, but pretended like he didn't, which we helped him do by not mentioning it when it happened. If I thought about it, maybe it was a weird arrangement, but how much weirder was it really than Dale and the rest of his family pretending that his dad was ever going to get better or people making believe that the Toronto Maple Leafs were going to win the Stanley Cup in our lifetime?

"I mean," Julie said, "none of us has ever visited her— ever—she's always come here. It doesn't seem fair really. She *is* our mother after all." This last line she delivered while looking at me. I suppose I was old enough to fall in line as Julie's co-conspirator—two impish teenagers united against the fun-crunching adults—but I lowered my eyes to my bowl of Raisin Bran and picked my spoon back up and shoveled away so I wouldn't be able to use my mouth for anything else, like talking.

When my father finally looked up from the linoleum, his expression wasn't anything I either expected (pinched-lipped, furrow-browed anger) or Julie was hoping for (panicky, scrambling acquiescence); instead, he just looked old and tired. And sad. Sad that somehow we'd betrayed him. He walked by us without speaking into the living room with his newspaper. We heard him turn on the TV. The weather man was talking about a snowstorm.

"You could have said something, you know," Julie said. "You didn't have to just sit there like a little idiot."

"Why would I say anything? I'm not the one who wants to go to Toronto."

"God," she said, crossing her arms again, this time for my benefit. "You are such a little idiot."

"I know what you are, but what am I?"

"Real original, Tom. Real original."

I looked at the mushy mess in my bowl. If you didn't eat Raisin Bran quickly enough, it turned into a soggy disaster. I wondered whether I should write down what I had managed to eat, and if so, how to record it? As a quarter bowl? A fifth? Without using a hanging scale like they had at A&P to weigh your fruit and vegetables, it would be impossible to tell for certain. What was I supposed to do, scrape my uneaten cereal into a plastic bag and take it to the grocery store so I could weigh it? As ridiculous as that sounded, if I didn't write down exactly what I'd eaten as opposed to some eye-balled approximation, what was the point of writing down anything at all?

"Look at that," Julie said, looking at me as I contemplated the bowl. "You're not even hungry. You've wasted all that food. God. Who eats cereal after dinner?"

I nudged my spoon through the congealing flakes; gave up, left it sticking up in the bowl.

"Julie?" I said.

"What?" she snapped.

"Why are you mad at me?"

We'd learned in science class about the paradox of an unstoppable force meeting an immovable object, but now I knew what Mr. Bennett was talking about. Dad was Dad and what he said went, but Julie did what Julie wanted to do. This was rarely a problem, either at home or at school, as she usually only wanted what was right and respectable—to get along with Dad and me, to be a good student, to consider her long-term future and to make her decisions accordingly. But whether or not what she thought was right was deemed as such by anybody else didn't really matter. It was like the time she burned her draft card.

When I was five years old and she was ten, Julie decided she was going to burn her draft card to protest the United States' involvement in the Vietnam War. That we were Canadians and that Julie was a ten-year-old girl who didn't have a draft card to burn didn't matter. She confiscated one of my hockey card doubles and hand printed then pasted onto it what information she imagined a draft card might contain (her name, address, phone number, birthday, the name of her school and what grade she was in) before setting it on fire on the front porch of our house on Vanderpark Drive for the whole neighbourhood to see. When our mother caught her with the book of matches and the charred remains of what was once Jerry "King Kong" Korab's O-Pee-Chee 1971-72 hockey card, she pleaded her right to free speech as protected under the first amendment all the way to her bedroom, where she was sentenced to spend the remainder of the afternoon.

I knew that cautioning Julie about the hazards of going to Toronto without Dad's okay or the more general danger of hanging out with Angie would be less than useless—would likely only make her even more committed to following her conscience—but I needed to say, to do, something. She was in the bathroom with the door open, getting ready in front of the mirror for her evening shift at Dairy Queen. It was hard to imagine anyone wanting an ice-cream cone or a milkshake when it was cold and dark and snowing, but Julie was brushing the lint off her yellow polyester uniform as if it were important whether or not the teenager taking orders and making change behind the counter was fluff-free. The lint roller was Mom's; not as sticky as it should have been, but still around after all these years and still, apparently, getting the job done.

"When's the last time you talked to her?" I said, leaning against the bathroom door frame.

Looking at herself in the mirror, Julie exhaled through her nose with exaggerated annoyance. *Look how put-out grown-up I am*, it said.

"Who? When's the last time I spoke to whom, Tom?"

Since her threat to phone Mom, we both knew there was no other *her* I could have been referring to, but Julie had recently become aware of the proper grammatical use of the pronoun *whom* and couldn't resist a chance to parade its proper usage. Like the way she'd taken to ending sentences with the name of her interlocutor, or the concoction of red wine vinegar she now employed for her iceberg lettuce-and-tomato salad instead of the Thousand Island dressing we'd always used, I suspected Angie's influence. I wished she'd never moved to Chatham. Why couldn't she have stayed in Toronto where she belonged?

"Mom," I said. "Obviously. Duh."

Julie shook her head a couple of exasperated, oh-so adult times and concentrated on the job at hand, carefully running the lint roller down her right arm.

"At Christmas," she said. "The same as you, Tom."

"So you haven't been, like, talking to her all the time about stuff?"

"Which is it: do you want to know if I have been *like* talking to her, or if I've actually been talking to her?"

I ignored her linguistic nit-picking, which I thought was rather adult of me, and said, "You wouldn't really go, would you? To Mom's, I mean."

Julie began pulling pieces of hair and lint free from the roller which she let float to freedom in the sink. "Why shouldn't I? She *is* our mother. And this way he"—she said *he* like Dad was the villain in the Superman movie—"wouldn't have anything to get uptight about, I'd be doing what he's so obsessed with, staying with an adult."

"Yeah, but…"

"But what?" She attacked the arm of her uniform anew with the roller.

"But it's… "

"But it's what? Spit it out, Tom."

"It's not an adult. It's Mom."

Julie looked at the roller like she was daring it to talk back; smacked it down on the bathroom countertop and pushed pass me. Maybe she's thinking twice about what she's going to do, I thought. Maybe I got her to reconsider. And maybe I didn't know when to say *who* and when to say *whom*, but I felt pretty damn grown-up myself.

It was a weeknight, but I needed to try to collect from one of my customers, Ms. Davis, who wasn't just punctual about paying me every Saturday afternoon but who'd tipped me two dollars at Christmas and always asked me how I was doing at school. She was a black lady who lived by herself and worked at the hospital, and she hadn't been home for two straight Saturdays. If someone was too sick to stop their subscription or pay up, a member of the family usually stepped in and took care of things. I liked Ms. Davis—she was nice and her house always smelled liked she'd just vacuumed—and I didn't want to see all of those unread newspapers piling up on her porch, but I had to go, I needed to get paid. After I'd peed and washed my hands, I'd walk out with Julie on her way to Dairy Queen.

Before I could close the bathroom door, though, Julie was back. She had a roll of scotch tape in her hand and a smile on her face.

"Mom taught me this," she said, peeling off several inches. "I'd forgotten all about it." She looped the piece in two and dabbed at the parts of her uniform that hadn't been cleaned to her satisfaction.

"See?" she said, showing me the messy evidence on the tape. "Sometimes it just takes a little ingenuity to get the job done, Tom."

Well-Liked Chatham General Hospital Employee Now a Long-Term Chatham General Hospital Patient Herself

"Now That I Have the Life I Always Wanted, I'm Alive But No Longer Living"

SHE USED TO *do* things.

Be the first person in her family to graduate from college, for one, St. Clair College Class of 1974 with a diploma in respiratory therapy and a job at Chatham

General Hospital immediately after graduation, just like Mr. Washington, her John McGregor High School guidance counsellor, predicted. With her first pay cheque from her new job she bought him a Danish Scandi-knit winter cardigan ordered over the phone, 1-800 from Toronto—the poor man sniffled his way through every winter, so thin and so worried-looking all the time—in appreciation for all of his assistance in helping her get the right grades (solid Bs) in the courses (biology, chemistry, calculus) necessary for admittance into St. Clair's highly respected program. It wasn't just the glossy college brochures he pushed on her to take home and look at (and that eventually, in boring classes like English or history, she'd look at over and over again inside the book she pretended to be reading) or the exam-time pep talks he gave her or his help getting her a Saturday afternoon job volunteering at the Red Cross blood drive to plump up her resume.

It wasn't only what he did, it was also—and maybe this more than anything else—who he was: a Coloured person who didn't say "ain't" but did have an office with his name on the door; who didn't swear every other sentence but did have a university education; who didn't just live somewhere but owned his own house and called everyone he met, even if they were just a student like herself, Mr. or Mrs. or Ms.; who didn't own a television but who did have a complete collection of not only the *Encyclopedia Britannica* but all eleven volumes of something called *The History of Western Civilization,* and not because he had to have them for his job, but because he wanted to read them. She loved her mother and her brothers and sisters and even the father she couldn't remember, and if "Black is Beautiful" never sounded quite right—sounded, no other word for it, *rude*—she was proud of the colour of her skin and the people of Colour she knew about from books (like Frederick Douglass and Rosa Parks and Dr. King) who made her want to work hard to be a better person and have a better life than the people whom she loved. But Mr. Washington did what black squiggles on a white page couldn't—was a walking, talking reason to be proud of who she was and to keep moving forward toward who she wanted to be. She was. She did. In time, she was that too.

And so what if she loved Mr. Washington? And so what if he—although, of course, like her, never saying it or showing it because he was her teacher and she was his twenty-years-younger student and it would be wrong, wrong wrong wrong—loved her? When love is what love should be—I am because of only you only ever wholly me—it doesn't need to be spoken or shown or consecrated by the government. Her sister had three children with three different men, two of whom she was (however briefly) married to; was what she'd had more real, more right, than what she and Mr. Washington shared? Mr. Washington never married, and so neither would she. People—her sister, her brothers, the world—were all sex-mad anyway. Virginity was no secret shame. Pure heart, pure life.

And now that now was finally now—she had a wonderful job to go to and a lovely little house to come home to and a handful of worthy charities and church work and friends to keep her mind clean and clear, now she couldn't go to the bathroom by herself. Now she—twenty-four-year-old old she—needed a new liver or she was going to die. She—who'd never drunk alcohol in her life because three of her siblings were unrepentant alcoholics—had suffered acute liver failure brought on by autoimmune hepatitis and now lay in a private hospital room at Chatham General, no less, watching people she knew do their jobs like she used to while wishing she had something useful to occupy herself with other than hoping someone young and healthy died in a car crash so that she could have their healthy liver. So that she could have a twenty-five percent chance of staying alive for another year or so.

Mr. Washington heard about her condition from another ex-student and came to the hospital to visit, but she was asleep and he didn't want to disturb her. He came again the following week and the nurse at the desk said that that there had been bleeding in Ms. Davis' gastrointestinal tract and that she was in emergency surgery. Did he want to leave a message for her?

He didn't know what he wanted to say—he'd only wanted to drop in and say hello—but, Yes, he said. It wouldn't seem right not to.

He wrote that he hoped she would be feeling better soon and that he remembered how hard she worked in high school once she set her mind to the task and that he knew that she would work just as hard now during her successful recovery.

She never read it.

"If you say anything—*anything*—to Dad to make him freak out, I'm serious, I'll never talk to you again, Tom, I won't have a brother anymore."

"He's going to freak out anyway when he finds out that you're gone."

"No he won't. I'm leaving him a letter that explains everything. He won't find it until I'm on the train to Toronto."

"No letter is going to keep him from going nuclear."

"Don't you worry about that. You just make sure you don't say anything."

It wasn't snowing the morning of the afternoon Julie's train left for Toronto. And when it did begin to snow, it was only steady flurries, it didn't seem like the start of a full-blown snowstorm. But each blizzard begins the same way. Buried underneath every avalanche is the very first snowflake.

It started to snow during first period English. It began to snow harder and the sky to change from gym-sock white to old wool sock grey during second period, geography. By the end of third period, math, Mr. Cole gave up trying to teach us about integers and joined us as we watched the world outside the window become erased in sky-belching white and listened to the wind warn us not to go outside. Recess was cancelled, and rumours of the school shutting down and everyone getting to go home early dominated lunch. Ten minutes into the afternoon's first class, the announcement came over the intercom that because of the storm, school was closing and foot-commuter students should begin their way home immediately and the buses for the students who came in from the country would be arriving shortly. We were in history, Mr. Brown's class, and he came to my desk and told me he had to stick around until the school was empty, so to stay where I was, it shouldn't be too long.

School being cancelled was obviously the big news, but Mr. Brown conferring with me about our departure time got some attention too. I didn't hide the fact that I got a ride home from him most nights, but I didn't brag about it either, not like Harry Martin did about how his dad the chiropractor played golf all the time with our principal, Mr. Yates. No one said anything, but I could tell from the looks I got after Mr. Brown went back to his desk that they weren't looking at me the same way. I pretended I didn't notice. I was used to people thinking they knew things about me. At least I knew that this thing was true. This was probably how celebrities felt all the time, I thought.

We drove home our usual way, but that was the only thing that was the same. We went slow—although after awhile it didn't feel like it because everyone else was traveling at the same reduced speed—and Mr. Brown would pump his brakes long before he wanted to stop. I'd thought the streets would be chaos, like in a Godzilla movie when everyone's in a panic to escape the city and the monster, but even though the schools and the factories and most everything else were closed or closing, people still obeyed the rules of the road and were letting other people into traffic ahead of them more often than usual, and with big exaggerated hand gestures and even the occasional thumbs-up. There were already a few cars marooned by the side of the road, their skid marks long erased, but there were also people whose cars were still running who were standing with the disabled cars' owners and waiting with them for help, or else the stranded cars were locked-up and abandoned, someone having rescued their distressed drivers and delivered them home. I had imagined that people would be scared and panicky nasty, but it seemed as if they were especially helpful and sort of excited.

You could only see the road clearly for a moment, in the instant after the wiper made its pass over the windshield and before it popped back up to do it again the other way. It was almost better not being able to see; to see how hard it was sideways snowing and blowing and how little of anything else was visible. I looked at Mr. Brown peering hard though the windshield like he couldn't find what he was looking for. He pushed his glasses up his nose and I wondered how bad his eyesight really was. The *squeak pause squeak, squeak pause squeak* of the windshield wiper and the blowing dash heater were the only sounds inside the car. "It's really coming down," I said.

Mr. Brown flipped on his turn signal although there wasn't anyone behind us. "I've never seen it go up," he said.

We both laughed, and I knew we were going to make it home okay.

What I'd find when I got there was what I was worried about now. How angry would Dad be? What would I say if he asked me what I knew, how long I knew it, why I hadn't said anything? I pictured policemen in the kitchen, I wondered if Dad was going to follow her to Toronto, I didn't want to think about what would happen if he found her.

The shop was closed, just as I expected, and I stomped my feet at the bottom of the stairs several times and climbed them as slowly as I could and still be actually moving. I listened for yelling or weeping or voices I didn't recognize. The kitchen radio was on—a weather update, of course—and I pictured Dad discovering Julie's note and rushing out of the house without shutting it off. I dropped my Adidas bag and started taking off my coat.

"Tom? We're in here," I heard Dad say.

He didn't sound too upset. Maybe whoever was with him—Angie's parents? A sympathetic cop?—had convinced him that Julie was okay, that she'd be back before too long. I'd still need to explain my bystander role in her escape, though. "Be right there," I shouted from the hallway.

Dad and Julie were sitting at the kitchen table eating Oreos right out of the box and laughing. Julie saw my surprise, locked her eyes with mine. "What's so funny?" I managed.

"Sit down, son, join the party." Dad pulled a chair back. "It's not funny, it's just…"

"Stupid," Julie said. And they both laughed again. I was so happy they were both happy, I didn't care that I didn't have a clue why.

"Julie's friend Angie, she taught Jewel"—when Dad was feeling particularly good, he called Julie "Jewel" and me "son"—"the damndest—"

"The stupidest," Julie said.

"Okay, the stupidest, but also the best way to eat Oreos. Get a load of this." He picked up a can of whipped cream from the table and squirted some onto an Oreo. "Voila," he said.

"Gross," I said, but I was smiling.

"Go on, try one," he said.

"No way."

Julie took the can and made her own Oreo hors d'oeuvre.

"Okay, your loss," he said, popping the whole thing into his mouth. Chewing while he spoke, "You might want to get used to them though," he said. "They said it's going to keep snowing for the rest of the day and all through the night and pretty much everything but the hospitals are closed. Who knows? We might have to live on these for the next couple days." He laughed and licked some chocolate goop from his moustache.

Snow: it was going to snow all night, and all the dead stars in the sky that were what our sun was going to be like one day wouldn't be visible. They'd still be there—frozen, mute, barren—but for tonight, at least, no one was going to see them.

"Even VIA is shut down," Julie said, handing me a white cream-topped cookie. I took it but didn't eat it. "No trains in or out."

"For how long?" I said.

"Who cares?" Dad said. "I won't have work and we've got nearly a whole can of whipped cream left."

"Yeah, who cares, Tom?" Julie said. "Get with the program. Eat your Oreo."

Chapter Six

Newspapers piling up on a customer's front porch could mean a few things. Someone went away on vacation and forgot to suspend their subscription. Someone moved and neglected to do the same. Or something bad happened and today's and yesterday's and the previous day's *Chatham Daily News*-delivered news can't compete with the family's very own home-grown headlines of disapointment and despair. Like when Mrs. Thompson came home from work one day after picking up her son from pre-school and discovered Mr. Thompson floating face down in the vacationing next-door neighbour's swimming pool.

Some people said that Mr. Thompson drowning like he did—in the middle of the morning when he should have been at work, when the early May weather wasn't really warm enough yet for swimming, in the pool of his neighbour with whom he didn't get along because his neighbour used to complain about the Thompsons' grass needing cutting because it attracted mosquitoes—was fishy, but the obituary in the newspaper said only that he passed away "suddenly" and that he would be deeply missed by his wife and son, his mother and father and three siblings and five nephews and nieces, and his colleagues at Aldershot Accountants, where he'd worked for eleven years.

"What was he like?" Dale said as we approached the Thompsons' house. It was Friday and he was sleeping over so I had company while I did my route. He was sucking on an extra-long orange Mr. Freezie he'd gotten at the convenience store near CCI. Dale wasn't allowed Mr. Freezies at home, only the frozen orange-juice pops his mother would make and keep in the big freezer they had in their basement. I'd wanted one too—the trees were beginning to bud, it was becoming Mr. Freezie weather—but after recording everything I put in my stomach, I'd come to realize that the less I had to remember and write down, the simpler my life was. Plus, Dale didn't know about the eating and drinking chronicle I was keeping. We had our favourite sayings and teacher-nicknames journal, but he wouldn't understand this one.

"What do you mean?" I said. I'd gotten to be a pretty good newspaper tosser—the key was concentrating on where you wanted the paper to land, not how hard you hurled it—but I walked up the Thompsons' sidewalk and placed today's newspaper in the mailbox. Someone had finally brought in the old copies that had started to turn yellow on the front step and I didn't want to start that somber chain of events all over again. Unread, unfurled newspapers left to slowly rot in the sun and the rain made me sad. It was an occupational hazard of being a paper boy.

"I don't know," he said. "Did he seem like... I don't know. *You* know."

I wished I had some secret knowledge, some special insight into Mr. Thompson's mind, but the truth was,

Mrs. Thompson was usually the one who paid me when I collected, and I could only remember her husband being a normal-looking, normal-acting man—not too young, not too old, not too much or too little of anything—the kind of person you'd probably forget five minutes after meeting them. It didn't seem like enough. It was the same as when people wanted to know what it was like when I'd gotten lost in the sewer and returned from the dead. It felt as if I'd be letting them down if all I told them was the truth.

"He was quiet," I said, once we were back on the sidewalk and out of earshot.

"Oh yeah?" Dale said, pushing his Mr. Freezie up in its clear plastic wrapper with his thumb.

"Yeah."

"What else?"

I shrugged. "There was just something about him."

"Like what?"

I waited until I'd tossed a newspaper onto the front step of the house three doors down. "Just *something*. You know what I mean?"

"Yeah," Dale said, and tilted his head back and jammed down a length of Mr. Freezie.

"You're going to get a Mr. Freezie headache," I said, pitching a newspaper onto another front step.

"No I won't."

"Yes you will, you'll see."

We kept walking down Pine Street. "Maybe he didn't even do it," Dale said.

As awkward as it was trying to make things up about Mr. Thompson to make him sound more interesting, it felt worse thinking that he hadn't killed himself, like when you watched a car race on TV and no one crashed.

"He did it," I heard myself say. "In the obituary, it said he died 'suddenly.' That's what people say when they really mean suicide but they don't want to come out and say it." I'd been talking to Julie in the hallway outside our bedrooms about Mr. Thompson—she'd briefly taken piano lessons from Mrs. Thompson when she was younger—and Angie, who was laying down on Julie's bed with her hands behind her head, overheard us and set us straight, said that that was what happened all the time in the obituaries in the *Toronto Star*.

Dale finished what was left of his Mr. Freezie in one uninterrupted suck and swallow. I pulled another newspaper out of my bag and gave it a toss. Dale stopped walking and bent over, hands on his hips, groaned.

"I told you," I said.

"Yeah, yeah," Dale said, doing the only thing a Mr. Freezie headache sufferer can do, rubbed his temples and waited for the pain to go away.

"I told you," I said again.

Man Found Drowned in Next-Door Neighbour's Swimming Pool

"I Didn't Necessarily Want to Die, but I Didn't Want to be Alive, Either"

ONCE HE KNEW he was going to do it—that this time, he really, really was going to do it—he felt a temporary stillness of spirit, call it an almost-calm, that had eluded him since... since he'd been him, he supposed. That dubious rumour of peace of mind he'd heard about for so long and wanted so badly finally confirmed as true, he could himself now actually corroborate in the affirmative. Too bad it took deciding to kill himself to do it.

He wouldn't leave a note. Not that kind of note, anyway. He'd write something short for his wife saying he was sorry and that he loved her and that she should never for a moment blame herself, and that he loved their son more than he loved himself, as he knew she did too, which was why she had to be strong and raise him right for both of them. Tell him I was unhappy and that now I'm not. And don't let him believe he had anything to do with it.

Which was a lie, which wasn't, which was why he wasn't going to leave a note. Explain what? Your life? Your pathetic body, your tangled brain, your poisoned past, your empty present, your nervous future? Your loveless parents, your niggling siblings, your (at best) oblivious spouse, your grasping (if naturally forgiven) child, the idiot people you work with, the annoying people who live next door? His mind was an upside-down telescope: you could see what was there, you just couldn't make out what it was. And you get tired of straining your eye looking, always looking. Look too long and squint and strain too hard, and the eye grows as confused as the instrument.

The eye *becomes* the instrument; I, me, mine all of the time (religion and well-meaning fool philosophers regardless) and all of us so important to ourselves. Not even an exception for that superlative self-denier, the suicidal. Self-hate is self-love disenchanted. My sour mood the world's sulky *Weltanschauung;* feeling a little gassy today, *ergo* everyone is full of hot angry air.

No telescopic inversion resulting in exasperating meaning-loss blurriness or scornful soul shadows when you're asleep, though. And notice how easily a puffed-out ego is expertly punctured empty by a good long nap. The blaze of selfhood instantly extinguished with a mere forty winks. One brave moment and then an eternity of consciousness-cooling slumber.

Brave? A gun or a rope or a tall bridge would be brave. Efficient and resolute: estimable quasi-ethical compensation for the leftover corporal mess. But a failure even as a fucking suicide. Softness—he craved softness, it had to be soft. Like his will. Like his intellect. Like his life. Forgive me.

He'd wait until his wife was at work and his son was at pre-school and when the family next door was away on vacation. As soon as his house was empty and he was alone, he'd put on his swim trunks and swallow the sleeping pills and let himself into the neighbour's fenced-in backyard (he remembered how you had to raise yourself up on tip-toe and stick your hand over the wooden gate and feel for the latch) and step into the shallow end and slowly submerge up to his shoulders in the chilly water and wait for... what? He didn't know, but he knew that he'd understand.

He did.

School in the spring was hard. Sometimes you'd be sitting there trying to do the right thing—keep your eyes on the front of the classroom and your running shoes flat on the floor underneath your desk and listen to Mr. Brown talk about how the Family Compact in Upper Canada and the Château Clique in Lower Canada were the same shady thing, only different—but your eyes would drift in the direction of the window and the gushing green everything outside or the back of Kerri Hoffman's long white neck and your feet would *cha-cha-cha* all on their own and it was never as nice and sunny out in 1831 as it was today. History was black and white and everyone dressed funny and no one ever had to go to the bathroom.

"Yes, Tom?"

"Can I go to the bathroom?"

"Sure." I stood up. "As soon as you tell us what changed with the institution of responsible government." Everybody laughed, including Mr. Brown, so I laughed too. It wasn't like when, in English class the year before, I had to read aloud from our mythology textbook and mispronounced "Zeus," the father of the Greek gods, as "Zaius," the head orangutan on the Planet of the Apes. We were less than two months away from the end of the school year so I could take a joke.

"Okay," I said, "but I can't be held responsible for what might happen if it takes too long." I got an even bigger laugh than Mr. Brown, but he didn't mind, was in a good mood all the time these days, ever since the Ontario Heritage Foundation had made that offer to help pay for the incorporation of Harrison Hall into the mall developer's plans.

"Basically," I said, still standing at my desk, "responsible government meant that the men who controlled the business, the politics, and the religion of both Upper and Lower Canada weren't in charge anymore because people got to vote for the people they wanted, so it wasn't just rich people who were friends with each other who ran things."

"Things were democratized, yes, very good. The citizens began to decide what was best for themselves, not the plutocracy. Now off you go before I have to tell the janitor to stand by with his bucket and mop." Everybody laughed again, but it was alright, we were just having fun.

Plutocracy. Mr. Brown was always working words you didn't know into sentences full of words you understood, so it never seemed like he was trying to be a big shot, or that he was trying to get you to learn something. The words sounded weird, but normal weird, like the names of the planets until you heard them repeated enough that they became normal, were just the names of the planets. There were dictionaries at the back of most classrooms and, unlike when you wanted to take a leak, you didn't have to ask permission to get up and use one. *Plutocracy.* I'd look it up when I got back from the bathroom.

A deliveryman had propped open one of the glass doors and forgot to close it after he was done. All you could see was blacktop and a little bit of blue sky, but it smelled warm and soft and alive out there. The sound of busy lathes whirred from Mr. Laidlaw's shop class down the hall. I went to the washroom and tried to pee, but I had a hard-on and couldn't, and I hadn't even been thinking about Kerri Hoffman's neck or any other girl's anything. The more I tried to pee, the worse it got—my dick got harder and nothing came out and it actually started to hurt. I quit trying and zipped up and walked back to class. Someone had shut the glass door so the hallway didn't smell like anything now but chalk and floor cleaner and sour milk.

Mr. Brown was talking about the Rebellions of 1837-38 when I sat back down. A few minutes later, my hard-on had disappeared and now I had to pee again, only this time ten times as much as before. I knew I couldn't ask to go to the bathroom again, so I tried to concentrate on what he was saying and not to look at the clock and waited for the bell to set me free. It wasn't until class was finally over and I was almost done peeing that I realized

I'd forgotten to look up that word Mr. Brown had said. And now I'd forgotten it.

Elementary School Industrial Arts Teacher Dries Out

"It Was the Right Thing to Do. I Really Had No Other Choice. It Was the Right Thing to Do."

LACKING A HANGOVER to attend to, he found himself at loose ends.

He got his teeth cleaned—a plaquey mess and a mouth full of rinse-and-spit-please gingivitis, but only two cavities and one slightly cracked molar, not bad for seven years between visits. He went to an optometrist and discovered he was slightly near-sighted and was prescribed a pair of glasses for when he was driving. Who knew he wasn't seeing everything that was there? On a roll now, he made an appointment for a complete physical, something that would have been unimaginable a year ago, and was surprised and pleased to learn that—an understandably slightly enlarged liver aside—his biggest health concerns were a moderately high cholesterol count and an oddly shaped mole on his back. The mole was removed and declared benign and he was advised to cut down on greasy food and to work some cardiovascular activity into his schedule. He certainly couldn't say he didn't have the time now.

He could have decided to stop drinking when he awoke for work virtually every morning with a headache and a queasy stomach and a short temper. It could have been when the school principal—not just a colleague, but someone he considered a friend—asked him into his office and told him that what he did on his own time was his own business, and God knows he liked to have a good time as much as the next guy, but he simply couldn't have him show up at school smelling of alcohol, it just couldn't happen. It could have been when his wife finally took their three children and moved into her sister and brother-in-law's house and said she wouldn't even consider coming back unless he joined AA and quit for good. It could have—should have—been any of these things; in truth, it took all of them. His health, his job, his family. He liked to drink—he liked to drink until the day he stopped; had all along kept drinking and hoping that there was a way he could somehow hold it all together and still keep drinking—but he wasn't so wet-brained that he couldn't see how this particular story was going to end up. Better a boring movie without much plot and unconvincing acting than no movie at all.

So he quit.

And remembered what it was like to sit in the backyard and do nothing but listen to the breeze in the trees. To watch the seasons change. To have a 32-inch waist again. To take the kids camping and laugh that none of them caught any fish. To remember that his wife made the best key lime pie he'd ever tasted. To lie on the living room couch in the afternoon and savour the gurgling coffee maker's serene domestic music; the dog scratching her ear, shaking her collar; the mailman's steps on the porch; the refrigerator reliably coming on and going off and coming back on; the reassurance of his wife's voice when she answered one of the children's questions.

So what was missing?

Never an escape drinker, it wasn't the soothing illusion at the bottom of a glass. He hadn't been to a bar in years—the music (disco!), the smoke, the sex chatter—and there weren't any fellow imbibing enablers he missed, he'd always preferred to drink alone, in the dark, in his easy chair, when the house was asleep. All he'd ever wanted from life was what he got—to be married, to have kids, to be a teacher—so no booze was required to fool him into feeling right about how things had turned out.

So what was missing?

The dark, his easy chair, the house asleep.

So what was missing?

The Chatham Jaycee Fair was a big deal. The anxiety its annual arrival engendered and the palpable relief provided by its eventual departure were hardly offset by the clanky, vomity rides and foregone games of chance and the overpriced, overly greasy food. But the Chatham Jaycee Fair was a big deal, no one over the age of twelve could deny it.

By the time you were a teenager you were supposed to ask a girl to go with you. When I was a kid I went with my parents and sister. For awhile it was just Julie and me, big-sister sentenced to look after her little brother and hoping she didn't run into too many of her friends. In the last couple of years Dale and I had gone on our own, but although we were best friends, we weren't ideal carnival companions. Just watching a rollercoaster rise and fall made me nauseous, so I'd wait by the ticket booth while Dale had fun scaring himself, just like he'd have to put up with me trying to toss a ring over a peg or knock the bowling pins over with a ball. You rarely won, and when you did, the prizes were mostly cheap plastic crap, but it was important to spend all the money you'd diligently saved for the fair somehow. You could only eat so many onion rings and corn dogs and candy apples before your stomach felt like you'd ridden the Zipper or the Salt-and-Pepper Shaker without ever having left the ground.

Besides, we were thirteen years old now, and going with your best friend to the fair was suspect, like sitting next to a guy friend at the movies instead of leaving an empty seat between you. I couldn't wait to turn thirteen, but being expected to ask a girl to the Chatham Jaycee Fair wasn't one of the teenaged things I'd been looking forward to. Not because I wouldn't have wanted to show up on Saturday night with Lisa Evans or Jennifer Peterson or even her younger, less attractive sister Nancy, bumping into people I knew and acting cool about it, like, *Hey, man, what's going on? Lisa or Jennifer or Nancy and me are just checking out the fair, what's going on with you?* But for a girl to agree to go with you to the fair, you had to ask her. Which meant having to actually talk to her. Which was the problem.

Which was stupid, I knew, I wasn't stupid. I talked to my mom (or at least I used to). I talked to my sister every day. I talked to teachers, women to whom I delivered the newspaper, cashiers, crossing guards, and even old ladies I passed on the sidewalk with a hello because it seemed like no one had said anything to them but *Get out of the way* for the last forty years. But you didn't feel the sweat run down your back and into your butt crack when you said good morning to Mrs. Ginsberg, the elderly school secretary at school or tempt humiliation if your sister said no when you asked to borrow her copy of *Sgt. Pepper's Lonely Hearts Club Band*. It was easy for Dale to tell me to just ask someone, anyone, so we could still go together, only this time with dates—*he'd* already been asked, by Sarah Smith, the daughter of one of his dad's law partners. It wasn't just the professional connection—Dale had feathered blond hair that parted naturally in the middle and blue eyes that all the girls said made him look like Leif Garrett, a comparison he pretended to dislike but I could tell didn't—but it still didn't seem right. Just because my hair was straight and stringy and wouldn't do what I told it to and my eyes were matching boring brown and I didn't look like anyone but myself, that shouldn't have meant he didn't have to do what I was so afraid of doing; not if we were really best friends. *Don't be a chicken, just go up to somebody and ask them,* he counselled. It was like when I was five and still occasionally wet the bed: it was usually people who had never done something who were the ones most eager to advise you how to do it.

It was Saturday and I was at Coles Bookstore, which was two doors down from Murray's Smoke Shop and right next to the big brick Bank of Nova Scotia building on the corner. My dad had set up a savings account for me when I began my newspaper route (getting me started with a twenty-five dollar deposit), and every month during the hockey season there was the *Scotia Bank Hockey College News*, which was glossy and free and always contained a two-page fold-out poster. I'd made my deposit and picked up two copies of this month's edition—one for reading and keeping, one for plucking out the staples to remove the poster of Steve Vickers so I could hang it on my bedroom wall. I wasn't a New York Rangers fan, and an article in last year's *Hockey Digest* listed Vickers as one of the NHL's ten most overrated players, but the poster was colour and eight-by-ten inches and nicer to look at than white paint. The bank was one of the buildings slated to be demolished for the mall. Mr. Brown said it had been the home of *The Chatham Daily News'* predecessor, *The Chatham Planet*. When the time came for it to come down, I hoped I wouldn't have to go too far to get my copy of the *Scotia Bank Hockey College News*.

"What's going on, Tom?"

I looked up from the selection of notebooks I'd been considering to find Angie standing beside me. *What's going on, Tom?* was her customary greeting. I didn't know if the way she always made sure to rhyme my name with *on* was supposed to sound nice or nasty. Maybe that was the point.

"Reading outside the curriculum, I see," she said. "I'm impressed."

"I'm just looking for a book," I said. No one but Mrs. Wakowski knew about my Journal of Consumption, and I hadn't intended for her to know, it just happened.

"Well, it's a bookstore, so it looks like you're in the right place."

I'd never seen her without my sister, so it felt strange, like running into a teacher at the grocery store. Although it was every day milder and drier and generally nicer, most people weren't ready to commit to summer yet, still wore light jackets and boots and carried around umbrellas. Angie wore black high-top running shoes and black tights underneath blue-jean cut-offs and a white T-shirt with THE VILETONES stencilled across it. What she wasn't wearing was a bra.

"They're a Toronto band," she said, mercifully misinterpreting my lingering eyes.

130

"Are they punk?" I said. Their name sounded punk.

She rolled her eyes. "Punk is dead. As dead as mohawks and safety pins. The Viletones play rock and roll. Real rock and roll. Loud, fast, and hard."

Punk was dead? I'd only recently discovered what it was—primarily through the records that Angie loaned Julie—and now it was over? What's the new *punk*? I wondered. I'd have to remember to try to find out.

"Don't sweat it," she said. "You wouldn't have heard of them."

"I might have. I think I might have actually heard one of their songs on the radio."

Angie laughed. Not exactly like she was making fun of me, but as if she were amused by what I'd said. "Believe me, you did *not* hear one of the Viletones' songs on the radio. Not on any of the shit stations you get around here, anyway. *Gawd...* " She noticed the coiled notebook in my hand.

"What's with the notepad? Are you a narc in training or something?"

"No," I said, putting it back. Even if I'd known what a narc was, I couldn't have been more emphatic that I wasn't. "I told you, I'm looking for a book."

"Really," she said, folding her arms across her chest. "Which one?"

I almost said Farley Mowat's *Never Cry Wolf*—Angie was always loaning Julie novels, and it was the only one I'd ever read, earlier that year in English class—but I remembered a writer's name that she and Julie repeated a lot, so assumed it must have been a favourite. I only hoped I'd pronounce it right.

"Eric Jong," I said, pretending to peer over Angie's shoulder in search of the *J* section. "I'm really not sure if that's how you say his last name. It's kind of a funny name, to tell you the truth, and I've only read it on his books, you know?"

Angie nodded a couple of times; looked at her running shoes; wiggled her toes and looked at them. Finally raising her eyes, "Yeah, he's pretty good," she said. "But you know who else is good?"

"Who?"

"J.D. Salinger. Have you ever read *Catcher in the Rye*?"

"I don't want a sports book, I want a novel. I like novels."

"It is a novel. It's about a guy around your age. I think you might like it."

"Oh yeah?"

"Yeah."

"Do you think they've got a copy here?" I said. "It *is* Chatham, you know."

"Maybe we'll get lucky," she said. "There's only one way to find out, right?"

We didn't get lucky. Staring at the row of S's, where *Salinger* was supposed to be, "This is ridiculous," Angie said. "Every bookstore carries *Catcher in the Rye*." Every bookstore but this one, apparently.

"The manager might know," I said. "Maybe we should ask her."

"There's no point. She'll just tell us they don't have it." Angie stuck her thumbs in the pockets of her cut-offs. I did the same in the pockets of my cords. She drifted to the end of the fiction section.

"No way," she said, pulling a book down from the shelf. I joined her in front of the small poetry section.

She showed me the cover of the paperback in her hand. "*Spoon River Anthology*," she said. "We read it last year in English class. Some of it, anyway."

Strikes one and *two*, I thought. First, it's poetry. Second, it's a school book.

"It's not like regular poetry," she said. "I mean, it is, but it's not hard to read. It's pretty cool, actually. It's by this guy, Edgar Lee Masters, and it's about all of these people who lived in this same small town, who talk about what their lives were really like—their secrets and stuff—when they were alive."

"You mean they're, like, zombies?" I said. Now she had my interest.

"No, they're not like zombies, doofus. It's like…" She handed me the book. "Just read it."

It was poetry and a school book and it cost $2.25.

"Go on,' Angie said. "Have a little faith. Take a chance. Live a little."

I brought the book to the woman at the cash register and took out my wallet.

Water Finds its Level: Bookstore Manager and Failed Poet Discovers Something not Unlike Happiness
"Did You Ever Look at an Old Photograph and Have a Hard Time Recognizing Yourself?"

SHE READ THE right biographies and could recite from memory the best poems and didn't make the sensible mistakes everyone advised her to make. She didn't go to teacher's college after completing her English degree—she was going to be a writer, not an over-qualified babysitter, and didn't want to be distracted by responsibilities and respect. Once she received her master's degree, she didn't enter the PhD program because a lifetime of playing pin the tail on the literary reference wasn't why she was put here; she was a writer—of poems, mostly, but her ambitions certainly didn't stop there—and faithful to her vocation. The world was a swindling flirt who lied. All it had to offer was what it was, and that wasn't enough. She wanted something else, something more. What exactly "it" was, she wasn't sure, only knew that it wasn't anything she'd seen or heard or felt so far.

She moved to Toronto and did what young poets who move to the city do: met other poets and had love affairs (not all of them with other poets) and wrote poems and collected rejection letters and lived in a series of damp, under-heated basement apartments and served people food for minimum wage and tips like most of the young writers and actors and musicians who come to the city and it was alright because the best thing about being young is not having to arrive, not yet. Being young is Becoming. And if you're not becoming what you want to be quickly enough or not even at all, it's okay, that's alright, you're young, there's plenty of time.

Until you aren't anymore and come home to your shitty apartment and still have to hear *We regret to inform you* from the *Tamarack Review*. She was sad of course when she found out that her mother was going to die, but it was almost a relief that she had to move back home to take care of her. Returning to Chatham wasn't what she wanted, but it was at least better than not getting what she did.

The cancer was bad but quick and she was a good daughter but slow to leave town when the ashes were in the ground and all of the seemingly endless paperwork had been completed. An only child, she inherited the house and seven thousand dollars and enjoyed living above ground and having a bathroom window to open and not having to ask anyone if they'd care for more water or if they were ready to start thinking about dessert. When the money ran out, she got a job at Coles bookstore and told herself that it was a kind of adventure in normalcy that would broaden and enrich her work and that this wasn't her life, was only a weigh station on the road to where she wanted to be. Was *going* to be. Someday.

She kept in touch with a few of her Toronto friends until there were fewer and fewer reasons to bother and kept writing poems and waiting four-to-six months to usually hear *No Thanks*. Being around books all day, even if only as a seller and not as an author, was a pleasant change. It wasn't long before she was made manager and oversaw a staff of four and discovered that she was good at what she did. It felt good to be good at what you did. When she was thirty-five she met and married Jerry, a dentist who'd also attended the University of Western Ontario, and he encouraged her to join the Chatham-Kent Literary Society where her time in Toronto and her handful of published poems immediately made her the indisputable star of the group.

She discovered she was pregnant. She was nearly forty years old, but was in excellent physical condition and had a wonderful family doctor. She gave birth to a healthy, seven pound, six ounce baby girl. She didn't write a poem about it.

It was voluntary, but you had to do it. *I* had to do it. I think I had to do it.

Mr. Brown said he wanted to make it absolutely clear to the class that this was not an official school field trip—no permission slips would be distributed or collected, no attendance would be taken—and that no one should feel pressured to be there, it was entirely up to each individual whether or not he or she would join him at the next city council meeting to debate the proposed demolition of Harrison Hall. The Save Harrison Hall Group's successful courting of the Ontario Heritage Foundation had made city hall and the prospective mall builders nervous enough that ominous warnings about Chatham's long-term economic health were everywhere. Pro-business editorials in *The Chatham Daily News* and affable interviews with pro-mall politicians and businessmen on CFCO became commonplace enough that Mr. Brown and his conserving colleagues felt that simply showing up at the latest meeting and presenting the same arguments wouldn't be compelling enough, that they needed something more dynamic. This was where we, his grade seven history students, came in.

"It's one thing for us to talk about how we're trying to protect some of Chatham's history for future generations," he said. "It's another thing entirely if the community can actually *see* what we're talking about. *You're* Chatham's future, people. And by standing there in solidarity with us in council chambers two weeks from now you'll make that fact as clear as the noses on the faces of everyone present." He was sitting at the front of the classroom on a chair turned backwards, his chin perched on his forearms, as if to illustrate that this was all off the record and wasn't something between teacher and students, but between concerned citizens. Then he told us the part about how we weren't obligated to go, how democracy worked best when people acted on their personal beliefs and not according to what they thought so-and-so would think of them, and the bell rang for lunch.

I packed my binder and books into my Adidas bag, careful not to squish my wax-papered tuna sandwich. To save time, I'd already recorded it (plus an apple, four chocolate-chip cookies, and a can of apple juice my dad wrapped in tin foil to keep cool). Every day now, by usually no later than a quarter after twelve, there was a baseball game underway until lunch period ended. Yesterday's game had been suspended just as I was due up at bat.

"What are you going to do?" Allison Hamilton said, stopping at my desk.

Allison had a dark, dime-size mole on her chin and wasn't very pretty, but she was captain of the girls' basketball team and the 1500- and 800-metre track-and-field champion and had long, lean legs and tight muscular calves that went up and down when she ran. Running or jumping weren't like scoring goals or hitting home runs—there weren't any heroes in track and field like there were in hockey or baseball. There was Greg Joy, the Canadian high-jumper who won a silver medal at the 1976 Montreal summer Olympics, but he was only famous for a little while, and then only because, winter sports aside, a Canadian winning a silver medal was roughly the equivalent of an athlete from any other country earning gold. If track and field was your favourite sport, it wasn't because you were inspired by what you saw on television or because you wanted to be rich and famous. I liked it that Allison was dedicated to something that you only did because you liked to do it.

I also liked her because she'd saved me from having to ask a girl to the fair by asking me during gym class if I was still going now that Dale was going with Sarah, her best friend. I said I didn't know, and she said that was stupid, that we shouldn't miss out just because those two thought they were Lee Majors and Farrah Fawcett, and suggested that we should go together, as friends. I knew she was telling the truth about the going only as friends part when, later on during our dodge ball game, she nailed me in the face with the rubber ball. She caught me rubbing my reddened left cheek as we were filing out after class and said she was sorry, though I noticed she was half-smiling as she said it.

"I don't know," I said. "What about you?"

Allison's dad ran Hamilton Plumbing and Electric, which was just down the street from my dad's shop, so she knew what I was up against, that our fathers wouldn't be pleased to discover that their offspring had chosen to be cheerleaders for the very people the local merchants were warring with. But she liked Mr. Brown too—he was the cross-country coach as well as the girls' basketball coach, the one who'd named her captain—and didn't want to let him down. Plus, what he said about preserving Chatham's past made sense. Just as long as you didn't think about what everyone else said about Chatham's future.

Allison shrugged. "I don't know."

"Yeah."

Because it was lunch and we weren't stuck in our seats, Dale and Sarah were holding hands, class time the only time they seemed not to be limb-entwined. Allison scratched her bare left thigh and we watched them walk out of the classroom together. You could tell summer vacation was coming because girls would sometimes wear skirts or flowery shorts to school, but Allison wore her shiny red nylon running shorts as soon as the snow was off the ground. If red hadn't been our school colour and she hadn't been our best female athlete, she probably wouldn't have gotten away with it. But it didn't seem like she was wearing tight red shorts because she wanted anyone to notice her; it just seemed like she really liked wearing them.

"Well, you know those two won't be showing up," she said.

"Nope." Dale and Sarah's fathers' law firm was representing the developers. If it wasn't a good idea for us to attend the Save Harrison Hall meeting, it wasn't a good idea for Dale and Sarah to even think about it. Not that they would have been. They were both too busy thinking about each other.

"It's not fair, you know," Allison said. "Mr. Brown is just trying to make sure that there's still a town left when we get to be his age. He doesn't have to be doing all this Harrison Hall stuff. We've got cross-country practice every day after school and he never gets somebody else to fill in for him, he's always right there running with us every day."

"Yeah." I knew he did, because I didn't get a ride with him anymore and had to take the bus home. I wished Allison would scratch her leg again.

"Well, I'm going to go," she said. "For Mr. Brown. He deserves it."

"Yeah…"

"My dad talks as if everyone doesn't do exactly what those stupid mall people tell them to, we're all going to end up in the poorhouse."

"My dad too." It was funny—I didn't think my dad even knew Allison's dad, but they sounded like the same person.

"I'm going to talk to everybody on the cross-country team. I bet I can get at least four or five more to come."

I nodded and looked inside my Adidas bag. Not only had I already recorded everything in my lunch bag and was therefore responsible for eating it, I was hungry.

"What about you, Tom? You want to help Mr. Brown, don't you?"

It was also my turn at bat. If I didn't hurry up and eat and get out to the diamond, I'd lose my spot.

"Sure," I said. "I want to help Mr. Brown. I've got to go now. I'll see you later."

Leading Chatham Lawyer Says the World Is What it Is; Nothing More, Nothing Less
"With the Right Legal Representation, However, it Can be Made to Resemble What You Want it to Be"

GENERATIONAL RESPONSIBILITY. Architectural integrity. Historical appreciation. All fine phrases, yes, except that none of them is the point. That's precisely what people like the Save Harrison Hall crowd don't understand—there *is* no point. At least not of the histrionic type they imagine exists from watching black-and-white Gary Cooper defending the good and innocent white ones from the bad and guilty black ones. *That* is the point. If the world ran on reason and righteousness, if life were suffused with sanity and sense, it wouldn't need the law and lawyers. Right and wrong don't exist, therefore the firm of Smith, Dalzell, and Russell does. Someone has to decide what is true and false, *ergo* here we are, and conveniently located in downtown Chatham, Ontario, where there's always plenty of free parking.

Only a fool goes to law school believing he's going to graduate and set the record straight, liberate the truth from the lies, separate the wheat from the chaff. Life is dark and lawyers shine a little light. The world isn't illuminated—the world is as murky as a lake is wet—but, for an agreed upon fee, enough temporary brightness can be provided to get you from X to Y and to get things done. Ask anything more and you're buying the lies the fool world tells itself so it can sleep at night. Lies are for children and those who think they should be able to see in the dark. An adult doesn't use the word *should*.

Socrates called the sophists "those who make the weaker argument appear the stronger." (Think a lawyer only knows torts and precedents and golf? Think again.) A lawyer makes other people understand why his arguments in favour of his client are the strongest. And because whoever's arguments are accepted best tends to get what he worldly wants, a lawyer is compensated by his client very worldly well, thank you very much, he couldn't say he didn't deserve every last penny. Go back, go way back, and whoever bow-and-arrowed the most animals during the day had the most meat to eat at night. No one begrudged the guy in the bearskin with the best aim because he and his family ate well and were warm in the winter and dressed in the best animal furs.

He had a beautiful wife five years younger than he was and a thirteen-year-old daughter who, mercifully, looked like her mother; he had a three-story house on leafy Victoria Avenue and a winterized cottage right on lapping Lake Erie; he owned a sensible Saab for sensible family driving and a gleaming Maserati just for the hell of it, just for him; and he wasn't done yet. His daughter

Sarah was going to attend either UofT or McGill and study whatever she wanted, he'd help make sure she was successful at whatever she did. By the time he was fifty and the firm could afford it, he and his wife were going to spend two months every winter at their own Florida beach house. He knew nothing about boats, but promised himself he would learn. He liked the idea of captaining his own ship.

Shakespeare was another one—said, "The first thing we do, let's kill all the lawyers." The same guy who used words—words, mind you, nothing but words—to make people see what he saw, to think what he wanted them to think, to feel what he wanted them to feel. His biggest concern, once he'd finished his last play and set down his quill for good, was to get an official family crest and a big, comfortable house in Stratford and enjoy being a bona fide gentleman. We know all this because he needed a lawyer to help secure the crest and purchase the house. Lawyers tend to keep good records.

Who showed up; who said what; who sat where: who really cared? Mr. Brown said that in addition to aiding the Save Harrison Hall cause, we'd also gain valuable insight into the democratic process. I didn't know about the democratic process, but I did learn that I never wanted to attend another town hall meeting. The people who wanted to knock Old City Hall down cheered when someone from their side made a speech and the people who wanted it to stay cheered when someone from their side made a speech and no one, as far as I could tell, left the meeting thinking anything other than what they thought when they arrived. The same people on both sides of the argument did most of the talking, and when someone else had the floor you could tell that all they were thinking about was what they were going to say when it was their turn again. I wished I'd brought my notebook. I hadn't had time to record that night's supper before slipping out to the meeting, and no one would have known that I was writing down *meat loaf (two pieces)* and not something somebody had shouted at somebody else.

After I did the dishes I told Dad I was going over to Dale's house to watch TV and that I'd be home by ten. Dad didn't go to things like town hall meetings. I was glad of that, because it meant I could go and support Mr. Brown and not have to worry about Dad seeing me there, but I didn't understood why, if he was so concerned about what was going to happen, he didn't want to be part of the democratic process. Now I did. The democratic process was a pain in the ass.

Not to Mr. Brown, though. Apparently he wasn't one of those ordained by the Save Harrison Hall group to do any of the speaking—mostly it was their lawyers talking at the other side's lawyers—which seemed like a waste since he was so smart and cared so much and we were so used to him talking over every aspect of the whole thing in class. But if he minded being a back-row cheerleader he hid it well, was beaming when it was all over two hours later and he invited Allison and James Dawkins and me, the sole members of our class who'd made it out, to join him at the Satellite for fries and Cokes, his treat. James' dad was the Reverend Dawkins, the minister of Saint Andrew's United Church, who would have been there himself to support the SAVE side except he was in

Toronto for a meeting, this one about the church's stand on homosexuality. Everyone knew that being a lawyer or a minister was better than being a tattoo artist or a factory worker, but people with important jobs spent a lot of time going to meetings. Sometimes Dad's neck and upper back would get so sore from working in the same position for hours on a difficult tattoo that he'd have to spend the entire evening with the heating pad wrapped around his neck like an electric scarf, but at least he didn't have to go to any meetings.

"Well, gang, what did you think?" Mr. Brown said. We were sitting in one of the Satellite's red vinyl booths, James and I on one side, Mr. Brown and Allison on the other. "I think we came out looking pretty good, wouldn't you say?" Mr. Brown looked at each of us in turn. The waitress hadn't brought us our order yet, so there was nothing to occupy our mouths, someone had to say something. *Someone* had to say something. Someone had to say *something*.

"It was interesting," James said.

James was only there because his dad was on the committee with Mr. Brown and it wouldn't have looked right if the Reverend's only child stayed home, where he would have undoubtedly preferred to be. James was chubby and wore thick glasses that were always smudged and was president of the Dungeons and Dragons club. Even though he was invariably chosen last for sports, no one picked on him because he didn't appear to care that he was fat, near-sighted, and a nerd. (Contentedly wore a shrunken white T-shirt during gym class, for instance, that prominently displayed his premature pot belly.) As long as he had his chocolate milk and peanut butter and jam sandwiches with the crusts cut off at lunch and could surreptitiously play with his purple Crown Royal bag of marbles under his desk during class he was happy.

Mr. Brown rested his elbow on the table, cradled his chin in his hand. "Interesting how, James?

Man, this is like class, I thought. It's nine o'clock at night and this is like class. I liked Mr. Brown—I'd shown up, hadn't I?—but school was for in school. And now I had to not only record what I'd eaten for supper, but whatever I ended up eating tonight, and I didn't even have my notebook with me.

"Just, I don't know, interesting. Like the issues and stuff."

Allison rolled her eyes at me, the waitress arrived with our french fries and Cokes, and thankfully James was spared being asked to please expand upon his concept of "issues and stuff." We ate and drank and got around to talking about what we were all going to do this summer and thanked Mr. Brown for paying for everything and walked out into the warm spring night. Being out after dark on a school night felt funny, like you were seeing a part of the city you knew existed but had only heard about.

"Smell you later," James said as soon as we stepped outside, Allison and I going east, James waddling west. Allison's family lived downtown as well, but in a house near the high school. All of her older brothers and sisters had gone to Indian Creek, so she made the trek across town to go to school there, too.

Once we were alone, "He's weird," Allison said.

"Who? James? He's okay."

"What's okay about him?"

"I don't know. I just know he doesn't bother me."

"That makes him okay?"

"That makes him different, anyway."

Every shop we passed was closed and there wasn't anyone else on King Street. The Capitol Theatre was still open, but the late movie hadn't let out yet. You could hear the buzz of the street lamps and the occasional moth bumping against them. One of the lawyers said at the meeting that downtown Chatham would be transformed once the mall was built, that it would be rendered unrecognizable from all the "residual foot traffic" that would result from increased business activity. I supposed that was a good thing.

"Do you know where Sarah and Dale were tonight?" Allison said.

"No."

"At the movies."

"Which one?" Ads for *Alien* had been playing on the Detroit TV stations for months and Dale and I had been talking about going to see it once it came to town for just as long. Then Sarah had asked him to the fair and they started going out and we didn't talk about it anymore even though now it was finally here.

"I don't know which one," Allison said.

"You can bet it's not *The Apple Dumpling Gang Rides Again*, I know that much." Now I'd have to go see *Alien* alone. Getting frightened by yourself wasn't nearly as much fun as with someone else.

"Who cares?" Allison said. "The point is that their fathers were both *there* tonight and those two couldn't be bothered to show up, and yet we showed up even though our dads would have flipped out if they'd seen us sitting with Mr. Brown and his anti-mall group."

"I guess. I hadn't thought of it like that." I stopped at the red light even though there wasn't any traffic. Allison kept walking. I looked both ways and caught up.

"God," she said, "they're both so selfish, it's unbelievable."

"I know. It's not like they couldn't have seen it some other time. Unless tonight's its last night. Which I seriously doubt."

"What are you talking about?"

"The movie—*Alien*—if it's not done showing tonight—and I don't think it is, it's a big hit and supposedly awesome, so there's no way it would be gone after, like, five days—they could have seen it some other time. That way they could have come to the meeting. The meeting tonight, I mean." We stopped at the Cenotaph, which was near the bridge that took you through Tecumseh Park to CCI and Allison's neighbourhood.

"I'm talking about our supposed best friends turning into total a-holes since they started playing kissy face and you're going on about—what?—a monster movie?"

"I think it's more like a supernatural space story," I said. "I mean, I've only seen the ads on TV, but I think it's more like an evil life force than an actual, specific monster."

"I'm going home now, Tom."

"Okay."

"Okay."

I was noticing how I could hear my feet on the sidewalk, how it was only when there was no else around that you realized you were really, actually there.

"Tom?" Allison said, calling my name from the bridge.

"Yeah?"

"You're weird."

I didn't know what to say, so I didn't say anything. I listened to the sound of me all the way home.

Chapter Seven

Allison liked to jog in the cemetery. During cross country season she and the rest of the team ran around and around the track at school or in and out of the enveloping maze of indistinguishable suburban streets, but now that the school year was over the cemetery was where she did most of her training.

"Why are you still running?" I'd asked one day not long after summer vacation started and I was delivering her family's newspaper. She was in the driveway on her ten speed and wearing a blue track suit. There was a white plastic water bottle attached to the underside of the bike. She shrugged, made sure the bicycle clip on her right pant leg was fastened properly.

"Why should I stop?" she said.

I put the newspaper in the mailbox. "Are you going to the school?"

She shook her head. "The cemetery."

"Why do you want to jog there? It's creepy."

"People say that, but it's not, that's just something people say because everyone else says it. There are lots of trees and a big creek. And it's quiet, no one bothers you."

I remembered a joke I'd heard on Big Chuck and Hoolihan the week before. "Do you know why they put fences around graveyards?"

Allison zipped up her track suit jacket. "Not really."

"Because people are dying to get in."

Allison rolled her eyes. "See you later," she said, standing up on her pedals as she bicycled away.

Dale and I used to watch Big Chuck and Hoolihan on Friday night and The Ghoul on Saturday at midnight together, making fun of the scary movies that weren't scary and memorizing the hosts' jokes that made up for not being very funny by our not having heard them before. But even though Sarah couldn't sleep over at Dale's house like I used to do, that didn't stop her from spending nearly every night with him, either going to the movies or the roller rink or watching ON TV on his family's big television. ON TV was something new, a cable service out of Detroit that, for a monthly fee, allowed you to watch *on your own television in your own house* big Hollywood movies that had just come out as well as Red Wings hockey games and Pistons basketball games and concerts by comedians who were actually funny, like Richard Pryor and George Carlin. If you weren't a subscriber, the station was just noisy fuzz, so they could show whatever they wanted, and the movies and concerts were full of nudity, violence, and lots of swearing. Really late on the weekends, like at two o'clock in the morning, they even showed blue movies that were better than the ones that played on the French station, and not just because the actors spoke English, but because they didn't speak much at all, were too busy being nude and doing it. I'd never actually seen one myself—Dale's family only became subscribers around the time he and Sarah started going out—so I only knew what Dale told me.

When I delivered Allison's family's newspaper the next day, I looked for Allison but she wasn't there. She wasn't there the next day either, so the day after that I changed my route so I'd be at her house half an hour earlier than usual. She was wearing her track suit again and getting her bike out of the garage.

"Hey," I said.

"Hey." Her water bottle was in her hand.

"Going for a jog?"

"Uh huh."

"In the cemetery?"

"Yep."

She climbed on her bike. Her track-suit jacket wasn't done all the way up and I could see a yellow tank top and white chest underneath.

"Do you ever jog with anybody else?" I knew Sarah wasn't a jogger; she didn't play any sports at all, which was weird considering she was supposedly Allison's best friend.

"You mean like now? When I'm not training with the team?"

"Yeah."

"Not really. Why?"

"I figure I should probably start getting ready for football and I know you said the cemetery was a good place to jog—quiet, I mean, so nobody bugs you—so…" I pretended to be looking for something at the bottom of my newspaper bag.

"What football?"

"Junior football."

"You mean high-school football?"

"Yeah. I mean, I know it's not until next year, but I want to be in good shape when tryouts start. I hate jogging, but I thought if I did it with someone else it might not be so boring."

Allison climbed on her bike. "If it's so boring you shouldn't do it then." Her brow furrowed as she squirted a drink from her water bottle into her mouth. It was as if I'd said *she* was boring.

"No, I like jogging—I didn't say I didn't—it's just that, you know, sometimes it can get—"

"If you want to jog with me, fine." Allison stuck her water bottle in place and zipped up her jacket. "I'll help you get into shape"—she said it like it was her duty, that that was the only reason she was doing it—"but when I jog, I don't chit-chat. I jog because I'm serious about it, okay?"

"I know you are, that's why I—"

"And I'm doing it as a friend, right?"

"Yeah, I know."

"You're a nice guy, but I haven't got time for that kind of stuff right now. Next year is a big year for me—for you too—and I want to focus on my running. I want to win All-Ontario."

"I know it's a big year. I'm not going to beg you, though. If you don't want—"

"Put a sock in it," Allison said. "I'll meet you here at four o'clock. Ride your bike and don't be late."

Voice From Beyond the Grave Offers Otherworldly Counsel to the Living
"I Know No One Is Likely to Listen, But I Feel as if It's My Duty to Offer a Few Do's and Don't's Anyway"

ANYONE WHO'S DEAD can tell you what you were supposed to do when you were alive. ____

_____, for instance, born _____, died _____.
Easy as pie, in fact.

As an infant, exult in the indivisibility of mother and offspring. (All your life you'll uselessly search for Oneness with the World, Authentic Connection with Another, Communion with All-Knowing God, and yet burrowing deep into warm mother-flesh is what you're missing and looking for and will never know again.)

As a child, bounce a ball against a wall, over and over again, expecting nothing more than that it bounce back to you. (Later, every dream you dream, every success you strive for, every achievement you actually attain will never be enough, will never be what you thought it would be, and only the *thump catch throw thump* of the ball will never disappoint, the doing of whatever you set out to do all that ever matters and mattered.)

As a young adult, enjoy the gluey goodness of woman, the honesty of a hard cock, the stupid, corporeal strength of steaming youth that screams that you're immortal and that the world only exists because you open your eyes in the morning and will it to be real. (Formaldehyde-breath and animal rot is your final reward; and the world never cared, hardly even knew you, has already forgotten you.)

As an adult grown, love your spouse and love your children and love your dog and any other two-legged friends *now*—not later, when you'll have more time and be better able to do it (sure you will) but *now*—and endure what needs to be endured to help them be happy and healthy and to lighten their load as they, loving you, will (hopefully) do too. (Dying in your sleep holding your dear one's hand surrounded by all of your other dear dear ones is pretty to think so, but cold hospital sheets smelling of sweat and piss, and tubes and permanent pain and noise in the hallway are what await, here's your nice little medal waiting for you at the finish line.)

As an adult old, try to stay alive until you're not. Keep: loving, hating, learning, wanting, doing, listening, looking, wondering, shouting, hoping, trying, and, yes, even fucking (or something like it). Make that sonofabitch in the black hood with the shiny scythe earn his belt notch when he takes you. (You've done nothing to earn anyone's respect by simply growing old; no special wisdom or spiritual peace necessarily accompanies white hair and arthritic knuckles; there's only one real retirement, and you don't get a gold watch, just a stopped clock.)

Of course, if you're dead, you already know all of this. If you're still alive, you'll listen and agree and nod yes yes yes and not do it anyway, or only do it halfway. No matter. It makes no difference to me. It's your funeral.

We didn't have a mailbox, only a cold, dead radiator at the bottom of the musty staircase where the mailman would leave us our letters, so one of us would grab that day's delivery and bring it upstairs and put it on the kitchen table. Because Dad was right there at work all day and Julie got home from school first, it usually wasn't me, but the day that the box addressed to Mrs. Walker was sitting on the radiator was one of the days that I got to the mail first.

Even if it was sunny summertime the hallway would be dark, so all I could see was the box, not who it was addressed to. Ordinarily, all we ever got in the mail were bills and junk mail. Lately, there'd been university catalogs for Julie. She knew she wanted to go to UofT, but you needed to list two alternate schools on your application in case you didn't get into your first choice, so every once in awhile, mixed up with a Bell Canada or a Union Gas bill and an offer from Lucky Dragon for one free egg roll with every ten dollars (before tax) spent, there would be a plump 8 ½ x 11-inch envelope postmarked Halifax or Kingston or British Columbia with the name *Ms. Julie Buzby* on the front. I never got any mail. There were birthday cards and Christmas cards from Mom, but you knew when they were coming and who they were from. I never got any *real* mail.

I carried the box upstairs and placed it on the table. That's when I saw Mrs. Walker's name. We lived at 48 William Street South and Mr. and Mrs. Walker lived at 148 William Street South and we'd gotten their mail before by mistake just like they'd gotten ours. The Walkers lived in a tidy little blue house with white awnings near the funeral home and Mr. Walker sold State Farm insurance and had a moustache and was fat. Mrs. Walker didn't do anything and must have been six inches shorter and a hundred pounds lighter.

I usually dumped my books in my room and had a cold drink of something and a pee before grabbing my newspaper bag, which I kept on a hook by the door, and going back downstairs and opening the bundle of newspapers that were left for me outside our front door and starting on my route. I had the drink (Tang Orange Juice, One (1) Glass) and the pee and put my hands on the box, intent on bringing it to the Walkers' house along with their copy of *The Chatham Daily News*, when I set it back down. I don't know why. Maybe because all of the other times the mailman screwed up, it had always been mail addressed to both of them. Maybe it was because I was taught to always put your return address on anything you mailed, and the box only had Mrs. Walker's name and address. Maybe it was because it was just a medium-sized brown cardboard box and when you shook it you couldn't hear anything identifiable, just a swishing sound and a slight thud. All I know is that I set it back down and poured myself another glass of Tang and sat at the kitchen table and looked at the box. Until I couldn't just look at it anymore and had to open it. I took out the pocket knife I used to cut the black plastic binding that bound the newspapers and tried not to make too much of a mess.

On top was an invoice from *Lover's Lullaby Clothing and Toys (Your Always-Discreet, One-Stop Adult Mail-Order Shop)*. I pulled away the delicate white packing tissue and removed the first item. It was a pair of red satin lady's underwear but with a hole in the crotch where there should have been more red silk. Underneath another layer of tissue was a matching red bra with a similar lack of fabric at the tip of each cone about two inches in diameter. I poked my finger through the hole in each of the bra's cups then placed it on top of the underwear, where I also laid the black garter belt, black silk stockings, and black blindfold. Underneath these must have been what thumped when I'd shaken the box. It looked like a red plastic banana, although not quite as curved. Then I noticed the banana-length embossed lines that looked like human veins and I knew what I was holding in my hand. I placed it on the table beside the clothes. At the bottom of the box was what appeared to be a baby soother, but it wasn't for a baby. Whatever it was for, it was for the kinds of things the other things were for.

I'd gone to the bathroom for another pee when I heard the key in the door. The bathroom was on the third floor, the front door on the second, so to attempt to beat whoever was there to the kitchen was a foregone failure that would only amplify my guilt. I washed my hands, something I rarely did, and stuck them in my pockets and started down the stairs. Julie and Angie's shared shriek of laughter stopped me on the steps halfway down.

"Hey, check this out," Angie said.

"What is it?"

"You really don't know?"

"Not really," Julie said.

"Here. Take it."

"Is it, like, the world's smallest dildo or something?"

"Something like that. Imagine a little bit further south. And to the rear."

Silence. I started back down the stairs.

"Ew!" Julie screamed, tossing the thing that wasn't a baby soother into the air like it was a hot coal, just as I entered the kitchen. It bounced, landed, lay at my feet.

Like one of those winter days when it hurts your lungs to breathe and your face feels like someone just slapped it and you've turned the corner and hit the open street and braced yourself for the wind's razor-blade hello, I steadied myself for the smack of ridicule I knew I was due. Julie was who I should have been most upset to know what I did—she probably wouldn't say anything to Dad, but now she'd have a bullet in her gun if she ever had reason to use it—but it was Angie's eyes I couldn't meet. I didn't care that she knew I'd opened mail that I shouldn't have opened; I couldn't look at her because she knew I'd seen the same thing she'd seen—sex stuff.

"I assume this is your handiwork, Mr. Buzby," Angie said, hand on her hip, smirk on her face.

Staring at the thing that wasn't a baby soother on the floor in front of me, "I didn't know whose box it was," I said. "I didn't know until—"

"You saw the crotchless panties and the butt plug?" She and Julie laughed, but it didn't hurt—was warm and easy, not hard and sharp—and I laughed too.

"Yeah," I said. "That's when I thought it was Julie's."

"Good one," Angie said, bending over to pick up the thing that wasn't a baby soother. Her top fell open and I could see the tops of her breasts. Her bra was lacy red like the one in the box. "Who knew you had such a shit disturber for a brother, Jule."

"Not me, that's for sure," Julie said. She was smiling as she said it.

Shit disturber. Shit disturbing. So that was what I was doing.

Chubby Hubby Drives Erotically Neglected Woman to Purchase Fancy Underwear

"We Still Love Each Other—We Love Each Other More—It's Just... Different Now"

HE WAS TALL and strong and handsome, but that's not why she fell in love with him. It wasn't even because he was tall and strong and she was short and petite and when she was in his arms it felt as if he'd picked her up and placed her in his pocket and no one and nothing could ever harm her. She fell in love with him because he knew what he wanted.

He wanted to sell insurance. He wanted to sell insurance, he said, because providing people with peace of mind was a wonderful thing to do with your life. She'd never known anyone who cared about doing something wonderful with their life. Just: get out of school, get a job, get married, have kids, get a house, go on vacation, get old, have grandkids, get ready to die, die. When they were first married and he'd leave the house in the morning for work—so handsome in his new Brooks Brothers suit, so obviously pleased to be doing what he was doing—she thought, *Proud—I'm so proud of him.* This is what it will be like when they had children of their own and she would see them off to school so healthy and happy and eager and she would be so proud of them too.

They were already trying. But why did people use that silly expression—"trying"? As if letting a piece of dark chocolate melt in your mouth took effort. Like slowly sinking into a warm, enveloping bath was hard work. They made love. Not fucked, not screwed, not copulated—she and he made love. Constantly. At night when the darkness was an encouraging ally; in the daytime when, surprised by their own need, they didn't bother to turn back the blankets and let the sunlight see; whenever and wherever a gesture, a look, a word, a touch sparked what was already always there.

New trees grow too slow, old dogs age too fast, the future is always the day after tomorrow. Maybe. She never got pregnant. They made love less and less often. He was promoted again and again and got fat. It wasn't as if yesterday he wasn't overweight and today he was— he was still himself everyday, the same man she never stopped loving, that's why she didn't really notice it until one day, when he was in their bedroom in his underwear bending over to take off his socks before bed, she saw him in profile and thought, He's fat. She was honestly surprised, like she suddenly realized he'd started to go grey. The next time she put her arms around him she panicked because she couldn't find his waist. She pulled herself tighter to him, she dug her fingers into his back, she ran her hands over his chest and arms, but it was gone. She used to brush her fingertips back and forth across his ribs when they'd make love and he was on top. His ribs had disappeared too. Now when he was on top, sweat would drop onto her face and she'd have to use a pillow case to wipe herself dry. Once, they'd even had to stop because a drop of his sweat fell into her eye and it stung and she had to go into the bathroom and flush it clean. He wasn't the man she married.

It wasn't even so much that she didn't find him as attractive as she had before—love has a way of softening the focus, of blurring the bad and highlighting the good—it was more that he wasn't as interested in *her* anymore. She knew he worked very hard, she understood that they were older now, she realized they were no longer honeymooners, but everyone needed to feel loved and not just to know it. She knew he still loved her; she wanted to feel it still. So she changed his Sunday morning bacon and eggs to Bran Flakes and a banana and switched from homogenized milk to two-percent and he griped at first but ate and drank what was put in front of him and eventually thanked her for looking out for his health. She instigated evening walks in Tecumseh Park that he initially said he was too tired to take but soon came to enjoy as much as she seemed to.

160

He lost a few pounds and lowered his cholesterol, but a kiss on the cheek goodnight and a monthly perfunctory peck, stroke, and pump was all she got in return.

She was getting her hair done when she saw the advertisement at the back of the magazine she was flipping through while waiting underneath the dryer. The company looked to be satisfactorily reputable, tactful, and sympathetic to the needs of married individuals and loving couples looking to revitalize the amatory aspect of their lives. What could have been, at best, uncomfortable, at worst, embarrassing, was, under the admittedly awkward circumstances, a relatively simple and decorous process: you mailed away for their colour catalogue, you checked the boxes of the items you wished to purchase (they carried a variety of clothing items and adult accessories), you mailed the completed form with your cheque to the Montreal post-office box, and you waited four-to-six weeks for your package to arrive. Satisfaction was guaranteed, your money cheerfully refunded (minus the cost of shipping and handling) if you weren't entirely satisfied. And, of course, it was all entirely discreet.

She hoped and waited for the mailman.

SPECIAL TO THE *CHATHAM DAILY NEWS*: 'Chubby Hubby' Responds to Charges of Erotic Anemia

HARD TO HEAR, good to know, so it goes...

It wasn't as if he thought she was wrong. Not when tying his shoes in the morning was a daily challenge. Not when two flights of stairs was his own Mt. Everest. Not when his favourite pair of blue jeans didn't button up anymore and there are only two possible explanations: either he was getting bigger or his pants were getting smaller. Her telling him—with her usual tact, compassion, and because she wanted him to be healthier and happier—was only putting into words what he didn't need words to know.

But this other thing—the thing between her and him and who they used to be and the things they used to do and what could be done to make it more like it was—wasn't the same as cutting down on before-bedtime snacks and taking the stairs and not the elevator whenever possible. It would be easier if he didn't love her anymore, but he did. Both of them knew they were among the fortunate few and that it was the extraordinarily lucky who were left alone as devastated elderly widows or widowers, a few years of stunned grief in exchange for half a century or more of having someone in your life worrying when you're not home yet when you were supposed to be.

So he didn't feel like fucking much anymore. It wasn't about her—he didn't really want to have sex with *anyone*. Maybe it was his weight. Maybe it was sage nature just saying that at his age his sperm wasn't required anymore, so no more itchy urges down below for you, Sir. Maybe he'd simply had enough, maybe it was like Saturday night roaring with the guys: what once had seemed so essential becoming just one more thing he couldn't really remember when he'd stopped or why, he just had. Maybe it was the existential essence of what people meant when they said they didn't give a fuck.

But he'd keep fucking. Fucking, after all, was living. He'd keep fucking until there wasn't any living left for him to do.

Girls were like that. They weren't supposed to be as strong as boys—and sometimes, when it didn't matter, they weren't—but if they cared about something they would try harder and stick with it longer and you'd hear yourself say that whatever it was they were doing was dumb and you didn't care about it anyway. Jogging in the cemetery with Allison was like that. She was on the cross-country team and I wasn't, so I knew I might be rusty, but I wasn't prepared to have to stop so the pain in my side would go away while Allison jogged in place waiting for me to catch my breath. And she wasn't even trying to make me feel bad—was only doing what she needed to do until I was ready to jog again—which only made me feel worse.

I needed help. It wasn't enough to build up my wind; I had to build up my body, too. My muscles. Boys had more muscles than girls. Or at least bigger ones. Potentially, anyway. I needed help building my muscles.

Even though the fate of Harrison Hall still hadn't been decided, construction had begun on what was going to be the mall's main parking lot, goodbye Marks and Spencer's and Eaton's and Walker's Clothiers. How they could build a big parking lot without knowing for sure if there was even going to be a mall, at least where they intended it to be, didn't make sense, but there were piles of bricks at the construction site free for the taking after dark, perfect makeshift dumbbells. But I needed more than weights. I'd never been inside Garden of Eden Health Foods before, and I didn't know what I was looking for, but I knew I'd have a better chance of finding it there than anywhere else.

The first thing that was different about it wasn't what was on the shelves or the salesperson behind the counter selling it, but what was playing on the stereo. It was what people called "classical" music, the kind of thing you heard snatches of in movies or radio commercials or on TV, Elmer Fudd intent on killing the wabbit to the melody of "Ride of Valkyries" my introduction to symphonic music, just as the theme song to *Good Times* was my first foray into the world of gospel and the title tune to *Barney Miller* where I heard jazz for the first time. But there were no cartoons or sitcoms to accompany this music, no interruption of what it was for the sake of something else. The woman at the cash register with the long straight silver hair and the amulet around her neck and the man in the turtleneck sweater pushing the miniature shopping cart seemed to be actually *listening* to what was playing. I walked to the rear of the shop trying to look as if I knew what I wanted while also attempting to listen to the music, but it kept sliding away because there weren't any lyrics for my mind to sink into.

"Can I help you find anything?"

I hadn't even noticed that the woman behind the counter wasn't behind the counter anymore, was standing in front of me. The amulet had a black stone in its middle shaped like a human eye. It and the two eyes in her head were watching me, waiting for my answer.

"Do you have anything to help a person… I mean, if a person wanted to get stronger, say, stronger as in, like, weight-lifting stronger, is there anything you might have that might help a person get that way if they wanted to?"

The woman was tall and thin and might have been pretty except, I noticed, she wasn't wearing any makeup, not even lipstick. Her lips were a smile, though, while she considered my question.

"Are you the bodybuilder in question?" she said.

"Sort of. I mean, yeah, but I'm not really trying to be a bodybuilder"—the woman pursed her lips, nodded in understanding—"I just want to get stronger all around. I also jog a few times every week."

"That's great," she said. "I'm a jogger too. Where do you go?"

"The cemetery."

"That's interesting."

"People say it's weird or creepy, but it's not. It's quiet and there are ponds and stuff and no one's there to bother you."

"I'm sure."

"Yeah." I looked around at the surrounding shelves, at row after tidy row of pill bottles and mineral water and books on yoga and fasting and meditation. The music had changed while we'd been talking; it wasn't a symphony anymore, only a single piano with just a whisper of identifiable melody so that, once again, I couldn't catch it and own it and say I know it like I could with a rock song. The way it rose and swelled and fell, however, the way it twisted and teased with meaning, made it impossible not to try keep trying.

"Do you know what this music is called?" I said.

She tilted her head and shut her eyes. "Bach," she said.

"Bach," I repeated. It sounded the same as the word that you used when a baseball pitcher got caught pretending he was going to throw to the plate.

"I know it's the *Goldberg Variations*," she said. "And I'm pretty sure it's Glenn Gould. I'm not positive—my business partner is the classical music nut around here. I'm more into jazz."

"I thought you said it was"—I sounded the word out in my head— "Bach."

"That's right."

"So… who's the other guy?"

"Glenn Gould, you mean?"

"Yeah."

"Bach is the one who wrote the *Goldberg Variations*—in the eighteenth century sometime, I think—but Glenn Gould is the one playing. At least I think it's Glenn Gould. If Judy were here, she'd know. She's in Toronto visiting her mother. Which is where Glenn Gould lives too, now that I think of it."

"He's"—it sounded funny to say it—"Canadian?"

"Uh huh. I'm pretty sure he was born in Toronto, but I'm positive he lives there now. We saw a documentary on him last year on CBC."

The CBC was Hockey Night in Canada on Saturday and Disney movies on Sunday and Mr. Dressup and his puppet friends Casey and Finnegan in the morning.

"Okay, well, thanks," I said. It was nearly five o'clock, but it was Saturday, Sam the Record Man was open until six. I didn't know if they had any Glenn Gould records or even any classical music. I'd never noticed before.

"Don't you want what you were looking for?" the woman said.

"No," I said. "I mean, maybe, but I've got to get something else first. Thanks for your help, though. Thanks a lot."

Girl Leaves, Woman Returns, This Is Her Home

"Why Should What I Do or Don't Do with My Genitals Define Who I Am as a Person?"

WHY SHOULD SHE be the one to leave? She, who loved this place as much or more than they did and who performed her civic duty as well or better than they did

166

and who wanted—yes, there was that—to show them that she deserved to be there just as much as anyone else. Of course, thinking about *them* the majority of the time couldn't be what life was about—anger spat always eventually blows back—but how could she, even now (a business owner, a homeowner, in love: happy) not occasionally understand herself in relation to *them*. Even before she knew was gay (she always knew), there was her and there was *them* and who they said she was.

She was a tomboy: would rather play baseball with her brothers and their friends than with the boring, dead-eyed dolls her parents bought for her.

She was difficult: wouldn't wear the nightgowns her grandmother gave her for Christmas, a pretty lace collar a sandpaper choker chain.

She was weird: volunteered to work the door at the Friday night high-school dances and didn't seem to care that she wasn't inside the gym with everyone else where all the fun was.

She got good grades and she had big plans and she went away to McGill and was never coming back, not to stay, anyway. A big city like Montreal allowed little you to hide away and be nobody, which is exactly what you need if you're ever going to be somebody some-day and not just something that someone else says you should be. She studied biology and fell in love (a couple of times for real) and learned to love to row (misty river rude early morning freshness, the pleasant ache of abused muscles all day long) and four years later she was gay in the same way that she was a Scorpio or had brown hair. Maybe she'd take a year off after graduation to travel (she just might be able to afford it, having worked part-time at a health food store near the university her last two years at school), maybe she'd apply to graduate school to study nutrition, the things she learned at the store about alternative healing and diet ultimately more interesting than her biology textbooks and boring labs. Or maybe she'd… but that was the point. A question mark can sometimes be the answer.

She didn't end up going to graduate school, she did work for a decade at this health-food store and that one, always bumping her head on being the manager but never the person who really ran the place or the person who made more than a barely-living wage. She turned thirty as a Montrealer of more than ten years, and love something or someone long enough and you'll likely grow to occasionally loathe it, too. *Haute couture* oh so what, spending a week's pay on a pair of boots you might wear twice and fashion magazines that smell better than you do are not the summit of cultural sophistication. She could speak French okay—could order her fresh bread across the busy bakery counter and even ask for directions if need be—but for some francophones, speaking French wasn't enough, you had to *be* French, had to be born there (and your parents before you) to be accepted, and at what point does the understandable need for self-determination become a linguistic license for out-and-out discrimination? She was no puritan, that was for sure, but for someone who didn't eat meat, smoke cigarettes, or drink more than the occasional glass of wine, the obligation to sit through a two-hour lunch or risk being considered rude was a bit much. She started to miss Chatham. She started to miss home.

Chatham: home: how funny was that. Since she was a kid at university, *not* calling Chatham home was one of the ways she knew who she was. She hadn't belonged there, she'd moved somewhere where she did, she'd made her happiness happen. And now, the first grey hairs flecking her long brown hair, having successfully marooned herself in Montreal, here she was feeling sort of... homeless. God, life was funny. Was something, anyway.

So she moved back. And met Susan. And they opened Garden of Eden Health Foods together. And because they were the only such shop in town, they managed to make a living, a life, the life she knew she was supposed to live. And if she never advertised her relationship with Susan, she never hid it, either. This was the woman she chose to spend the rest of her life with and this was where she was going to do it and she wasn't going anywhere, so they'd better get used to it. Whoever *they* were.

Dale called—he never called anymore—to ask what I was doing, did I want to hang out. Turned out that Sarah was away for a week with her parents in South Carolina so her dad could golf and her mom could shop, so suddenly he had time on his hands, had time for me. I tried not to sound too happy to hear from him. "I guess I've been pretty busy," I said when he asked me what I'd been doing since summer vacation started.

"Oh, yeah, doing what?"

"Well, I've still got my paper route every day. Every day but Sunday."

"Right." He sounded contentedly bored, like he was relieved that I hadn't been busy after all and that nothing had changed since he'd started spending all his free time with Sarah.

"And I've been jogging," I said. "Three times a week, at least." In truth, never more than three times a week, but technically, anyway, I wasn't lying.

"Really?"

"I'm just trying to get in shape for football. I know it's not for awhile, but I want to be ready."

"How far do you go? I mean, where do you do it?" He sounded sort of panicky. Somehow this made me feel calmer.

"The cemetery," I said.

"Really?"

"It's quiet and kind of nice actually. Nobody bothers you. We like it there."

"Who's *we*?"

"Allison and me. She's actually the one who told me about it."

"Allison Hamilton?" He laughed as he said it, but it wasn't a happy laugh and I didn't feel happy hearing it.

"What's so funny?" I said.

"Nothing."

"Something's funny or you wouldn't have laughed when you said Allison's name."

"I didn't, I didn't laugh."

"I don't care if you did, I was just wondering why."

"I told you, I didn't laugh."

"Okay, fine."

"Geez."

"I said *okay*."

"Okay."

The phone pressed to my ear didn't emit any noise, but I knew he was still there, I could hear him willing me to say something. I could wait just as long as he could. If necessary, I could wait forever.

Sometime before then, "So what are you doing today?" Dale said. "Do you want to come over? *The Abominable Dr. Phibes* is on the Creature Feature at one. We haven't seen that one in, like, ages."

I knew he was trying to be nice, and it really had been ages—six months, at least—since the last time we saw Vincent Price being hilariously abominable as Dr. Phibes, but, "I can't," I said. "I'm meeting Allison at one. We're supposed to go jogging." I wasn't and we weren't, but unlike sometimes when you lied, I didn't feel bad saying what I said.

"Okay," Dale said. "Talk to you later."

"Yeah. I'll talk to you later."

Chapter Eight

Allison wasn't my girlfriend, I knew that. I didn't know what she was. Worse, I didn't know what I wanted her to be. I *should* have wanted to be her boyfriend. I'd be entering grade eight in a couple of months and a girlfriend would be a good thing, like the moustache I was hoping to have by high school. Jack "Hacksaw" Youngblood, the Los Angeles Rams' All Pro linebacker, had a Fu Manchu moustache like Dad that made him look even fiercer than he already was, and the drummer in Pink Floyd wore the same thing, only on him it provided a sort of whiskery wisdom. To be somebody you needed to have things. All I had was a paper route and a journal where I wrote down everything I ate that I couldn't tell anybody about.

Allison was undeniably good girlfriend material: was smart but didn't act like it; was good at sports but wasn't a ball hog or a *prima donna*; was well-liked but not in any danger of being considered popular. What she wasn't was who I told myself not to think about when I went to bed at night and couldn't go to sleep because my body wouldn't let me. I told myself not to think about long-legged Bailey from *WKRP*. I told myself not to think about Mrs. Stanton, the office secretary at school, whose hair was black and long and who wore earrings that were silver and long. I told myself not to think about Angie, sunbathing with my sister on the roof outside Julie's bedroom window.

But Allison was nice. Not icky "Isn't she nice?" nice; nice for real, nice to me. Nice because she let rookie me run with old-hand her, nice because she waited for me when I needed to stop and catch my breath, nice because she gave me pointers (like to stay loose but in control when I jogged) without seeming like she was lecturing. But she wasn't just nice. Nice is never enough.

Once, when we were jogging in the cemetery and saw James' dad, the Reverend Dawkins, addressing a group of black people standing around a freshly dug grave, I said, "I wonder why those people don't have their own minister."

"That's stupid," Allison said.

"I'm not prejudiced," I was quick to answer. "I mean, like, maybe black people would want a person like themselves to do their funerals and stuff, is all I meant."

"They're not listening to him," she said. "They're listening to what he's saying."

We crossed the small wooden bridge that went across the stream dividing the old cemetery from the new section. Our running shoes thudded a surprising amount of noise—enough that a few people from the bowed-headed gathering looked up.

"The Bible, you mean?" I said.

"The Bible. And whatever else they need to hear."

I wasn't sure what she meant, but kept moving my feet and my clenched fists. Later on, taking a shower, I still didn't know whether she was right, but I couldn't come up with a reason why she was wrong, either.

United Church Minister Questions His Calling

"God Isn't Dead, He Just Doesn't Give a Shit"

HIS PARISHIONERS, HIS flock, his people—white, black, and otherwise:

Newspapers and television to tell them what to think.

Telephones to keep them busy babbling on about who's sick (or getting better) or what the weather's like (or will be later in the week) or who's coming to visit (or just left) or who moved away (or just moved in) or who's getting married (or divorced) or who had a baby (or just died) or Anyway, I just called to say… You know, I can't remember why I called; when I do, I'll call you right back—all to avoid even the tiniest temptation to use their heads for anything more than a human hat rack.

Sports to give them something to care about.

Politics to assure them that their opinions matter.

Marriages to avoid being alone.

Children to do the same, in addition to aiding in the illusion they'd actually accomplished something with their mortal lives.

Religion—that's where he and his church came in—to apply the metaphysical frosting to the whole festering fraud. Three out of four Sundays a month being dutifully bored in the third pew from the back and you're set for eternity, save the spiritual growth and wider ethical-awareness stuff for someone who's got the time, Holy Joe.

He'd worked his way through his undergrad at Queen's as a waiter; he'd gone to Harvard Divinity on an academic scholarship he'd earned by getting by on four hours of sleep and eating ketchup sandwiches and living at the library; he'd believed every word they taught him in graduate school about souls to save, consciences to salve, lives to enrich. He graduated in 1967 with high distinction and immediately secured his present position at Saint Andrew's United Church in Chatham, Ontario. Some people were calling it the Summer of Love. Some people weren't being facetious.

Was it really only twelve years ago that he came here?

And on the eighth day God wondered what the point was.

Ordinarily I would have forced Dale to listen to my new record, *The Goldberg Variations* by Johann Sebastian Bach as performed by Glenn Gould, Columbia Masterworks, $7.99. It was the last copy Sam the Record Man had. It was the only copy Sam the Record Man had. It sat in the same slim bin marked **CLASSICAL & OTHER** as Vivaldi's *Four Seasons*, Ravel's *Bolero*, *The Complete Nutcracker Suite*, and the soundtrack to the movie *A Clockwork Orange*. The guy behind the counter wearing the Doobie Brothers T-shirt studied me like he was going to ask me for identification, like I wanted to buy cigarettes or beer and not a record. Handing over my change and the plastic-bagged LP, "Enjoy it," he said. It sounded like a dare.

I took it home and listened to it (and listened to it), but I couldn't hear it; not like I had in the health-food store, anyway. Its wonderful, delicate strangeness had dissolved upon repeated listening into familiar bewilderment, the maddening simplicity of the music anything but simple to understand. But I kept playing it—while lying in bed reading, while sitting at my desk doing homework—because although I couldn't comprehend it, I could feel it. *What* I was feeling wasn't so obvious—calm elation, pleasant confusion, gentle, elevating sorrow—but something, anyhow, that made me feel good, made me want to keep listening. You didn't have to force yourself to do things that felt good.

I always listened alone. Alone was the best way to listen to a record or read a book—by yourself you were stuck with yourself, was just you and the music or the words and whatever emotions or ideas echoed around inside—but sometimes it was nice to borrow somebody else's ears or eyes to help to better understand what you'd heard or read. Like, when I'd take a Bach break and play Pink Floyd's *The Wall* or Queen's *News of the World*, why, even though my foot never stopped tapping the entire time they were playing, when the LP came off the turntable, did my mind feel like I'd chewed a piece of Double Bubble that had lost all of its flavour, that all that was left was pointless chewing and chewing? Chances were that Dale had never heard *The Goldberg Variations* by Johann Sebastian Bach as performed by Glenn Gould, but chances were that even if he had—if we were still best friends and he'd come over and I'd played it for him—he'd be hearing Sarah's voice and seeing Sarah's face, not the music. Being in love didn't leave much time for anything else.

I could have asked Allison to come over and listen—she wasn't my girlfriend, but I spent more time with her than with anyone else these days—but whenever I thought of it, something in my gut didn't feel right. It wasn't because I was nervous or worried that she'd say no; more like, if she said yes, she might be bored by what she heard or I might be bored by what she said about what she heard and either way it might ruin our running relationship. I liked jogging. I liked how when you were done for the day you felt sweaty empty yet filled up at the same time. I liked jogging in the cemetery. I liked how being around so many dead people somehow made you feel more alive. I liked Allison. I liked how, even though she was a girl, it didn't feel like it, we'd just run and some-times talk and then say *See you later* when we were done, just like two regular friends.

The only person I could imagine listening to Bach with was Mom. She'd never been musical, the radio was the only thing she played, but during the period she started spending as much time at the Cornerstone church as she had with us, one day she brought home a couple of cassette tapes Pastor Bob had loaned her.

I guess they were what are called hymns—choir music, men and women singing together to celebrate the glory of God to simple organ accompaniment—and Mom took to playing them over and over on the living-room stereo. It was the beginning of her being born again, and Dad, I think, put up with the nearly non-stop music because he didn't want to seem entirely negative about whatever she was going through. Maybe he thought that if he didn't push back too hard, she'd eventually get God out of her system. When God and Jesus and Pastor Bob became more important than Dad and Julie and me, however, he gave up sharing his house with the Holy Spirit and wouldn't allow her to play the tapes when he was around.

Dad worked long hours at the shop downtown and Julie and I would be home from school long before he'd return for our customarily late supper. The sound of voices raised together in song in praise of His great-ness would greet us as we came through the door, aural accompaniment to the milk and cookies Mom would have waiting on the counter. Julie would roll her eyes and take her after-school snack to her bedroom and close the door and usually put on *Tommy*, the album about the pinball kid who was deaf, dumb, and blind. I was six and didn't have my own stereo or records yet, so I'd sit on a stool at the kitchen counter and eat my cookies and drink my milk and watch Mom clean up or do her supper prep as she sang along with the music.

I didn't think of God or Jesus Christ or heaven while I listened—didn't see pictures in my head of an old white-bearded man in the sky or Jesus on the cross or billowy, cloud-pillowy heaven—I just felt…peaceful. Part of it was probably the cookies and milk, part of it was probably Mom being so happily-humming busy, but part of it was also the music, all of the different voices coming together like one great big voice, nothing jagged or sad or sour in the melodies and notes they sang, everything pushing upward, up, up, up. Mom would see me smiling and she'd look even happier, would hug me and ask me if I wanted another cookie and maybe some more milk. *Yes, please*, I'd say, and the music would keep playing.

Everybody was talking about it: an eclipse, a chance to see the sun disappear behind the moon. Or something like that. The weather woman on TV every night and an old man who hung around Mr. Coleman's antique glass shop next door seemed excited to explain what was going to happen, but I tried not to understand. I'd only come in to give Mr. Coleman his newspaper.

"So, you see," the old man said, "it can either be a full eclipse or a partial eclipse. People say 'eclipse of the sun' like it's the same thing, but it's not."

"Uh huh," I said.

The old man wore a mothbally cardigan over top checkered suspenders and a brown polyester shirt buttoned nearly to the top.

"And, you see, when the moon does block it, that's what's called 'occulting' the sun. I bet you didn't know that, did you?" He winked at Mr. Coleman who was busy cleaning a bottle with a rag and some smelly liquid from a can.

"Now, keep in mind, this can only happen during a new moon, when the sun and moon are what they call 'in conjunction' with one another. You follow?"

"Uh huh."

Not knowing something took almost as much concentration as its opposite, but in this case it was worth it. Reading in the newspaper that someone had died wasn't so bad if you didn't know them personally. The earth's life source might be a cosmic corpse in waiting, but that didn't mean I needed to become any more familiar with the deceased-to-be than I already was. Besides, if people knew what was going to happen when the sun vanished for real one day, chances were they wouldn't be so goofy-giddy about witnessing its phony disappearance now. The other big space story that year was the American Sky Lab, which was supposed to crash through our planet's atmosphere at any time and come hurtling to earth. It seemed kind of… rude—the Americans had put tons of steel and stuff up there, and now that it had done its job it was the entire world's problem when it came crashing down—but the scientists were now saying that all of that space junk was probably going to fall somewhere over Australia, so nobody I knew was too worried about it anymore.

I couldn't remember anyone actually buying anything from Mr. Coleman's store; people would come in just to talk and listen to the big band music he played on his eight-track machine and to suffer the stinky clouds of Old Port cigar smoke that puffed from his mouth. Everywhere you looked in the store there were old beer and whisky bottles with strange names like The Viking Brewery and J. Gundlach Wines and Brandies and pop bottles with embossed names like Azule Seltzer and Bay City Soda that you could feel with the tip of your finger, and smaller bottles, like the one Mr. Coleman was cleaning, that once upon a time had contained something Mr. Coleman called stomach bitters and health serums, and that had even weirder names like Dr. Harvey's Blood Cleanser and Dr. Henley's Eye Opener.

"Did any of those things ever work?" I said. I didn't really care, but I thought if I got Mr. Coleman talking, the mothbally old man might drop his unasked-for astronomy lesson.

"People kept making them, so people must have kept buying them." Mr. Coleman chewed on the white plastic tip of his cigar. He was an old man too, around sixty I guessed, but wore his full head of black hair greased back like a character on *Happy Days*. And he didn't wear old-man clothes—usually a very clean white T-shirt and blue jeans with rolled up cuffs and pointy black boots.

"Yeah," I said. "But did they work? I mean, did people get better after they drank them?"

"Oh, probably not." He picked up a squat, square-shaped bottle off the counter. "Take a look at this," he said. He handed me the bottle and I read the embossed name on its side: Burrill's Tooth Powder. None of these old bottles had paper labels like modern ones did. It must have been a lot harder to engrave each one as opposed to just slapping a piece of paper on it. I ran my finger over the name.

"How old is it?" I said.

Mr. Coleman took the bottle from me, looked at it, turned it around in the palm of his hand. "Turn of the century, for sure." He adjusted his cigar with his other hand so he could gnaw on its plastic tip. "A little haze, a little cloudy, but that's to be expected... the metal cap is a bit corroded... but no cracks, not even any chips or dings." He was talking to me, but it was as if he were talking to himself.

"I'll see you tomorrow, Coley," the old man said. "Don't work too hard." Some people, if they couldn't hear their own voice, didn't want to hear anything else.

Mr. Coleman didn't say goodbye, kept inspecting the bottle, kept chewing on his cigar. The bell on the door tinkled as the old man let himself out. I felt like I was intruding, that I should leave Mr. Coleman alone with his old medicine bottle.

Mr. Coleman set it down on the counter; readjusted his cigar so he could take a deep pull. He picked up his newspaper and exhaled smoke and sighed at the same time. "Let's see what kind of nonsense the world is up to today," he said. A pair of black reading glasses hung around his neck by a string and he placed them on his nose.

Before he could start reading, "How much does that bottle cost?" I said. He looked at me over his glasses.

"What do you want an old piece of glass for?" he said.

"I don't know." It wasn't much of an answer, but it was the truth.

Mr. Coleman looked at me the way he looked at one of his bottles. "How old are you?" he said.

"Thirteen. Almost fourteen"

"Almost fourteen. And how long... how old were you when you got lost? Lost down there."

"Seven."

"Seven years," he said. "You've been who you are now for just as long as you were before."

"I guess." Before *me* and afterwards *me* still felt like *me*—I wished it wasn't the case, I wished I was different and felt like somebody else, somebody transformed, but I didn't. But if Mr. Coleman needed to think there was that big a difference, that was okay too.

"Not everybody knows what it's like to be gone and then to come back, do they?" he said.

I just shrugged, but I knew it was enough.

Handing me the bottle, "Take it," he said.

"But it's old. It must be worth a lot."

"Take it," he said, almost smiling this time. "Or I'm liable to change my mind."

I took it and thanked him and placed it in my newspaper bag and was five minutes into my route when I realized it wasn't worth the risk, I had better go back home and leave it in my bedroom. It was nearly a hundred years old. There was no guarantee it wasn't going to break one day anyway, but that didn't mean I shouldn't avoid being careless when I could.

Motorcycle Crash Claims Life of Man's Son, His Marriage, His Reason to Live
"I Like Looking at Glass Now. I Like Looking at Old Glass"

HIS WIFE SAID to him that that was it, one was enough, if he wanted to have any more children, then *he* could have them himself. A little brother or a sister for one-year-old Barry would have been nice, but Barry was enough. Barry was better than enough. Barry was perfect. Taking a nap before his afternoon shift at Ontario Steel with baby Barry asleep on his chest, *So this is what happiness is,* he thought. Sometimes at work or cutting the lawn or filling up the tank of the Buick, he'd catch himself smiling and wouldn't be able to remember why he was supposed to be happy. Then he'd remember their son.

Babies, of course, learn to walk and talk and demand money for rock-and-roll concerts, but even when the boy wasted his allowance on gas money and a ticket to see the band *du jour* across the border at Cobo Hall in Detroit—paying for the right to be deafened: unfathomable—he was still a good boy, never came home high or drunk like some people's kids and always when he said he'd be back. When his son saw *Easy Rider* and caught the motorcycle bug his father promised to buy him a used Yamaha from a guy at work for his graduation (so proud, so proud; neither he nor his wife had managed to finish high school). His wife said no no no until the day it was parked in the driveway, the second day of summer vacation, June 11, 1970.

The day started the way it was supposed to—sunny, dry, a slight wind out of the west—but the weatherman hadn't said anything about rain. Barry had gotten his licence after taking riding lessons with the money he earned working part-time at a car wash, his father had brought the bike to a garage and had it fully inspected, repaired, and tuned up, and even his mother was somewhat assuaged when Barry promised to always wear his helmet when he rode. But the weatherman hadn't said anything about rain. It was only a light sprinkle—barely there even, almost a mist—but it wasn't supposed to happen, there wasn't supposed to be any precipitation at all.

The phone call from the police, the funeral, the first echoey empty days afterward: waylaying grief gave them a week or so of being too busy and bewildered to properly feel their pain. When it finally arrived, though, he wanted to howl like a tormented animal incapable of anything else. His wife began pouring her first water glass of Canadian Mist whiskey earlier and earlier each day, immediately washing the glass and putting it in the drying rack before pouring out her next drink twenty minutes later her sole concession to keeping up appearances. By the time he arrived home from work and they'd shared another silent supper she was drunk enough to begin reminding him whose idea the motorcycle was and what wouldn't have happened if he hadn't. What was once their home was now too big for just the two of them and too small for their shared sorrow, anger, and exhaustion. She kept the house, he moved into a large apartment downtown next door to a tattoo parlor, and there wasn't any reason for them to keep in touch. He didn't get a telephone installed, swore he'd never have another. If bad news wanted to find him in the future it was going to have to work a hell of a lot harder than simply traveling down a telephone wire.

Every abandoned shoe in the street was a tragic poem; every undercooked TV dinner he ate, every sour hangover he endured, every dull day again and again, all that he deserved. Until one day, putting out the trash, he spotted an old, squat bottle resting on top of the neighbour's overflowing garbage can.

Canadian Liquid Hair Dye

Prepared Only by Northrop and Lyman

Toronto Ontario

Warranted to Color Grey or Light Hair to a Beautiful Auburn, Brown, or Black, with All the Softness of the Original Hair.

1896

Just one more Buy me! Buy me! piece of bullshit no different from the same shit, different day products of today, but he stuck it in his pocket anyway and put it on his coffee table. One night after work, instead of turning on the TV, he drank a six pack and looked at the bottle. The next morning, *What the fuck is wrong with me?* he thought. A grown man doesn't do things like that.

Six months and an apartment full of old milk, medicine, pop, beer, and hair-tonic bottles later, he filled out all of the necessary paperwork for early retirement from the factory and rented out the empty store downstairs and Coleman's Antique Bottles became downtown Chatham's latest struggling business. He didn't care. The rent was next to nothing and his pension cheques from Ontario Steel, even at the significantly reduced rate he'd agreed to, were enough to see him through. The main thing was that he had enough room now. Truth be told, he got more excited about buying a new, rare bottle at a trade show in Toronto or Buffalo or Detroit than he did selling one out of his shop. Sometimes he'd wonder what had happened, how things had ended up the way they were. Eventually he quit asking.

———————

Things that people gave you, if they were good things, were things you could keep and call your own and could even become part of who you were. I'd never thought of being outside—of being in nature—as anything much but the opposite of being inside, where people usually were and therefore were supposed to be. But jogging with Allison in the cemetery made me like the surprise of a cool breeze on a warm day, to stop and stare at late-afternoon long shadows cast by summer-swaying trees, to sniff deep the dewy smell of early-morning earth just waking up. There wasn't any point to any of it—breezes and shadows and smells couldn't make you any smarter or stronger or put more money in your bank account—but I liked it anyway, I just liked it. That was another thing about good things: you never had to give a reason, you never had to come up with a convincing argument as to why they were good. Good was good because it was good.

But sometimes you didn't want to put on your running shoes and scurry in step with someone else's moving, maybe you just wanted to sit alone and read yet still be able to pause and look up at the sky's big blue nothing before going back to your book. I'd gotten a biography of Amelia Earhart out of the Chatham Public Library and taken it, a bath towel, and a can of C Plus onto the small tarpapered roof at the back of our building overlooking the parking lot. You could only get to it from Julie's bedroom window, but she was working at Dairy Queen and wouldn't be home for hours. I changed into my bathing suit and carried my supplies through the window and outside. I'd wrapped my pop in tinfoil to keep it cool, something Dad used to do with his can of beer when we lived on Vanderpark Drive and it was summertime and we'd play lawn darts in the backyard. Even your parents could give you something good that became yours.

Tarpaper wasn't grass, the roof of the building next door wasn't a sprawling weeping willow tree, but the sweet-and-sour sun was still up there—the mashed-potato clouds and the blue Mr. Freeze sky too—and the sweat that occasionally slid down my forehead and along my cheek and drop-plopped onto the page of my book testified that I was part of something bigger than just me and what I was reading. Outside, no matter where you were or what you were doing, you became a little piece of the puzzle of everything. It wasn't a bad feeling, not like you might expect, wasn't like being the last guy on the bench on a basketball team, the necessary eleventh man; was more like realizing there couldn't be a game without you even though it was all in your head, that there really wasn't any game at all. I was a frog on a rock on the shore of a lake, sitting and staring and sweating, just another stupid little amphibian whose stupid little amphibious brain was never meant to understand where all this water came from or what it was there for.

I skipped to the end of the book, the part where Amelia disappears over the Pacific Ocean while trying to fly around the world in 1937. The author said her plane hadn't run out of fuel and crashed and sank into the ocean like the government and the newspapers said, but that Amelia was a spy for America and that, after her plane crash-landed on a Japanese-held island and she was taken prisoner, she died of dysentery, and that the US government knew all about it but didn't do or say anything because they didn't want to be embarrassed and weren't ready to go to war with Japan or anybody else. I wondered how the government and the newspapers could have gotten away with lying to people, but before I could get all the way to the end of the book I fell asleep on my towel. When I woke up, I knew I was going to have more than a tan, and I was right. I soaked myself in Solarcaine, but I could still smell the sunburn underneath.

Chapter Nine

The Harrison Hall people put up a good fight, but the game was over, the mall people won, the city decided that old city hall could be demolished. Chatham council rejected the $150,000 offer from the Ontario Heritage Foundation, and when Mr. Brown and the rest of his group asked the Ontario Municipal Board to reverse city council's decision, the OMB said there was nothing they could do. The editorial in *The Chatham Daily News* said it was a victory for democracy and the entire town, so it had to be true.

Dad scored a victory, too, finally found a building he wanted to buy and thought he could afford, a realty hat trick: a permanent place of business for him, a brick-and-mortar legacy for his dependents, a home for all of us. And it would be a home, too, not just two floors of small rooms staring at William Street with a parking spot in the back for an extra ten dollars a month. It was still downtown, the new shop would still benefit from the shopper spillover that the new mall was going to supply, but it was near the nice old houses that cosseted CCI. Its floors were hardwood, not wall-to-wall linoleum; there was a gas furnace and heat vents in every room instead of steam radiators that constantly needed to be drained; there was central air-conditioning, which meant we could closet our two rotating fans and use our magazines exclusively for reading, not fanning; there was even a small backyard surrounded by a wooden fence. It faced Tecumseh Park, and if the wind was strong enough and blowing in the right direction when you stuck your head out of any of the building's three floors of large windows, you got a whiff of cedar as the trees waved and bowed in the breeze instead of a nose full of car exhaust. And trees were nicer to look at first thing in the morning than a garbage truck or a stumbling drunk stunned he'd run out of night. Even Julie was sort of impressed.

"At least the bathroom has a window," she said as we walked home from our first family viewing after supper one night.

"*Both* bathrooms," Dad said. He'd been there a few times already with the owner, who wanted to make sure he was serious about buying before he showed it to us. He was. The owner must have thought so too, because he let Dad take the key home. Dad said the man who owned the building didn't want to use a real estate agent. This way, Dad said, he could pass on some of the savings from not having to pay a commission to the agent.

"Living with two guys and one bathroom," she said. "I should get an award or something."

"Well, you'll only to have suffer for one more year," Dad said. We all laughed, even though it wasn't very funny. It was usually Julie who brought up how much better her life was going to be once she left for university, and generally only when she was sore about something she didn't get or something that didn't go her way. Hearing Dad making a joke about it, even a lame joke, made her leaving seem more real.

"I'll be back for Christmas and summer holidays," Julie said. "Don't rent out my room or anything."

Dad put his arm around her shoulder and pulled her close. "Don't worry, Jewel, wherever you go or whatever you do, my little girl will always have a place she can come back to whenever she wants."

Julie pulled away, gave him a playful poke in the shoulder. "I'm not anybody's little girl, Dad." We kept walking, and Julie slid back beside him, let him put his arm back where it was.

"The same goes for you too, son. Don't ever forget, you'll always have a home, no matter where you end up or whatever you end up doing."

"I know," I said.

We stood at a red light. A cool-looking car, like a car in a Steve McQueen movie, bulleted through the intersection. We were standing safely on the sidewalk, but couldn't help stepping back when it raced past.

"What kind of car is that?" I said.

Dropping his hand to his side, watching the car disappear down King Street, "The kind driven by an asshole," Dad said.

Julie and I looked at each other. "Hey, I know what we should do," she said.

Dad didn't answer; the light had turned green, but he was still scowling down King.

"What?" I said, even though she wasn't talking to me, not really.

"You know what we should do? We should celebrate. The new building, I mean. Let's go to Dairy Queen. My treat. What do you say?"

Dad looked at Julie, then at me, then smiled, was back to being Dad. "Don't you spend enough time there already?" he said. "You'd think you'd have better things to do on a nice summer night than hang around with your dad and brother."

"Who said I don't?" Julie said, smiling. "But let's go anyway. I can only use my employee discount card while I'm an employee. I won't always be able to save fifteen percent on ice cream cones, you know."

Downpayment on First Home or Very Own Dream Car? Rare Camaro Threatens to Drive Apart Local Family
"Who Am I Without This Car? This Car is Who I Am. Without This Car I'm No One"

"DOUCHEBAG" WAS A not infrequent appellation. That, and "freeloader," "waste of space," and, far less often, "Gary." She—and only she, and only when they were alone, and usually when they were making love or had just finished making love or were lovey-dovey leading up to making love—called him her "Gare Bear" or "Gary Gorgeous" or, for reasons neither of them could recall, "Bunny." Because they didn't know him. Didn't understand him. Not the real him. They didn't know what they did when there was no one around but the two of them and what they did. What he did to her. The happiness that he made happen. The delicious ache that only he could create and—so softly, so gently sometimes—end. The emptiness, the fullness, of afterward.

He barely managed to graduate from high school and she never earned less than a B. She'd been the setter on both the junior and senior girls' volleyball teams and a member of the Travel Club (they did the Europe's Greatest Hits trip during grade thirteen March Break; she sent him several postcards all signed, Love, Janice). He called the school's athletes (her excepted, of course) "fags" and anyone who served on student council or was in the Debating Club or the Investor's Club a "dweeb," a "wuss," or a "loser." His friends were all parking-lot smokers and lunchtime stoners and he didn't bother to apply to any universities or colleges. Worse, he didn't seem concerned about what he was going to do after graduation. "Relax, Babe, you'll live longer," he'd tell her when she tried to talk to him about his future. About their future. Sometimes it seemed as if he wanted to end up a… a nothing with nothing to show for his life, like he was trying to prove something or hoping to show somebody that he wasn't going to do what everyone always told him he was supposed to do.

Naturally, the summer before she was supposed to leave for Fanshawe College to study to be a dental assistant she became pregnant, they got married and moved into her parents' basement, and it turns out that the future ain't what it used to be. (Slight respite because A Baby! A Baby! It's a girl, a girl! A miracle, a blessing, a great big bundle of blah blah blah.) A year and a half later, she was a cashier at a drugstore and he was still looking for work and her parents were beginning to wonder aloud when they were going to get their rec room back. "Christ, I'm looking, what more do they want?" he said when she reluctantly brought up the subject. "How would they like to work in a fucking convenience store?" She didn't argue. What was the point? She had to get up early for work in the morning and didn't want to wake the baby.

Then he won the car. Bar-hopping in Windsor with some buddies because the talent at the Chatham titty bars was getting stale, he filled out a ballot at some place or another to win a car as part of a beer company promotion and for Godsake's he got the phone call at home that he won. The first thing he'd ever won, ever. And not concert tickets or steak knives, but a vintage 1969 Chevrolet Camero ZL1. Uh huh, uh huh, that's right, the muscle car of muscle cars: 435 horsepower, zero to sixty in under six seconds, look at everybody looking at me in my shiny, lovely robin's-egg blue 1969 Chevrolet Camero ZL1. He washed it, he waxed it, he used a toothbrush to scrub the engine clean. Eventually he didn't even drive it that much—too many a-holes out there to hit it or dent it or scratch it. Even her parents were mildly impressed—at least he cared about *something*.

Then she got pregnant again and the solution was obvious. Sell the car—he'd already had offers, good ones, without even putting it up for sale—and use the money to place a downpayment on a house. Her parents were so concerned about seeing them settled that they even offered to contribute a thousand dollars from their own skimpy savings. It wasn't like he'd earned the cash, but money was money, and as long as the table stands it doesn't matter how it got built. Her parents started circling reasonably priced homes for sale in *The Chatham Daily News* and leaving it on the breakfast table, right next to the cereal bowl his wife always put out for him before she left for work. You know Gary—he has to have his Sugar Crisp and glass of Tang first thing in the morning.

But he wouldn't sell it. Hell no he wouldn't sell it. He went along with the initial gentle joshing ("Kiss your baby goodbye, Gary, I'm gonna slip a For Sale sign on it tomorrow." "You mean Janice? I don't think she'll fetch that much." "Oh, Gary"). He endured their non-stop nagging ("But Gary, what are we going to do if you don't sell it? We can't live in my parents' basement forever." "Listen to me, son, my daughter and her children deserve to have a roof over their heads, a place they can call their own." "It's just a car, Gary, it's just a car"). He ignored their threats and all of their bullying ("If you can't take care of your family, maybe it's time for Janice to find someone who can." "You know I've never pushed you to do something you didn't want to do, Gary, but if you're not working, then at least maybe you could help out by getting some money from selling the car." "You're ruining my daughter's life, do you know that? I think you do, and to tell you the truth I don't think you even care"). He put up with all of their bullshit. But he wouldn't sell it.

In a way he felt sorry for them. None of them had ever owned anything as beautiful as he had. Owned as in "owned" as in his and his alone. They didn't understand.

Why? had come first; now there was also *What?* If you didn't know any better, it sounded like something Mr. Roberts, the grouchy old retired philosophy professor whose newspaper I delivered, might think about. But I knew better. I knew it was just about me.

Now that I'd filled an entire notebook with several months worth of what I'd eaten and drank, what was I supposed to do with it? The why of it had been easy. I wasn't who people thought I was. I didn't know what they thought I knew. I felt like a fake. I *was* a fake. Filling a red notebook with dates and the names of foods and liquids every day was the perfect punishment.

But something happened. Now the daily recording felt like something else, something different, something—I wasn't sure what—almost real. It was as if doing it was itself almost reason enough to do it.

So now what? Just a red notebook full of dates and the names of foods and liquids. I slid it into the middle drawer of my desk. I took out a fresh notebook from the bottom drawer and opened it up to the first page, pressed it flat with the palm of my hand. I entered today's date. I remembered and I wrote.

Decades of Dedicated Scholarship and Contemplation Fail to Prevent Ex-Philosophy Professor from Being Perpetually Pissed Off
"The Soothing Salve of Wisdom is a Steaming Crock of Shit"

SOMETIMES IT WAS good not to be angry. Sometimes music, wine, good prose, good weed, the cat's thank-you meow, a friend who called and something to do, someone doing their job effectively and with pride and without fuss, something, sometimes. More often than not, though, Plato was a fucking fool; this is it, this is what there is, truth, beauty, and goodness just things you read about in books when you're young, visions of Platonic sugar plums dancing in your empty head, no Form of the perfect anything floating around anywhere, no consoling peace of mind while you wait out your imperfect time down here.

A week-long sample list (79/08/07-14) of sundry items that stuck in his craw, that got his goat, that grinded his gears, that reminded him—as if at age sixty-seven he needed reminding—that sage philosophical detachment is as much a lacerating lie as the guilty getting what they deserve and the cheque being in the mail:

- The mouth-breathing man who lived next door and his preternatural ability to know to roar his lawnmower just when his neighbour had ventured out of his house for the first time in days to settle into a lawn chair with a book and a glass of iced tea.
- The cow-eyed wife of the man who lived next door whose perpetual mopping, dusting, sweeping, scrubbing, polishing, vacuuming, and hanging of basket after basket of laundry on the backyard line testified to her belief that a clean house wasn't just a place to live, but, indeed, a reason for living.
- The dirty, shouting, snot-dripping children of the man and woman who lived next door, whose own particular reason for existence seemed solely to consist of losing their tennis balls and basketballs over his back fence and in ringing his doorbell and demanding them back.
- The people of his city of birth, the city where he was going to die and spend earthly eternity, who had two hockey rinks and one bookstore, the POETRY section of the latter almost as large as the one containing PLUMBING (HOW TO).
- The newspaper of his city of birth delivering a different national or international poke to

his supposed third eye every day: the Three Mile Island nuclear meltdown; oil spills in the Atlantic and the Gulf of Mexico; an anthrax leak from a military factory in the Soviet Union that killed over a hundred citizens and was explained away by the government as merely an unfortunate outbreak of tainted meat; Mother Teresa of Calcutta the rumoured front runner for this year's Nobel Peace Prize, although presumably not for her condemnation of birth control for the overpopulated planet's poor, starving, swarming misbegotten; an amusement ride fire in Sydney, Australia, that killed six children because park officials hadn't budgeted enough money for sufficient fire safety; and in nearby Perth the stage collapsed at the Miss Universe pageant when contestants and photographers alike rushed to greet her Highness as she was tearfully ensconced on her cushy winner's throne.

- Him, because it wasn't supposed to be this way. He was supposed to know better.

I hoped that the radio reception at our new house was the same or better than on William Street. The new building was only a ten-minute walk from the old one, but radio signals were unpredictable—sometimes on a late summer night, a Cleveland or Cincinnati or New York station would inexplicably crackle into existence on my transistor radio before just as mysteriously vanishing the same way—and I worried that maybe all of those century-old trees in Tecumseh Park might somehow mess up the electrical recipe that allowed me to hear, however buzzy and briefly, what Dave from Toledo thought of that night's 7-6 Indians loss to the Red Sox, or what the overnight low in Central Park was going to be. It was only sports talk and weather reports, but it also wasn't, was what people who spoke with funny accents had to say to each other and what the temperature was going to be in places I'd never been.

The on-the-hour big news stories were pretty much the same in the south as they were in the north. Margaret Thatcher elected as the new British prime minister. The nuclear power plant accident at Three Mile Island. Ronald Reagan nominated as the Republican presidential candidate. Mr. Brown said it was important to be informed about the world, that we were all global citizens. The world was definitely out there, but we weren't the world. We were Chatham, Ontario, Canada, population approximately 33,000. We had our own headlines.

What I liked best were baseball games on the radio, the farther away the broadcast the better. Hockey was fast, so play-by-play guys on the radio had to stick to the game, could only try to keep up with the action. Baseball was slow and there were plenty of interruptions and delays, so baseball broadcasters told stories and jokes to help keep you interested. Sometimes the stories and jokes were the best part.

Better than lucking into a baseball game on the radio, though, was a baseball game taking place on the West Coast, the Cleveland Indians, say, on the road against the California Angels, the ten p.m. first pitch meaning I'd be cozy under the covers by the third inning with my teeth brushed and the alarm set so that I could fall asleep with the transistor radio turned low and resting on my chest and the game going on and on without me but with me still right here. And in the morning the radio was always switched off and sitting on my nightstand. I knew Dad put it there, and I knew that he knew that I knew, but he never said anything about it and neither did I. When I was little my mother would read to me before bed and I'd fall asleep and she'd turn off the light and we never talked about that either.

But best of all was a Detroit Tigers' game on the West Coast, for all of the usual late-night reasons plus the number one reason to listen to any of the team's broad-casts— whether early, late, or on weekend afternoons— Ernie Harwell, the Tigers' play-by-play radio announcer. I wasn't even much of a baseball fan. Fergie Jenkins and Bill Atkinson were from Chatham, but other than Mr. Allan, our gym teacher at school who'd played a couple of years in the minor leagues, that was about it for homegrown professional baseball players. Being born into hockey, I didn't have a choice what my favourite sport was, the just-across-the-border Detroit Red Wings, my dad's team, my team too. I played it until I was twelve, we watched it most Saturday nights on TV (even if it was always only the Toronto Maple Leafs), I read about it in *The Hockey News*, *Hockey Digest*, and wherever else I could. But that didn't matter because I wasn't really a baseball fan or even a Tigers fan. I was an Ernie Harwell fan.

Ernie had his Ernieisms that we all wanted to hear at least once per game. When Detroit turned a double play, it was "two for the price of one for the Tigers." When an opposition batter was out on a called third strike, "he stood there like a house by the side of the road and watched it go by." When a Tiger belted a home run, the ball was "looong gone." When someone fouled a ball into the stands at Tiger Stadium, we heard how "a man from Wallowa will take that one home" or how "a young woman from Ypsilanti has got herself a souvenir." Until I was older and Dad told me that Ernie just picked places at random, I thought Ernie Harwell must have been the wisest man who ever lived.

But amusing catchphrases weren't why anyone listened to Ernie Harwell. Ernie Harwell's voice sounded like life. Life the way it was supposed to be, not the way it ordinarily was. It was smooth and sweet—pancake-syrup smooth and sweet—but never sickly sugary like eating a whole bag of cotton candy at the fair, there was a gravelly rumble at its heart that reminded you that everything delightful is full of everything else too, that's how you can tell it's the real thing. Life was boredom then fear then excitement then uncertainty then funny then sad then confusing then scary then predictable then... A baseball game called by Ernie Harwell made sense. Some parts were better than others, sometimes you won and sometimes you lost, but that same sane, honeyed voice was always reminding you that it's a long season, 162 games, and even if it's unlikely that it'll all work out in the end, that's okay, today's game is all we can really know, so sit back, friends, enjoy, and let's see what happens.

Former Star Baseball Prospect Ends Up Teaching Gym
"Games. It's All About Playing Games, Isn't It?"

IT WAS ALWAYS only a game. Baseball was fun. A thirteen-pitch at-bat battle resulting in a hard-earned

201

passed-ball truce; the smack of a grounder safe in the pocket of the glove and a lazy laser to first base and *Out!;* that rare thing, the thing no hitter ever hears enough: sweet-spot crack of bat to ball and bye-bye and touch all the bases on your way home. But hockey was fun too; so was basketball, football, even track and field. He played them all and he played them well and if he hadn't been such a damn good line-drive hitter and a hit-thieving fielder he would have just kept playing them all until... Well, why would he ever stop? They were fun. And wasn't that the way it was supposed to be?

But he was good—very, very good. Could hit a curve ball when most other kids his age were glad to just get it out of the infield; was a skinny-legged vacuum cleaner sucking up fly balls in left-field; sometimes it seemed like he could steal a base whenever he felt like it. His coaches and his father and his conscience convinced him to funnel his time and talent and choose baseball as it had so clearly chosen him. He thought it might have been fun to try university—you heard stories about fraternities and keggers and girls who had their own apartments—but his coach knew someone who scouted part-time for the Phillies, and with his parents' blessing, arranged for him to complete high school in Windsor, where the competition was better and where American scouts were known to visit. It was only an hour away, and his parents rarely skipped a home game, but he missed his friends and his sisters and Chatham. Ended up batting .487, though, and earned a reputation as an outfielder that you simply didn't run on.

He wasn't drafted, but the Yankees inked him to a rookie contract that included a $1,000 signing bonus. He wanted to buy a car, but he didn't know how to drive. His parents convinced him to put the money in the bank and his father assured him that when he was a major leaguer he could buy the best sports car around. Hell, he said, he wouldn't need a car, could have his own limousine and driver if he wanted. He received a one-way bus ticket in the mail and rode the Greyhound for nineteen hours to Ft. Lauderdale, Florida, home of the Yankees single-A affiliate. The home of him now, too. He moved into a duplex that wasn't near the ocean with three other teenaged prospects. The guy from Alabama was hard to understand and chewed tobacco and left used-up, dried-up chaw all over the apartment. The black guy from New York, his roommate, was a good guy but snored so loudly he took to sleeping on the living-room couch which was two inches too short. The other guy, a Puerto Rican, didn't speak any English.

But he wasn't there to make friends, he was there to bust his tail, as his dad advised, and to force the Yankees to notice him and promote him to their Manchester, New Hampshire double-A team. He was too embarrassed to ask anyone, so he went to the public library to get a map to see where New Hampshire was. Wherever it was, it had to be better than Ft. Lauderdale, Florida. Everyone back home asked about orange trees and the ocean and girls in bikinis, but all he saw was the highway to the ballpark and the inside of the duplex and the crappy school bus they rode for five, ten, sometimes twelve hours at a time. And whoever thought you could grow tired of sunshine? Like a twenty-four hour snowstorm back home, but in reverse. And the humidity, God, the humidity, you couldn't take enough showers in a day to feel clean for longer than fifteen minutes.

But as his dad reminded him in a letter he wrote to buck up his homesick son's spirits, he wasn't there for the weather or to see the sights or to enjoy the scenery— he was there to put his nose to the grindstone, to put his shoulder to the wheel, to get his name in the newspaper. By the end of the year, he'd broken his nose in a home-plate collision (he was called out) sprained his right shoulder swinging and missing at a nasty sinker (he struck out), and by season's end his statistics, as published in the *Ft. Lauderdale Times*, read: Batting Average .209, RBI 11, Home Runs 1, Strike-Outs 89, Stolen Bases 4. He didn't embarrass himself in the field, but he didn't distinguish himself either, which at baseball's lowest minor-league level is almost the same thing. Show us something special or show yourself the door, son, there are plenty more hometown heroes where you came from.

He stuck it out for another season before his sore shoulder and aching ego sent him back home on another Greyhound, another one-way ticket. His father kept on him to stay in shape and keep his spirits up and not to give up on his dream. He also got him a job at Webster and Sons Roofing where he'd worked for 23 years and where everyone was a big baseball fan and had lots of questions about what it was like to play for the Yankees. "The Ft. Lauderdale Yankees," he'd remind them, and hammer in another nail. It wasn't Florida hot and humid, but laying down shingle on a tar roof at two o'clock in the afternoon in August sure as hell felt close to it. He might not have known what his dream was anymore, but he was pretty sure what his nightmare was: 23 more years of this shit. He still had his banked bonus money and used it to enroll in the University of Western Ontario.

Where he discovered that he liked school. He stuck to intramural sports—the shoulder had healed up okay, but he limited himself to beery touch football on Saturday afternoons and a bit of golf with some of the guys from his residence—and focused on his studies. He majored in political science, but what he really wanted was to one day teach physical education in high school. Of course. It was obvious. Why hadn't he thought of it before? Games: he could play games all day again, play games and pass on to others just how much fun it was to play games. After all, wasn't that the way it was supposed to be?

"Where's the towel?"

"I didn't take it," I said. I lifted my hands from the half-full sink of soapy dish water to confirm my innocence. "I'm doing the dishes."

"No shit, Sherlock," Julie said. "The *dish* towel. You know—to dry the dishes."

The evening dishes—washing *and* drying—were my responsibility, and I never volunteered to help Julie when it was her turn in the morning. People usually only did nice things for you when they wanted something even nicer in return.

"Goof," she said, taking the towel from my shoulder and lightly flicking me in the chest with it, locker-room style, "You'd forget your head if it wasn't screwed on." I moved over a few inches to make room at the counter.

You'd forget your head if it wasn't screwed on was something Mom used to say, and in the same gentle poking, joking way. Not bothering with the white plastic drying rack anymore, handing her the heavy crock pot to dry directly, I noticed how much Julie looked like Mom. She'd always had the same longish, thin face and high cheekbones and alert, blue eyes, but now, now that she was as tall or taller than Mom, I really saw it. My sister was beautiful. I felt sort of proud.

"Hey, remember last winter when you wanted to go to Toronto and you told Dad you might ask Mom if you could stay with her? Would you have really done it?" I said it like the question had just occurred to me between the clean crock pot and the dirty mashed-potato bowl and wasn't something I'd always wanted to know but never knew how to ask or when to ask it.

"Sure," she said. But her *sure* wasn't what it sounded like; too casual, too chirpily off-the-cuff to be either.

The kitchen radio was on, I must have turned it on, although I didn't remember doing it and couldn't give a good reason why. Who cared about the latest update on what was happening in Iran and who could be bothered with the kind of crappy music CFCO played? There *was* a dial, and it didn't have to stay stuck on Chatham's only station, there were others, better ones, like CKLW. There was even an FM switch that could be flicked and FM stations like the ones Julie listened to. But we left it on CFCO. CFCO was what always got played in the kitchen.

I kept washing and Julie kept drying, and I thought I caught her humming along to Kenny Rogers' "The Gambler," which was playing on the radio while she wiped. She noticed me noticing her. Instead of pretending she'd been humming something else, she laughed and sang along with the song, the part about knowing when to hold 'em, knowing when to fold 'em, knowing when to walk away, knowing when to run.

"What a lame song," I said.

"Yeah, and you know all the words to it, too."

"No I don't."

"Right." When the chorus came around again, she sang along again, this time singing at me, holding the potato masher in front of her face like a microphone.

"Cut it out," I said, but smiling, scrubbing the potato pot.

She closed her eyes and sang louder, the end of the song giving her a convenient chance to belt out the chorus twice. The song ended and the disc jockey started talking and she opened her eyes and we both laughed and she dried the masher. A commercial for a furnace company came on next reminding listeners that winter was just around the corner and now was the time to replace that old unreliable furnace or take advantage of their fall furnace check-up special.

"What was your initiation like?" I said. "When you started at CCI, I mean."

"What are you talking about?"

"The grade nines. They get initiated, right?" I let the water from the tap fill up Dad's coffee cup and then did it again. It was important to get the coffee stains out, but you didn't want it to taste like soap the next time you used it, either.

"Who told you that?"

"I don't care," I said. "I'm not worried. I just figure if I can find out what it's about, why wouldn't I want to know?"

Julie shook her head while she wiped. "Whoever told you CCI still had freshman initiation is full of it. Probably someone who never even went there, right?"

I shrugged. Dale had told me, back when we still told each other things. I really hadn't been worried—not like

207

math-exam worried—but couldn't help feeling better. The commercial break was over and another song came on, "The Devil Went Down to Georgia." It hadn't been a hit long enough for us to know the words without wanting to. "Remember those hymn tapes Mom brought home and played all the time?" I said.

"You remember that?"

"Yeah."

"You were so young, I mean."

"I remember."

All that was left was the silverware, which I had already washed and put in the drying rack before Julie showed up. She started in on the forks. "You've got Mom on the brain today," she said.

I was rinsing the sink, directing all of the little pieces of leftover food into the drain catcher. "Do you ever think… I don't know… that maybe we should have tried harder to get her to stay?"

Julie stopped wiping; looked at me. "You weren't old enough to know what it was like, Tom, not really. God, God, God, day and night, every day, all day. Did you know she wanted Dad to tithe twenty-percent of his income to that stupid church she belonged to?"

"I know, I remember."

"You couldn't have, you were too young."

"I said I remember."

"Do you also remember she was having an affair with Reverend Bob? Yeah, her and Holy Joe."

I removed the catcher from the drain and emptied it in the garage pail underneath the sink. It had seemed like one day there was Mom and Dad, the next day there was Mom and Reverend Bob, where and when the one started and the other began as unclear as why it happened.

I crossed my arms and leaned against the kitchen counter, looked at my running shoes. The song was still on and it made me mad that although it was a dumb song, I was starting to memorize it. How come you knew things you didn't want to know, but things that you wished you did, like the name of all the provincial capitals, you didn't?

"She left *us*, Tom, not the other way around."

"She said Dad told her to leave."

"Maybe he did, but that's not what I meant. And you know what I mean."

I kept looking at my shoes.

"Look, she's Mom and I love her too, the same as you do, but she's happier this way. And so are we."

"How do you know if she's happy?"

"When you talk to her on the phone, does she sound like she's sad?"

"I don't know."

"Yeah, you do. She sounds like somebody she's supposed to be. Just… love her and be happy for her. That's all you can do."

I'd finished scrutinizing my running shoes. "We haven't seen her in, like, three years."

"Love her and be happy for her." Julie hung the dish towel over the oven door handle. She went into her room and I went into mine.

Sometimes we'd sit on the grass for a few minutes after we were done our jog. There were acres of thick green lawn and plenty of tall shade tress and more chirping birds and fluttering butterflies than even in Tecumseh Park, but if you thought too much about where you were it could get in the way of having a good time while you were there. The blade of grass I was chewing while lying on my back looking at a cloud resemble a three-legged sheep got its extra-grassy greenness from the daily deposited dearly departed, the A-1 fertilizer otherwise known as fresh funerals. Funerals that provided rotting corpses that, in turn, provided nutritionally rich soil for, say, the blade of lip-hanging grass I was looking at with slight difficulty over my nose. Life, death, fertilizer, repeat. I spit the piece of grass out, but it landed on my bare thigh. I flicked it back where it came from, where it would begin being whatever it was going to be next.

"My grandfather is buried pretty close to here, I think," Allison said. Having completed her customary fifty post-jog sit-ups, she was watching as the late-afternoon sun created long vertical shadows on the trees that looked like someone had spray-painted them black. "We used to come here all the time and look after the plot and the flowers. It's been awhile now though." It was still August, but the shadows came out earlier every day. "My Grandpa had a big place near Charing Cross that used to be a small farm with lots and lots of land. He used to take me with him on his big riding lawnmower when he cut the grass. My parents were always all, 'Dad, no, she's too small, she might get hurt" and he would ask me, 'Allison, do you want to help Grandpa cut the grass today?' and I'd say yes, and he'd scoop me up and we'd ride around all afternoon. And when we were done he'd let me have a sip of his beer." Her palms were flat on the cooling earth behind her, her tan, muscled legs extended in front of her. "I still can't believe he's really gone, you know?"

"I guess."

"I mean, I know he's dead, but it's like—how can someone you know and love just be *gone* one day, gone forever? It's just… weird." *Weird* was Allison's favourite word.

"I know what you mean, but in a way, it's weirder that he was ever here at all. That any of us were ever here at all."

A breeze came up that was less summertime-refreshing than surprisingly chilly, and Allison tried to rub the goosebumps out of her thighs. "You don't know what I mean," she said. "You have to have lost somebody who was really important to you to know what I'm talking about, somebody who's been there your entire life."

"Don't you remember science class last year? How Mr. Bennett said that it takes a billion sperm to make one zygote?"

"So?"

"So, remember how he said that if there was one life preserver thrown into the ocean and there was only one turtle in the ocean, the odds of that one turtle sticking its head out of the water at the exact instant that the life preserver was thrown and its ending up around the turtle's head would be about the same odds as anybody being born as who they actually are."

Allison looked as if she were going to say something, but turned her head and studied the shadow-splattered trees instead. By the time I got home and showered and ate dinner and did the dishes it would almost be dark. The sun felt good on your skin and in your bones, but it was still going to die and everyone and everything with it. But if you talked about something else you could avoid thinking about it for awhile.

"Do you want to see if we can find it?" I said.

Allison paused before answering. "Find what?"

"Your grandfather's grave."

Allison looked at the trees. I'd said what I'd said so that she'd feel better, so she wouldn't be mad at me for talking about sperm and zygotes and life preservers and turtles instead of her grandpa. Now it seemed as if I'd made her even more upset, that she couldn't even look at me for fear of screaming or worse. In a quiet, calm voice, though: "So when you got lost in the sewer when you were a kid and everybody thought you might be dead but then you were all right after all—is that what made you think about things like that?"

"Things like what?"

She laid back and shut her eyes. "Like… I don't know, like things that are just… weird."

I thought Allison might have been the one. Someone I didn't have to lie to. It would have been nice just once not to have to tell someone what they wanted to hear—to be able to just say what had happened—that nothing had happened—but everyone, it seemed, needed me to tell them *their* truth. I plucked another blade of grass and stuck it in my mouth and pretended to see something in the distance that wasn't there.

"I was really young," I said, "so not all of it makes sense, not even to me." Allison's eyes were still closed, but she nodded. "But the main thing I remember is missing my mom. Not exactly *missing* her—I mean, I'd only been down there for half a day or so, so it wasn't as if I'd never been away from her for that long before—but it felt like… like it wasn't real, like what was happening couldn't be happening to me, and if my mom had been there with me it would have been… not okay, but normal, kind of."

"I can understand that." Her eyes were open now, she was looking at the sky.

"Really?"

"Sure. That makes complete sense. People you care about are almost… supposed to be there."

"Right, that's right."

She rolled onto her side and looked at me, head resting in her hand. "That's why you can talk about the odds of a life preserver landing around the head of a turtle and all the rest of it, but some people you can't imagine not being there."

"Even when they're not."

"Even when they're not."

I picked up my bike. "We better get going," I said. "We don't want to be riding home in the dark."

We used to have a car like everybody else, but that was when we lived on Vanderpark Drive, when we still lived with Mom. When Dad sold the house, he decided to sell the station wagon too, said that, between everything but my school now being within walking distance and the gas shortage meaning that filling the tank meant spending a small fortune, there wasn't any point paying for a car we'd have very little reason to use. He eventually bought a second-hand orange moped for when it was necessary to get somewhere too far away to reach on two feet, so it wasn't as if our automobile-less lives were all that much different than before. But it was different, was one more way Dad could make sure we weren't the same as we'd been when we were four instead of three.

Dad didn't use the moped much, but one day when I was at home by myself he called and said he'd run out of gas near the Wheels Inn and didn't have any money with him and that I needed to go downstairs and ask Mr. Coleman to fill a can with gas and drive it over. For some reason Mr. Coleman didn't have a telephone.

"What if he's got customers and he can't come?" I said.

"Just go," he said. "And tell him to hurry."

Mr. Coleman's shop was predictably empty except for him polishing a green bottle with a tiny white cloth no bigger than the size of a matchbox. When I told him what had happened and what Dad wanted him to do, he put down the bottle and cloth and picked up the cigar burning in an ashtray on the countertop. He puffed and blew a stream of blue smoke and chuckled. "So your old man's putt-putt went kaput on him, did it?"

"His moped, yeah."

He chewed his cigar and chuckled again. "Maybe he should switch to a ten-speed, they're even better on gas, I hear."

I didn't like it that Mr. Coleman called the moped a *putt-putt*. And what was wrong with trying to save money on fuel? Dad said that every time somebody filled up their gas guzzler they put money in the pockets of the kind of people who were burning American flags in Iran. Mr. Coleman was a jerk. What kind of person had a shop with nothing in it but old bottles? No wonder he never had any customers.

"Dad said to try not to take too long."

"Oh, well, we better get going then," Mr. Coleman said. "Let me slip the *Back Soon* sign in the door and grab my hat."

We didn't talk much in the car, neither on the way to Esso to fill up the red gas can he had in the trunk nor on the way to the Wheels Inn parking lot, where Dad had pushed the moped and was waiting for us. Mr. Coleman chewed on his cigar the entire way, a dog gumming an old sock. He drove with both hands on the wheel and sat so far forward on his seat that his nose nearly touched the window. When we'd had a car and it was only Dad and me, sometimes he'd steer with just a pinky finger. When we'd stop at a red light he'd wait, wait, wait, then snap his fingers and point at the light which would always change to green.

Dad was sitting on the curb with his helmet resting on the ground between his legs, his knees almost touching his chin. It was warm out and he'd taken off his jean shirt and tied it around his waist. With his tattoos and long hair tied back, he looked like an overgrown adolescent who'd been reprimanded for riding his bicycle too fast. We pulled into the parking space next to him and got out of the car. I wanted Mr. Coleman to open his trunk and get out the gas so we could just fill up the moped's tank and get going. Still chewing on his cigar, he walked around the front of the car to where Dad was sitting.

"Thanks for coming, Jack," Dad said, standing up.

"Not a problem."

They shook hands and looked at the moped standing upright on its kickstand. The sun was shining directly on it. It looked like it'd been painted with orange marmalade.

"I feel like a damn idiot," Dad said. "Never once ran out of gas in my entire life, not once."

Mr. Coleman lit up his cigar and peered at the moped. "That thing got a gas gauge?" he said.

"Not really. Full and empty, basically."

"Well, there you go."

"Yeah, but I should've known."

Mr. Coleman inhaled, exhaled, gave the cigar a good long suck while admiring the trail of smoke he produced. Some guy walked by whistling. People who whistled when they were alone seemed like they were showing off, like they were trying to convince everyone how happy they were.

"Not like you ride it every day, is it?" Mr. Coleman said.

"Hardly ever. That's what pisses me off. I finally do, look what happens."

"That's probably why you couldn't tell it was empty. Not used to it."

"Yeah, maybe."

"No maybe about it."

Dad hadn't said anything to me yet even though I was the one who'd answered the phone and went downstairs and told Mr. Coleman. If I hadn't been home he would have still been sitting there on the curb.

"Well, let me get that gas," Mr. Coleman said.

"Give Tom the key and let him get it. I want you to look at the brake light for a second."

"I don't know anything about these… *putt-putts*," he said, laughing.

Here it comes, I thought. *Look out now.*

Dad laughed too. "A brake light's a brake light. C'mon, just have a look."

Don't beg him, I thought. *Why are you begging him?*

Mr. Coleman took the keys out of his pocket and handed them to me. "The long silver one," he said.

I unlocked the trunk and got the gas and stood there in the parking lot waiting while they talked about the brake light.

Some Guy Who Was Sick, Happy Just to Not Be Sick Anymore

"It's Too Bad You Only Feel Fortunate to be Healthy Once You Haven't Been, If You Know What I Mean"

HE WAS SICK and then he wasn't and Oh my God. Praise Jesus, praise Allah, give the Buddha's belly a vigorous rub while you're at it. He didn't believe in any of them, but somebody or something needed to be thanked. When you're sick or hurt there's no such thing as young and old, rich and poor, beautiful and ugly, fat and thin, there's only you and every other lucky bastard who isn't. Six-foot-one, broad shoulders brain tumour. Cute as a bug seven years old she'll never walk again. Monogrammed his and hers this and that who gives a shit when your fucking back is killing you.

A rare form of leukemia, an excruciating spinal fissure, a really bad head cold: forget it, put away the how-to-be-happy manuals and all the rest of that mind-over-matter mumbo jumbo because aching bones and runny noses know what you really need. Healthy equals happy—even when you don't know it, even when it takes being not healthy to know how happy you actually are. Which, admittedly, is sad. In spite of what certain poets and other professional phonies will try to tell you, however, better sadness than an impacted molar or rheumatoid arthritis.

He whistled while he walked just because he felt like it.

The public library was a good place. The library at school was good too, but not only was it not open in the summertime, it was much smaller than the one downtown. Although I hadn't actually read every one of its books, as I got ready to begin grade eight it sure felt as if I had. Mrs. Wilson, the school librarian, wouldn't actually say anything discouraging when I'd sign out Stan and Shirley Fischler's *Encyclopedia of Hockey* again and again, but I could tell that she wasn't impressed by the way she looked at me as she stamped the return date on the card at the back of the book, not like she would act when, say, Sarah brought a copy of *Charlotte's Web* to the checkout desk. *Charlotte's Web* was one of those books we were "encouraged" to read (Mrs. Wilson had posted a long list of "Reading Suggestions" in black Magic Marker on white Bristol board), and when someone decided to take out one of them she'd smile and say something like, "Oh, this is a wonderful choice, Sarah, I'm sure you'll enjoy it," as if it had been the student's idea all along. When I'd bring up my hockey book or UFO book or shark book, I knew the only thing Mrs. Wilson would say was, "Due back in two weeks."

I didn't know the names of any of the librarians at the Chatham Public Library, but you weren't supposed to; that was one of the things that was good about it: you picked out whatever you wanted and all anyone cared about was whether you had your library card. We'd learned about the Dewey Decimal system at school, so you could also use the card catalogue to find things out. The year before, on my birthday, after I'd gotten off the phone with Mom, I'd gone to the library and looked up hydrogen sulfide gas. Twelve, I decided, was old enough to know what had really happened to me in the sewer. But books could only tell you facts. *If* there's a high enough concentration of gas, it said, it *could* be fatal. *If if if*: I already knew that. Facts couldn't tell you the truth. Only you could do that.

Most of the time, though, I spent in the sports section or where the supernatural titles were kept, but sometimes I'd come home with a book I'd never known existed until I chanced upon it looking for something else. *Things* I'd never known existed. Tracking down the Dewey Decimal System number that would lead me to the UFO cover-up book that I read about in another UFO cover-up book, I came across *Hell on Earth: 20th Century Atrocities. This looks promising*, I thought, pulling the oversized book from the shelf. It looked like a coffee table book, but instead of pictures of cats or muscle cars, presumably there would be photos of cool stuff inside. I flipped its pages while standing in the aisle.

But World War One soldiers without noses, just a pulpy crater in the middle of their faces like burned out candles, weren't cool. Neither were photographs of abused children chained to basement pipes or police shots of entire families lying slaughtered in their homes or skeletal concentration-camp survivors with eyes as big as their faces. I thought of Mrs. Wakowski and felt like I was going to puke. I stuck the book back in place and headed straight for the sports section. I left the library with Ken Dryden's *Let's Play Hockey* and a biography of Gordie Howe, but also with *Hell on Earth: 20th Century Atrocities*. I didn't want to; I had to. Not because it seemed as if I was doing the right thing, but because it seemed like if I didn't take it home and read it I'd be doing something wrong.

Books weren't the only thing you could find at the Chatham Public Library. There was also Chatham's youngest hobo, although Dale had told me that his mom, who was on a committee to raise money to help Chatham's poor people, told him that's not what they were called anymore, that they were supposed to be referred to as "street people." Except that you never saw Chatham's youngest hobo on the street—on a bench in Tecumseh Park when the weather was nice, or, if the weather was cold or it was raining, slumped in a chair with a book in the periodical section at the library. His head was shaved and he wore a long, thick black overcoat year-round, even when it was hot and everybody else was in shorts. He wasn't really that young—probably Mr. Brown's age—but compared to some of the grey-bearded old men you saw pushing rickety shopping carts down back alleys looking for pieces of discarded copper or going through people's garbage searching for returnable pop or beer bottles, it felt like he was.

Aside from how he smelled—a cross between pee and Kentucky Fried Chicken still hot in the bag—he seemed like he was doing okay. He didn't have a cart, didn't bother collecting things that could be sold, seemed to spend most of his time just sitting in the park watching squirrels burying their nuts or sitting in the library reading a book. I wondered what kind of books he read, or if he was reading at all (they were always thick hardcovers, but that was, I reasoned, because he never wanted to give the librarian a reason to say he was just hanging around). Once, when I saw him put his book down on the floor bedside his chair and go outside for a cigarette, I drifted over to the periodicals and, by standing and pretending to leaf through *Sports Illustrated*, managed to sneak a peek. All I could make out was the title: *Does God Exist?*

What would a hobo want with a big book about God? I put the magazine back and decided that it was probably part of his plan, that he was a pretty crafty hobo after all. Not only would any suspicious librarian clearly see that he was reading and not just taking up a seat and resting his feet, how could you kick someone out of the library when they were reading a religious book? If he was reading about God—even if he was Chatham's youngest hobo—he had to be a good person.

Chatham's Youngest Hobo Wasn't
Always a Hobo

"What—You Thought I Was Born with a Bindle
Over My Shoulder and Patches on My Knees?"

NO ONE DECIDES to become a bum. No one says,
when they're eleven years old, "When I grow up I want
to worry about where I'm going to sleep at night and
whether or not I'll have enough to eat." When he was
eleven years old he wanted to grow up to be like his
dad, over there in Korea killing communists and helping keep America free for people like his mom and him.
A picture of his father in his uniform taken in their
backyard in Kalamazoo, Michigan, at a goodbye barbe-
cue sat on his bedside table alongside his baseball-card
collection so that he could see it first thing every morning when he woke up. He brought his picture of his
father in his uniform to class for show-and-tell and got
the loudest applause of anyone, even more than Bert
Watson and his picture of the two-headed cow that was
still-born on his family's farm.

His Dad mailed him letters that were just for him—
"It looks like there's something for somebody in today's
mail," his mother would half-sing—and he'd tear the
letter from her hand and run upstairs to his bedroom
and sit cross-legged on his bed and read his letter with
his father's picture on his bedside table turned to face
him. When he finished and slid it back inside its envelope and put it with the growing pile of other letters
he kept together with a rubber band, he'd feel sad, of
course, because reading his father's words meant hearing his father's voice, meant missing him even more
than he already did, but it also made him feel secretly

guilty, because if his dad hadn't been 6000 miles away he wouldn't get letters in the mail covered with crazy-coloured stamps and people at school, and not just in show-and-tell, wouldn't think he was special.

A dead soldier is a different kind of hero—people lower their eyes and no one applauds. His mother eventually began dating the man who owned the bowling alley where she'd gotten a job because army-widow benefits weren't enough for her and her son to live on. He wasn't supposed to know, but sometimes the guy spent the night; even with his mother's bedroom door closed he could hear him in there snoring in the same bed where his father used to sleep. He still wanted to be a soldier and joined the Junior ROTC at his high school as soon as he was old enough, shined his shoes with purpose and learned to drill with admirable intensity. His Sergeant Major said he had real officer potential, and he might have stayed that way if he hadn't read *On the Road* and learned to like sniffing glue. Kerouac's book made him want to go places— any place at all, just as long as it wasn't Kalamazoo, Michigan—and because he wasn't going anywhere, a dollar tube of Testors airplane glue helped him get there. He liked to lie in bed on his side and sniff and nod, sniff and space out, and one Saturday afternoon he woke up with the tube stuck to his teeth. He snuck down to the kitchen and pulled out his father's tool box from underneath the kitchen sink and used the ball-peen hammer to separate the tube from his face. He stopped attending ROTC.

Huffing glue was good enough to get him through high school—and his mother's marriage to the bowling-alley guy ("You don't have to call me 'Dad' if you don't want to, son")—and pot was as pleasant a discovery as the books that weren't on his Western Michigan University freshman course syllabi: more Kerouac, of course, plus Jack's unbeatable Beat buddies Ginsberg, Burroughs, Whalen, and Corso. Not only could you retain what you were reading while smoking weed, it was a wonder drug when experienced while listening to Miles or Trane or Lester Young, a 3D sound facilitator with headphones on and consciousness blown wide open. He managed a semester and a half before his mother and step-father pulled the pecuniary plug on his "selfish, self-destructive lifestyle." He really didn't care; he'd been meaning to drop out anyway, just couldn't be bothered to go down to the administration building and fill out the necessary forms.

It was a chance to do what he'd always said he was going to do one day anyway: move to Detroit. Going to university was supposed to cure his hometown blues, but his glue-tainted grades meant Kalamazoo's own Western University was the only school to offer him admission. Now he could read what he wanted and get high when he wanted and meet people who were like him. He rented a room in a house near the Wayne State campus with a shared kitchen and bathroom and got a part-time job in the stockroom of an art-supply store and waited for life to happen. What happened was he met a girl working as a waitress at The Cup of Socrates, a Beatnik coffee shop near the university, and they fell in love, first with each other, then with heroin. A part-time stock boy and a minimum-wage waitress have a choice: either quit using heroin or start making more money. The guy at the café who'd initially turned her on offered them an alternative, set them up as his dealers around campus. They didn't make any more money than they had living on her waitressing tips, but they stayed high.

Every once in a while they'd talk about getting clean, about both of them going back to school, maybe even having a baby, but it took more than good intentions and possible plans to get straight. He was already so messed up on wine he missed his vein entirely, but she was always the better shot and fell over on her face a minute after the needle was out of her arm. They'd been excited to try the new stuff, been told that it was unbelievable. He didn't believe it until she was in the ground and he had to leave town because the police were looking for him. When he got his draft notice—different yellow people to kill this time, Vietnamese, but for the same no-good reason— it made it simple: he crossed the Ambassador Bridge to Windsor and told the customs officer that he'd lived in Michigan his whole life without once having visited Canada. The man told him welcome and said to have a nice weekend.

Weeks make up months, months make up years, sometimes your mind is made up for you: he hadn't planned to stay in Canada, he never made a decision when to leave, he just… lived. More or less, just like most people. Crappy, cash-under-the-table jobs, usually outside, hot in the summer, cold in the winter; crappy one-room basement apartments when he was lucky, a small room in somebody's house who doesn't want you there, only your money in their hands the first of every month, when not; wine, cigarettes, coffee, a book, sleep—what else was there? Eventually, it just seemed to make more sense not to give a shit.

The idea of living on the street was understandably hard to accept at first; after awhile, surprisingly easy. To him it was just what happened to him. To the people where he somehow ended up, Chatham, Ontario, a little town an hour north of Windsor, it was who he was. He could disagree, he could try to explain, but who would listen? And what would he say?

It was easy to forget to return a library book. Having anything long enough, being around it all the time, it begins to feel like it's yours even when you know it's not. But *Hell on Earth: 20th Century Atrocities* wasn't hard to remember to return. I read it—although looking at the pictures that adorned each smooth, oversized page was the most difficult part—and had it back to the library two days later.

Napalmed Vietnamese children. Wives with their throats slashed by their husbands. The tortured victims of serial killers. Where were their miracles? It didn't say so in the book, but I bet some of them prayed to be saved too. Prayed as hard or harder than I had when I was lost. Why hadn't God listened to them?

Chapter Ten

You knew it was spring when it rained and the earth smelled like worms. September smelled like school. Even if you never admitted it, even to yourself, the first day of school was exciting, everyone wearing their coolest new clothes but pretending as if they'd thrown on the first thing they'd found in their closet that morning, and friendships and flirtations interrupted by summer vacation instantly resumed on the playground before the first bell of the year rang. Rainy days excepted, there would always be a ball-hockey game going on, and this year was no different but for the fact that none of this years' grade eights—us—were playing, just a mixture of grade sixes and sevens. I saw Dale leaning against the red brick wall of the school watching the game. I walked over and leaned and watched too.

"Stevens is such a spaz," he finally said.

"Which one is he?"

"The kid with the fro and the big honker. Look! Check it out! Empty net and he kicks it a mile wide."

There wasn't actually a net—just the two metal posts that supported the basketball backboard and hoop—but Stevens, if that was his name, sent the tennis ball soaring off the blacktop with his running shoe and into the grass. Everyone stood around with their hands on their hips waiting for him to retrieve it.

"Here come Bennett and Wilson," Dale said. Eddie Bennett and Scott Wilson emerged around the corner of the school tossing a green Nerf football back and forth. I wondered when Dale stopped calling people by their first names; it seemed kind of rude, like swearing but getting away with it. I wondered if he called me by my last name when I wasn't around.

"Hey," they said.

"Hey," we said.

When he knew they couldn't hear him, "Did you see that?" Dale said.

"What?"

"A *Nerf* football? C'mon."

I shrugged, watched the resumed game. I suppose we'd made just as much noise, shouted and laughed just as much as them, but I couldn't remember, it was hard to tell if something was true after you were done doing it. It was hard to tell when you were actually doing it, too. It was getting closer to nine o'clock and more grade eights showed up, including Sarah and Allison, Allison saying something and Sarah laughing while they walked toward us. Allison was wearing the Adidas track suit she always wore. Sarah was wearing tight jeans and a white shirt with the top two buttons undone.

"Hi, guys," Allison said.

"Cutting it pretty close to the bell the first day of school," I said.

"I'm here, I'm here." Allison had been more peeved than disappointed when I told her I wasn't going to keep jogging when school started, or join the cross country team in the spring. She wasn't going to miss me—not much, anyway—she just hated to see anybody quit. Maybe I wasn't going to be a medal-winning long-distance runner, but it wasn't so weird to talk to girls anymore.

"Hello, Dale," Sarah said.

"Hi." When it was clear he wasn't going to say anything else, "Okay, see you guys later," Allison said.

"Did you guys have a fight or something?" I said.

"Who?"

I made a face.

"Sarah? We broke up. You didn't know?" He said it like I'd done something wrong.

I looked at my running shoes. We couldn't afford Converse or Nikes, so I'd gotten a new pair of North Stars. North Stars were okay, there wasn't anything wrong with them—it wasn't as if they were Chex—but they were mostly white with blue stitching and they looked too new on the first day of school, like I was trying to impress someone, and they got dirty too easily, like I was wearing the same pair I'd had the year before. So many things were either too little or too much.

"What about that time you got lost in the sewer?" Dale said.

"What about it?"

"What was it like?"

"I already told you."

"No you didn't."

"Yes I did."

I *had* already told him. I'd told him what he needed to hear about his dad. I knew he must have been feeling bad about breaking up with Sarah, but I'd already told

229

him what he needed to hear once already. Then the bell rang and it was time for school and there wasn't any time anyway.

I still got my morning and after-school ride from Mr. Brown most days, but we didn't talk as much as we used to now that Harrison Hall was slated for destruction. *Mr. Brown* didn't talk as much as he used to—I talked more, because he said less. I didn't like to hear the sound of my own voice so often, but it was better than hearing Mr. Brown saying nothing.

"So my dad says it'll be about the same amount to own our own building as it was to rent where we are now." *Our own building.* I didn't mind hearing myself say that.

"Uh huh."

"And even if it is a little bit more expensive because of property taxes and other stuff, there'll be more people downtown because of the... you know, more people downtown, so he'll get more business and he'll make more money."

Not even an *Uh huh* this time, and I knew why. There were going to be more people downtown and more business for Dad and more money for us because of the new mall. The mall was one more thing Mr. Brown didn't talk about anymore. I wasn't thrilled about Harrison Hall getting knocked down either, but now that the fight to save it was officially over, why couldn't Mr. Brown be happy that people were going to do better, people like Dad and us? Mr. Brown, I decided, was selfish. Some people just couldn't stand other people being happy.

We were almost home as we passed by the big empty space that used to be the old stores that had come down to make room for the mall's main parking lot. There was a crane with a big wrecking ball hanging from it that hadn't been yesterday. I hoped that when they used it on Harrison Hall I'd be there to see it. You didn't see something like that every day.

I wanted stuff—who didn't want stuff? Birthdays were mostly about getting things, and for my fourteenth there were a few things I was counting on. Julie was always good for a record or two, although she decided what I wanted to hear and what I wanted to get so I never bothered dropping any hints otherwise. It bugged me a bit that she thought she was giving me good taste as much as she was doing her sisterly duty, but because she was usually right—it had been hard listening to REO Speedwagon after she'd introduced me to The Ramones, like going back to walking after you've travelled on a rocket ship—I didn't complain. Ever since we were seven or eight years old, Dad always gave us cash for our birthday. One year, I'd use the money for a Phantom Mustang airplane model, the next for a Farrah Fawcett poster. I always got a birthday card from Mom, and although it was nice to find a letter in the mailbox with your name on it, the card itself wasn't much, the ever-present five dollar bill tucked inside along with the same insipid inscription (*Tom/ Best wishes on your big day/God bless you/Love, Mom*). But Mom would also phone me on my birthday, the same time every year, 7:43 p.m., the exact moment I was delivered into the world. Everyone knew to stay off the phone on September 30 when the hands on the clock were praying together 7:43.

Julie was at work and Dad was somewhere else. Whenever he knew Mom was going to call, he tried to be somewhere else. The phone rang *ring-ring* and I was officially fourteen years old and the *tick-tock* countdown to fifteen had already begun. I cleared my throat and lifted the receiver from its mount on the kitchen wall.

"Hello?" Answering the phone like you didn't know who it was when you actually did felt dishonest, but if I said, *Hello, Mom*, that would have felt showoffy. You did things the way everybody else had always done them not because it was necessarily right, but because it was just simpler that way.

"Hello, Tom, it's your mother!" Ever since Mom found God, you could hear exclamation marks at the end of her sentences.

"Hi, Mom."

"Happy birthday!"

"Thanks."

"Do you know what time it is?"

Every year she asked me the same thing. Every year I answered the same way. "7:43. When I was born."

"To the minute, that's right. You didn't think your mother would forget, did you?"

"No." It was what I was supposed to say, but I really didn't think she would forget. I *knew* she wouldn't forget. She'd left us for Jesus and Toronto, I hadn't seen her in a long time, we talked on the phone only a few times a year, during which she always said she really needed to get back to Chatham someday soon to visit us, but I knew she would call me on my birthday, to the minute. Maybe that was what people meant when they talked about faith.

"How's school?" she said.

"It's alright."

"You're in grade eight, king of the castle now."

"Yeah, I guess so."

"And now you're fourteen. You're a real teenager now."

"At least it'll be easier to get into good movies." Without having to lie quite as much about my age, I meant.

"I'm sorry, Dear, what do you mean 'good movies.'"

"It's just—" It's just that it would be easier to gain cinematic access to naked boobs and the bloodiest of murders "—just movies, that's all."

I could hear her nod. I could hear her thinking of something else to ask me. I could hear the phone hum.

"How's Silver Wings?" I said.

"Oh. Well. As a matter of fact, there *have* been some very interesting changes going on, and not just in our little company but in the whole courier industry itself, at least in the bigger urban areas like where we are. I say that—'little company', I mean—although with a full-time employee now plus the several part-timers that work for us on and off—and that's not including Bob and me, who work *more* than full-time, believe me—we're not really a little company. But anyway, what I was saying was, we've started using bicycle couriers now, can you believe that?"

"Oh, yeah?"

"Yes, and it's actually surprising that no one thought of it before. With all of the traffic and general congestion down there around Bay Street, it's amazing that it never occurred to anyone to give it a try, it really is. Bicycles can get around so much easier, you see, and you don't need to look for a parking space and you don't need to pay for gas."

"That makes sense, I guess," I said.

"It really does."

I thought of telling her about how I cycled to the cemetery this summer and jogged with Allison, but she was interested in telling me something and it didn't feel right to be interested in anything else.

"And another thing about bicycle couriers," she said, and another thing and another thing and then another, until I heard the door open and someone in the hallway.

"I guess I better get going," I said.

"I can't believe it's nearly eight-thirty," she said. "Have I been talking too much? We were supposed to be talking about your birthday."

"No we weren't. We were just talking."

She God blessed me and told me to take care of myself and we said goodbye and it was Julie who'd come home, still in her Dairy Queen duds. If being an NFL player didn't work out, I wasn't sure what I wanted to be when I grew up, but I hoped I wouldn't have to work for a courier company or have to wear a uniform and serve fast food. What you didn't want to do with your life seemed almost as important as what you did. I put the receiver back in place on the wall.

"Your annual Mom birthday communication?" she said.

"Yeah." I went to the refrigerator and got a C Plus. "You want one?" I said, holding up my can, the fridge door still open.

"Since when do you share your sacred stock of C Plus?"

"You want one or not?"

"I'm okay," she said. She watched me pop the tab and take a drink. "It was so dead tonight. I had more slushies than any person ever should plus a couple of Dilly Bars because I wasn't already enough of a pig."

I faked the laugh that was expected of me and said I was going to my room.

"Don't you want your birthday present?" she said.

"Sure."

"Wait here." She went upstairs to get it while I stood there drinking my C Plus. When she came back down she'd changed into jeans and a faded blue T-shirt and had a sealed record album in her hand.

"Welcome to fourteen," she said, handing me the record. "It only gets better."

We didn't bother wrapping each other's gifts. Thirty seconds more of surprise in return for a hassle for you and a bunch of garbage for them. I set my can on the counter and took the album. "Thanks," I said. "Although of course I don't know who they are." The band was The Undertones, and that must have been them on the cover, just a bunch of ordinary-looking guys with short hair sitting on a brick wall staring at the camera.

"I knew you were going to say something like that, so I was going to get you the new Blondie record because I know you like the one I got you last year, but it sucks, they've totally gone commercial."

"Thanks," I said, putting the LP under my arm and picking up my pop. "I'll listen to it tonight."

"Trust me, you'll like it. Play 'Jimmy, Jimmy' first. You won't be able to stop singing it. If you listen to the words, I won't tell you what it's about, but it's actually really sad, but you won't be able to not sing it."

"Sounds like fun."

"Just play it. Trust me."

"I do."

"I'm serious, you wang."

"So am I."

I don't think she knew what to say to that, which made sense because I didn't know why I said it, so I took my pop and new album and went upstairs. Halfway up, "Happy birthday," she said.

Average Guy Lives Average Life
"It's Not That It's Bad; It's Just That It's Nothing"

DON'T MISUNDERSTAND: HE never felt as if he were destined to do something special, to be someone important, that he deserved to live a life of unremitting interest, ease, and pleasure. Even as a boy he knew he wasn't the sharpest knife in the drawer. He recognized he'd never burned with ambition. He acknowledged he was average. Acknowledged it and was okay with it. What was wrong with being average? Not everyone can be someone. Better to be happy with who you really are than unhappy trying to be somebody you're not. Say what you wanted about him, he always knew who he was.

Forty-seven years old, he knew he was fucked. How many years already of: an hour to get ready for work; half an hour to get to work; eight hours of work; half an hour to get home from work; an hour to wind down from work; set the alarm for work; sleep; an hour to get ready for work; half an hour to get to work; eight hours of work; half an hour to get home from work; an hour to wind down from work; set the alarm for work; sleep; an hour to get ready for work; half an hour to get to work; eight hours of work; half an hour to get home from work; an hour to wind down from work; set the alarm for work; sleep. How many years more of the same?

Of course, it wasn't *all* work. His high-school football team finished second in the county his senior season and he had a good seat on the bench to watch the march to runner-up. There'd been almost three semesters at the University of Windsor before he realized he was in over his head and dropped out. There were two marriages and just as many divorces and a couple of kids he rarely saw. There were several funerals and weddings, a few stays in the hospital, 1,537 hangovers. Eighteen more years of work and he could retire and wait for the cancer that was going to kill him.

He never expected his life to be exciting. He never wanted to be the center of attention. If life was a movie, it was all right to be a supporting actor or even an extra, every film needs those too, not everyone can be a star. But he never imagined that life was like the same movie, every day the same goddamn movie—being in it, seeing it, seeing yourself being in it—the same goddamn movie.

There's the alarm; hit the snooze button, just five more minutes, just five more minutes. There's the alarm.

Halloween used to be easy. What could be easier than dressing up as your favourite superhero and holding open a pillow case for people to fill with free candy? But fourteen was the gateway age to hanging up your costume: too old to put on a plastic mask and tights and pretend to be Spiderman for the night, too young to be content to stay home and be the one handing out the candy. Content or not, though, you couldn't trick or treat when you were fourteen. Dale, for instance, was vice president of the student council—how would it look if the vice president was seen begging for miniature Snickers bars while wearing a rubber Frankenstein mask? Grade eights simply didn't trick or treat.

This year Halloween fell on a Friday and Dale and I were spending it at my house. Dale's parents made as big a deal about making their house Halloween-menacing— cardboard tombstones on the lawn, a glow-in-the-dark plastic skeleton hanging in the front window—as they did ensuring that, come Christmas time, they were Ho-Ho-Ho-certified (wooden cutouts of Santa and his reindeer on the roof, every inch of the house brightly lit and dependably blinking). Dale's TV was bigger and got more stations than ours, but if we were at his house he'd have to help his mother give out candy. Because we lived over top of dad's shop, no costumed, sug-ar-searching children ever came calling on us. Dad said that next year, after we'd moved into our own building, Halloween would be like it used to be when we lived on Vanderpark Drive.

"Why are we listening to this?" Dale said.

It was too early for a horror movie to be on TV, and I'd slipped on my Glenn Gould album after the Alice Cooper record Dale had chosen was finished. I shrugged and pretended like I didn't know what he meant. "Yours was over so I put this one on." I didn't want him to think I was trying to get his attention, but I wanted him to notice what I'd put on, for him to ask me questions so I could tell him what I knew. I picked up the empty record jacket and looked at its cover.

"Did you know that Glenn Gould is Canadian?" I said.

"Who's that? The guy on the cover?"

I nodded. "He's the piano player."

"They're called pianists."

"Just because you don't like classical music doesn't mean you have to be a jerk."

"They *are*," Dale said. "My sister studied piano for, like, five years. Somebody who plays the piano is called a pianist."

"Yeah, and somebody who plays the violin is called a scrotum, I bet."

"Not *penis*," Dale laughed. "*Pianist*." He picked up the LP jacket and looked at it. "Oh, yeah, I know this guy. My sister has tons of his albums."

"I doubt it," I said.

"Why?"

I didn't like it that someone else owned a Glenn Gould record. I didn't like it that someone else knew about Glenn Gould before I did. I didn't care that it didn't make any sense. "There was only one of his records at Sam the Record Man," I said.

"So?"

"So I doubt if they ever had more than one. Two at most, maybe."

Dale put the record cover on top of one of my speakers and stretched out on my bed; yawned. "She probably got them in Toronto," he said. "Her and my mom used to go there all the time when she was serious about playing. That's where the Royal Conservatory is. You know what that is, right?'

"Duh," I said, sitting at my desk now and with my back to him, busy pretending to be looking for something in the messy middle drawer.

"What is it then?"

"What? The Royal Conservatory?"

"Yeah."

"What does it sound like?"

"That's what I asked you."

"Duh."

"You already said that."

"Whatever."

"Because you don't know, do you?"

"Whatever."

"You already said that too."

A single scream, two people laughing, a thump, footsteps in the upstairs hallway. "Is that your sister?" Dale said.

"Probably."

"Who's that with her?"

"Probably her friend Angie."

"Oh, man, you mean that one with the black fingernail polish and the green hair who was here that time before?"

"It was only green for a week. She dyes it whenever she's bored."

"She's hot. Weird, but definitely hot." Lady's man Dale. Goes out with a girl for four months and all of a sudden he's Burt Reynolds. And not just that: Dale talking about Angie's hotness bothered me the same way his talking about his sister knowing all about Glenn Gould bothered me.

A knock at my bedroom door; I got up to answer, and Angie on the other side wearing padded hockey pants held up by suspenders, a thin, white, virtually seethrough T-shirt, and bare legs and feet. Even for her this was a bit much. Then I noticed that the hockey pants were mine, Pee Wee discards from years ago. I laughed. Then she laughed and I laughed some more.

"Just hurry up and ask him," Julie yelled from her bedroom.

"Ask me what?" I said. "How you ended up looking like a hockey hobo?"

"*Hockey hobo*—that's pretty good, actually. Did you make that up all by yourself?"

"Me, myself, and I."

"Just ask him!" Julie shouted. "We're going to be late because you have to flirt with every single person you talk to."

"Yeah, like I'm flirting with your little brother," Angie yelled back.

"Just ask him and let's go."

Even if I knew she wasn't flirting with me, I liked it that someone thought she might be. I crossed my arms and leaned into the door frame.

"Have you got any more hockey equipment?" she said. "Julie found these"—she plucked the suspenders with her thumbs—"but I need at least a stick or something."

"What's going on?" I said.

"It's Halloween, Dummy. Don't you have a calendar?"

"Yeah, Dummy, but I'm also not ten years old. We're hanging around here tonight."

Angie popped her head inside. "Who have you got hiding in here?"

"Dale, this is Angie. Angie, this is my friend Dale."

"Hello, Dale, friend of Tom's."

Dale was sitting up on the bed, knees up to his chin, hands cupping his knees. "Hi."

Angie and I looked at him. He looked at us. Angie turned back to me.

"So. What else have you got?" she said.

"Nothing. I haven't played hockey in a million years. I don't even know where Julie got those."

"C'mon, you've got to have something." We both looked around my bedroom.

"What's this music?" she said.

"Glenn Gould. It's Bach's *Goldberg Variations*." I wished I remembered Bach's first name. At least I didn't call him a *penis*.

"I didn't know you actually had any musical taste," she said. "You're okay for a squirt."

"Take a look in the mirror: you're the one going trick or treating, not me."

"For one thing, it's a Halloween party, and for— A hockey puck!" Angie spotted the commemorative Chatham Maroons Senior A hockey puck they gave out the first year the Seniors were back in town. I'd kept it because the team folded again a couple of years later and someone said it might be worth something someday. "Can I borrow it?"

"Sure," I said. I grabbed it from the top of the dresser drawer and handed it to her.

"What are you going to do with it?" I said. "You can't just walk around with a hockey puck in your hand."

She thought for moment, tossed the puck in the air and caught it. "I don't know yet, but I promise I'll bring it back."

"You better," I said. "Have fun."

"Thanks again."

I closed the door and turned around and Dale was still sitting up on the bed looking like he was waiting for someone to tell him he could stop.

"What time is it?" I said.

Dale looked at his watch. He'd gotten an expensive Timex for his fourteenth birthday, the kind like in the ad on TV that took a licking and kept on ticking. Whenever you asked him what time it was he usually answered "Time to buy a watch" before eventually telling you. This time all he said was, "Almost 9:30."

I looked where the hockey puck used to be. The spot where it had sat on the dresser was a shiny perfect circle of not-dust. "Still two hours until The Ghoul."

"More like two and a half. They moved it to midnight."

"Really?"

"Yeah."

More laughter from Julie's room. I wondered what she was dressing up as. I should have asked when I had the chance.

"It's your turn to pick a record," I said.

"Okay," Dale said, but he didn't move.

I lifted up the dustcover, turned over the Gould, and dropped the needle.

The better Dad's mood, the more likely we were to eat takeout. Who wanted to plan a meal and shop for it and cook it and clean up afterwards when there was so much excitement going on? William Street Tattoos wasn't doing any better—business was even slower than usual, in fact, probably because, if there wasn't much incentive to go downtown before, jackhammers and wrecking balls and the taste of demolished-building dust provided even less—but Harrison Hall was coming down and the mall was going up and, along with it, Dad's expectations for the local tattoo trade. He hadn't signed any papers yet, making the new building officially ours—the owner always seemed to be at his house in Florida golfing or fishing—but that was just a formality.

"How about some egg roll with your plum sauce, Tom?" Julie said.

"Bite me."

"Hey," Dad said. "We're eating dinner, all right?"

"She started it," I said, crunching into my favourite part of the Lucky Dragon's Dinner for Four. You needed lots of sweet plum sauce to compliment the crispy fried dough if you wanted to maximize all of its Chinese goodness, the same way that doughy chicken balls were best enjoyed saturated in warm orange sauce.

Forking a squiggly helping of chop suey onto his plate from the tinfoil dish, "I don't know why we always order so much chinky food," Dad said. "We'll never eat all of this."

Julie set her fork down. "I think it's called *Chinese* food."

"What did I say?"

"*Chinky* food."

Dad chewed, looked at Julie while he chewed, swallowed. "It's just an expression, sweetheart."

"A prejudiced expression."

"If I'm not prejudiced—and you know I'm not—using a word doesn't make me prejudiced. It's just a word." He must have known he was losing the argument because he looked at me when he'd finished.

"What about a really bad word," I said, "like—"

"Okay, that's enough," he said. "I don't know why we always order so much *Chinese* food." Julie picked up her fork, Dad shook his head, I squirted some more plum sauce on my egg roll.

We always ordered too much food because there was Dinner for Two, Dinner for Four, and Dinner for Six, but no such thing as Dinner for Three.

"I'll have the other egg roll if no one else wants it," I said.

"I bet you will," Dad said. "Eat something besides the chicken balls and we'll see."

"You won't be able to keep up with your girlfriend next time you're out jogging if you don't eat your vegetables, Tom," Julie said.

I was supposed to be bothered by the insinuation I had a girlfriend, so even though I wasn't—kind of liked it, actually—I made a face. Because Dad's mouth was full of chop suey, he could only look from me to Julie, and we dropped it, concentrated on filling our own mouths.

If Dad decided we were going to eat takeout at home, it was usually either Chinese food or fish and chips, never just burgers or pizza. When Julie and I were kids and there were still the four us, Friday was grocery day, and after we were done shopping and the trunk was packed with brown paper bags full of next week's necessities, we'd stop off on the way home to eat somewhere, usually A&W. Dad would park beside the speaker and we'd tell the scratchy voice on the other end what we wanted and then the girl would come out and attach a tray to the rolled-down driver's-side window and bring out our food, which Dad would distribute around the car. I didn't like it when Julie and I would get our usual Teen Burgers to go with our fries and root beer and Dad would order the Papa Burger, but sometimes, instead of getting the Mama Burger, Mom would order a hot dog. She wasn't supposed to do that. She was supposed to get the hamburger that was the hamburger just right for her and be like the rest of us.

It was Saturday night and the windows of the apartment were open and we all had somewhere to go and something to do. I'd collected for the week and homework could wait until Sunday night and I was meeting Dale at the Capitol Theatre where a new horror film, *When a Stranger Calls*, was playing. Angie was coming over later and she and Julie would spend a couple of hours scuttling between the bathroom and Julie's bedroom getting ready to go to some party at somebody's house whose parents weren't home. Dad still had use of the owner's key to our building and liked to take his tape measure over there after dinner and jot down the dimensions of rooms. And even if the movie wasn't any good, and if you asked Julie and Angie about the party afterward and they invariably said it sucked, and even if Dad had already recorded the square-footage of everything there was to record by now, he always came home whistling, and sometimes with donuts from Wiersema's Bakery. They'd be there on the kitchen counter whenever you got home and you knew they were for the family, you didn't have to ask if you could have one. I'd put two on a plate and pour myself a glass of milk and eat them in my room. The next morning, the empty plate and the dirty glass would remind me I'd forgotten to write them down before I went to bed.

"Who wants more chicken fried rice?" Dad said, white cardboard carton in one hand, fork in the other.

"I'm stuffed," Julie said, pushing away her plate, leaning back in her chair. "Beyond stuffed."

"Tom?"

I didn't say anything, but he knew what I was thinking.

"Go on, take it," he said, pushing the last egg roll my way. "Unless your sister wants half."

Julie tossed a plastic package of plum sauce in front of me. "How could I deprive a growing boy of his egg roll?"

"Thanks," I said, tearing open the top of the package with my teeth.

"Just don't eat the container," she said.

Dad laughed, I smiled, and there was going to be lots of leftovers for tomorrow.

Illegal Chinese Immigrant Rises to the Top of Business World Through Hard Work and Dedication

"Knowing in Your Head How Something Should Be Isn't the Same as It Actually Being That Way"

NOT THE COLD or the smell (cheesy plastic, or maybe it was plasticky cheese) or the casual bigotry or the people who all looked the same and talked the same and did the same, all the same—solecisms were what he minded most about his new country, insults to his adopted idiom that weren't the weather's fault or the fault of his faintly odorous samey hosts but obviously only his.

"Bawss, you call me?"

That's not right, you know that's not right. "Call" is the present participle; "called" is the correct form for past tense. You know that. Try it again.

"Bawss, you called me?"

You mean "Boss."

"Bawss."

Better, but…

"Bawss."

Forget it. Just get a mop and pail and clean up the puke some kid just made at table six.

Both of his parents were doctors in the military, so it hadn't been exceptional for him to join the People's Liberation Army when he was fourteen years old, where he served nearly five years on the northeast border with Russia. He was admitted to university just before the Cultural Revolution shut down the schools for a decade and Chairman Mao's Little Red Book was all anybody needed to read, but his subject of preference—medicine—was ignored and he was assigned to study engineering instead. He was never very good at math and he didn't want to build bridges or buildings, but he did what he was told because that's what he was told to do.

He graduated and was working on a project that took him to Taiwan for a conference on tailings dams when he took a taxi to the airport in the middle of the night and got on a plane and flew to Canada. It might have been America, it could have been Britain, but there was a flight leaving immediately for Toronto so it was Canada. He called his father a week later and his father told him that not only was he a widower, he now had no son, and hung up. He didn't call back.

Toronto and its Chinatown was the obvious choice, but he ended up in Chatham, Ontario, because of a job interview for an engineering firm (the only one he managed to gain in two months of dedicated trying, and only because the company was small and just starting up and couldn't afford to pay much) that led to the realization that his weak English and foreign degree were double strikes against him ever being employed in the only field he was educated to work in. He'd used up most of the remaining money he'd managed to bring with him to Canada to get his only suit dry-cleaned for the interview and buy a roundtrip ticket, and after the man had shaken his hand and thanked him for his interest in the position and wished him good luck with his job search, he walked where his feet took him downtown, and wondered how he was going to pay next month's rent. It was only a small room in a house overcrowded with seven other Chinese illegals—shared bathroom, shared kitchen, shared oxygen—but it still cost money, money he soon wouldn't have. He kept walking.

He saw a Help Wanted sign in the window of one of Chatham's two Chinese restaurants and an hour later he was the Lucky Dragon's newest dishwasher. The job came with a room over the restaurant and he only had to share the bathroom with the two waiters and one of the cooks. He didn't have a God to thank and he didn't believe in fate or destiny, so he settled on considering himself lucky. Lucky to find the Lucky Dragon. He did believe that life was strange.

It's not a lie, but it's rare, and it happens so seldom that it lacerates like a lie to those whose lives have been bet on it and who lost and wished they'd never been born to play, but it's not a lie—the American Dream, even slimmed down to modest Canadian size, does sometimes, intermittently, exist. Existed for him, anyway. Went from: dishwasher to kitchen staff to waiter to manager to (work work work, save save save, work work work, save save save) sweat-equity investor to ten-percent owner to full partner to actual owner, 57 years old and always attired in an open-neck white golf shirt, freshly pressed grey slacks, and with silver-streaked black hair Byrlcreamed and parted sharp to the right. He didn't need to do it, he could afford to have someone else do it for him, but every evening he liked to answer the phone for an hour or so, just to hear his own voice.

"Good evening, Lucky Dragon, may I take your order, please?"

"Yeah, hi, uh, can I, uh, get the dinner for four, I guess."

"Certainly, sir. Will that be pick-up or delivery?"

"Delivery. 48 William Street South."

"And the last name, sir?"

"Buzby."

"Thank you, Mr. Buzby."

And someone else would cook it and someone else would deliver it and at the end of the night someone else would clean up, but he'd always count the money. He was never very good at math, but he was the boss, that was what the boss did.

"There they go again," Dad said, talking to the television as much as he was to me.

"Who?"

"Who else? The damn Soviets. Putting their noses where they don't belong. Again."

You tried to avoid the news, but sometimes it just wasn't possible. It was Friday night and Julie had skipped dinner, was out with Angie somewhere, and Dad and I were eating dessert in front of the TV. The only condition he applied to television-watching while eating—in this case, a fat hunk of Sara Lee chocolate cake—was that the channel be turned to the news and what kind of mess the planet had gotten itself into since yesterday's broadcast. I would have preferred *Hogan's Heroes*, but eating cake on the couch was worth putting up with the world for a few minutes.

The anchorman said that the Soviet Union had long been aiding Afghan forces fighting against fundamentalist insurgent groups with names I couldn't pronounce who were, in turn, being funded and aided by, among others, the United States. Millions, maybe billions, of dollars were being supplied by each side, but the anchorman never said why, so I asked Dad.

"Because the USSR wants to take over every country it can get its hands on and make them communist, that's why. And the US is just trying to stop them, trying to spread democracy."

"The anchorman said that the guys the US are supporting are Islams, though—aren't those the same kind of guys in Iran who took the Americans hostage?" Every news program began with an American hostage update. Behind the broadcaster would be a big black number saying how many days it had been since the hostages had been taken prisoner. Today was Day Eleven.

Dad took the last bite of his cake; looked at his plate while he chewed. He set his fork on the plate and placed it on the coffee table. "It's complicated," he said.

That part I was pretty sure of. That's why I'd asked him what I did. "Isn't it kind of crazy for both sides to spend all that money—and now they're saying the Soviets might send soldiers to Afghanistan too—just for, you know, an idea."

"Some people hate freedom, some people love it," he said. "Seems pretty simple to me."

You just said it was complicated, I wanted say. I ate what was left of my cake instead.

We were learning about the Cold War in history class, the jittery game of nuclear chicken the two most powerful nations in the world had been playing off and on since the end of World War Two. Mr. Brown told us about 1961 and the Soviet ships on their way to Cuba stocked with nuclear-tipped missiles that were intended to be pointed at the US and the United States' insistence that they turn around or else. Everybody knew what *Or else* meant. *Or else* didn't happen that time—the Soviet ships circled back and headed home—but if the USSR followed through on their threat to send troops to Afghanistan and the Americans decided to do the same, maybe this time it would. All of a sudden the sun blowing up millions of years in the future didn't seem as scary as it used to. I told Dad I was going to my room.

"What do you say we finish off that cake?" he said, winking.

"I'm stuffed," I said.

He looked at his stomach and gave it a couple gentle taps. "Probably best if we save some for your sister anyway." He handed me his empty plate and I took it and mine into kitchen and grabbed a can of C Plus.

I tried to read, but my eyes wouldn't stay stuck to the Teflon words. Even Glenn Gould and Bach couldn't stop me from thinking about *Or else*. Then I remembered I hadn't recorded dinner in my Journal of Consumption yet and I felt happy. I pressed the pen hard to the page as I entered each item; I could feel the white paper soaking up the blue ink, something that hadn't been there only an instant before now looking as if it *had* to exist, had *always* existed. When I was done, I felt sad until I spotted my can of C Plus on the corner of my desk and I wrote down that too.

When Dad heard me in the kitchen and asked me what I was doing and I said I was getting another piece of cake, "I thought you said you were full," he said.

"That was before," I said. "Now I'm hungry again."

Chapter Eleven

Dad made his living giving other people tattoos and had plenty of tattoos himself, but he never talked about tattoos, not like, say, Allison's dad, who somehow always managed to work drain-cleaning or valve installations or sewer replacement into every conversation, even when he was just talking to the paperboy. There hadn't been any new tattoos in a while—all the ink that covered Dad's arms was there when I was old enough to notice: a shining star on his left bicep; a flaming Phoenix rising from its own ashes on his right; a moon rising in the mist, a tiger poised to pounce, Julie's name and mine in flowing fancy script. And Mom's name, too, where his right arm became his shoulder. You never saw it unless you caught him with his T-shirt off, shaving in the morning or stepping out of the shower, but it was there.

"I'll be out in just a minute, kiddo," he said, his Fu Manchu moustache freshly trimmed and his razor put away and just the foamy white excess left to deal with. Dad wasn't like Julie—was an in-and-out of the bathroom user—so "just a minute" wasn't just an expression to keep you from pounding on the door again.

I was standing in the bathroom doorway in my pajamas and bare feet. "It's okay," I said.

He looked at me while he toweled off his face and neck. "Won't be long until you'll be keeping your old man waiting while you're shaving."

"I guess."

He kept looking at me like he was trying to spot evidence of an incipient teenage moustache. If he was, he was wasting his time—I'd already tried the same thing and it didn't work. I looked at Mom's name on his arm and wanted to ask him why he still had it, but knew I'd better not. He didn't offer tattoo removals himself although I'd overheard him tell some of his customers that it happened all the time.

Instead, "When did you get that star tattoo?" I said.

"When I was young and stupid."

"Not as young as me, though."

"No, not that young. And don't get any ideas—you know the rule."

The rule was no tattoos until I was nineteen, the same age as anyone coming into his shop. I wasn't even sure I wanted one when I was old enough—anything your parents did couldn't be all that great.

"Why'd you get a star?" I said. Getting an eventually-exploding star stencilled on your body made about as much sense as carrying a calendar around with you everywhere you went—why would you want to remind yourself of Time's ticking hand?

Dad blasted the water from the faucet and used his hand to rinse the remaining whiskers in the sink. "Would you believe me if I said I don't remember?"

"Not really."

Dad laughed. "I don't blame you, but trust me, it's true. I suppose I just liked the way it looked, plus it was different. Everybody I knew back then that had a tattoo had either an anchor or *Mom* or a crummy-looking motorcycle, so I guess a star seemed kind of unique." He turned off the tap and wiped the sink dry with a piece of toilet paper he folded in two. "Besides, a star is pretty cool, don't you think?"

I didn't tell him that I thought a star was about as far from cool as the earth was from the sun, the someday-to-be-expired sun. "When did you get the tattoo of Mom's name?" I said. I was as surprised to hear my question as he seemed to be.

He pulled on the white T-shirt that had been hanging on the back of the bathroom door and bye-bye Mom. "A long time ago," he said.

"Like when you guys met?"

"I forget, kiddo."

This time I knew he wasn't telling the truth. I knew because he didn't ask me to trust him. I'd come this close to the sun without burning up, what were a few more inches? "Did you ever want to get rid of it?" I said.

"How about pancakes?" Dad said.

"What do you mean?"

"What do you mean 'What do you mean'? Your dad is going to make us pancakes this morning, how's that sound?"

"Good."

"Good. Now get cracking on that shower. They'll be on the table by the time you're done and dressed."

It was cold—the kind of cold that keeps you from going outside. Or, if like me, you had to be outside—it was Saturday after all, and assaultive winds and skin-pinching temperatures or not, *The Chatham Daily News* needed its money so I needed to make my collections—you hurried from house to house hoping that whoever opened the door wouldn't have that week's payment ready and would let you inside for a few minutes so you could at least partially thaw out before having to step back outside again. But everything was okay now. I was at home on a Saturday night doing nothing while the rest of the world was out somewhere busy doing something, but that was okay too.

Even though it was even colder than it had been that afternoon, I was lying on the couch in the warm living room eating a bag of Lay's barbeque chips and watching a midnight horror movie on channel 50. Even better, the movie was showing on *The Ghoul Show*, hosted by The Ghoul himself, a self-confessed "sicko" ("Stay sick," he'd encourage his viewers) who wore a light blue lab coat and a curly blond wig and a fake black moustache and goatee and dark sunglasses with one lens missing. He looked like the kind of person who'd periodically blurt out his most famous catchphrase, "Hiya, gang. Hiya, hiya, hiya." During breaks in the movie—always bad, but so bad it was usually good—he'd make corny jokes and blow up model cars and food with firecrackers and sometimes even a plastic frog named Froggy whom he took pleasure in physically and verbally assaulting throughout the show. The only part I didn't like was when his voice would suddenly interrupt the movie itself, commenting on how phony a flying saucer looked or how implausible a plot turn was. For a bad movie to be a good movie, the people making it—the writers, the actors, the prop people—had to have tried to succeed. It wouldn't have seemed ridiculous if they hadn't been sincere. If you treated it like a joke, it wasn't as funny.

Julie and Angie were at a dance at CCI and Dad was at the new building, where he went when he wasn't at work or at home. Although the deal had been delayed again—the owner had broken both his legs skiing in Colorado—it hadn't stopped Dad from increasing his presence in the place. His latest project was refinishing the hardwood floors, first sanding them all down and then coating them with polyurethane. He'd go to work then come upstairs and eat and then head over to the building immediately after dinner, coming home several hours later covered in wood dust or smelling like sweet poison, but always happy, exhausted but happy. He'd drink a bottle of beer standing up in the kitchen, too wound up to take a shower first or to even sit down.

It was a supposed-to-be-scary scene in the movie—the skulking monster could see the smooching couple parked in the moonlit convertible but they couldn't see it—so it was quiet and I heard Julie and Angie come up the stairs.

"You mean you've never heard the expression 'Laughing at children'?" Angie asked.

"I think that's 'The laughter *of* children,' Julie said. "'Everyone loves the laughter *of* children.'"

"Are you sure?"

"I'm pretty sure."

"Wow. That's not how I remember it."

Julie stuck her head into the living room. "Hey," she said.

"Hey."

"Dad burning the midnight oil with William?"

William was our nickname for the new building because it was on William Street.

"I guess so. He left here with two new paint brushes, anyway."

Angie walked into the middle of the room and stood there, looked at the TV with her arms hanging at her sides. Both of them still had their coats on. Angie wasn't wearing a hat and her long hair—red this week—was still specked with melting snow flakes.

"What's this?" she said.

"*The Hoofing,*" I said.

We all watched the monster creep closer to the unsuspecting couple.

"Is it going to attack them?" Angie said.

I knew better than to answer. Obviously she was setting me up.

"Is it going to hoof them?" she said.

Is it going to hoof them? I looked at Julie. She just rolled her eyes. *Maybe she's drunk*, I thought—they *had* been at a high-school dance. But drunk people slurred and stumbled and shouted, and Angie wasn't doing any of those things.

"C'mon, Ang," Julie said. "Let's make grilled cheese."

"Wait a minute," she said, holding up a single finger. "I want to see how this turns out."

We all watched the monster—obviously a tall thin man in a crappy-looking lizard costume—wave his arms in the air and make a lot of groaning sounds and chase the couple into the woods. Then The Ghoul came on with a bag of apples in one hand and a bunch of firecrackers in the other. "Hiya, gang. Hiya, hiya, hiya."

"Ang, c'mon," Julie said.

Eyes still stuck on the TV, finger in the air again, "Hold on," Angie said. "Who's this guy? Is he with the hoofer?"

Obviously, she was either making fun of me or the cold had frozen her brain and it hadn't defrosted yet. Either way, I didn't want to risk saying anything. Julie stepped into the room and touched Angie's arm—barely enough for her to feel it, but enough that she'd know she was there.

"Let's make grilled cheese, Ang," she said.

Lifting her finger and pointing at the television, "He's going to light those firecrackers."

"He blows up stuff all the time," I said.

"He *blows* things up? He *blows things up all the time*?" Angie put her face in her hands and slowly shook her head back and forth, softly moaning like the monster in the movie. The snow in her hair had all melted now; it looked like her hair was crying.

"It's just The Ghoul," I said.

Angie removed her hands from her face and stared at me; looked like I'd just told her that the hoofer was in the other room.

"Okay, that's enough," Julie said and snapped off the TV. The picture faded to a single silver point then disappeared. This time she put her arm around Angie's shoulder and gently but firmly guided her out of the room. "I'm taking Angie home," Julie said. "Before Dad gets back."

I was going to say something like *Bundle up*, but that would have sounded lame, like something Mom would have said to us when we were kids. "Okay," I said, waiting until I heard the door slam downstairs before turning the TV back on. The Ghoul's set was littered with blown-up apples, but he was yelling at Froggy for making such a mess, so I knew there'd be at least one more explosion later. And I still had half a bag of barbeque chips left and the Hoofer was still on the loose.

Dale got another girlfriend so I had no choice but to try and kiss Allison. Joanne Scott was nothing

259

special—average everything with the added irritation of laughing at anything anybody said that she thought was supposed to be funny, whether it actually was or not—but Dale had dropped me for a girl again. We weren't the same friends we'd been before he'd started going out with Sarah, but since they'd broken up he was at least someone to go to the movies with, stand around with at recess, make fun of the teachers with. Now he and Joanne ate lunch by themselves, held hands at recess, passed notes back and forth during class. It wasn't like I really wanted to do any of those things—not with Allison or with anybody else—but no one wants to get left behind like Charlie Willard, who had to repeat grade seven.

Most of the time, I only saw Allison at school. But because we both lived downtown, sometimes we'd run into each other and I knew that because of basketball practice she took the city bus home on Tuesday and Thursday nights, the last bus of the night pulling into the terminal not too long after I wrapped up my paper route. It was cold and already getting dark even though it was just a little after six p.m. I'd timed it perfectly; my surprise at seeing Allison just as she was leaving the station was convincing.

"Hey," I said.

"Hey."

I'd rehearsed what I was going to say, but the words stayed stuck in my mouth. Allison noticed the empty newspaper bag sagging from my shoulder.

"I thought you finished up your route over by CCI," she said.

I'd prepared for this. "I've got a bunch of new customers over near the Fifth Street Bridge. They're not supposed to be on my route, but what the hell are you going to do about it?" I'd thought the inclusion of *hell* was a nice touch, would add an element of pissed-off authenticity.

"Okay, well, see you," Allison said. She flipped her Adidas bag over her shoulder and walked away.

"Hey, I forgot," I said. "I've got the key to our new building. My Dad wants me to check something we've been working on. Want to come with me?"

I had the key because I knew Dad wouldn't notice—business had gotten so slow, he'd taken to keeping William Street Tattoos open until eight p.m. Thursdays, Fridays, and Saturdays—and the closest I'd come to helping him was being there when he'd bought the sandpaper and mop and polyurethane.

"Now?" she said.

"Why not?"

"It's dinner time. My parents will freak out if I'm late."

I swung my paper bag from one shoulder to the other; looked down at the ground as I spoke: "Right—family dinner. Since Dad started putting in extra time at the shop we haven't had too many of those." I kicked a piece of ice skidding down the sidewalk. The final bus had come and gone; the depot was empty.

"Where is it again?" she said.

"It's on the way to your house. It's near the Granite Club, right across the street from Tecumseh Park."

"Right, you told me. I guess I do go right past there on my way home."

"I know, right?"

"Okay," she said. "Just for a minute though, I've got to get home for supper."

"Yeah, just for a minute."

On our way over I learned that Sarah was also going out with someone new, resulting in Allison being dropped again too. "It's gross," Allison said. "They're not even in high school yet and they both think they're such hot shit."

Allison rarely swore, so I knew she was upset. Allison was rarely upset, so I knew Sarah dumping her was a big deal—bigger than Dale blowing me off to be with Joanne.

"Just wait until next year," I said. "There'll be more people—better people—to hang out with." I knew she was going to CCI too.

"I wasn't talking about new people. I was talking about Sarah."

"I know, but—"

"Is that your building?" she said.

It was, and there we were, but as I pulled the key from my pocket I wished I'd given it a test drive. I hoped it would fit in the lock and the handle turned on the first try. It did, and we were inside and part one of my plan was complete. I remembered where one of the first-floor light switches was and flicked it on, revealing a large empty room with particle-board walls and shiny, freshly polyurethaned floors and an empty bucket and mop. Also, thankfully, Dad's portable eight-track player, obviously left over from his last floor-restoration session. I'd never had a girlfriend, but I'd watched enough movies to know that seduction usually included music.

"I guess this'll be your Dad's new shop," Allison said.

"Yeah. And we're going to live upstairs."

"Just like you do now."

"No. Right now we rent. When we're living upstairs here it'll be *our* house. And there's a backyard. That'll be ours too."

"Neat," Allison said. "What are you supposed to be checking? I should get going."

"Just a sec," I said, pushing the eight-track into the player, "Bad Moon Rising" in mid-song jumping out of the tiny, single speaker. I wished it was something a little more… make-out friendly, but I was glad it was Creedence. It was Dad's favourite tape, and I liked them and Julie liked them and even Angie, who ordinarily didn't approve of any music not made by somebody with a safety pin stuck through some part of their body, liked them. Creedence Clearwater Revival was like french fries: anybody who didn't like them was either lying or a jerk.

"Want to see where my room's going to be?" I said.

"Is that where the thing you've got to check on is?"

"Yeah." Lying was like anything else: the more you did it, the easier it was.

"Okay, but let's make it quick."

"We'll be quick, don't worry." If everything went according to plan, we *would* be quick: hand on her hip, my lips to her lips, and a kissing virgin no more. And Dad had said we could order a pizza from *Mike's* tonight, extra-large with whatever toppings we wanted. I led Allison up the dark stairs to the second floor and what was going to be my bedroom.

"What are you doing? What's the matter with you?"

I rubbed my shoulder where Allison pushed me; pushed me with the palm of her hand hard enough that I stumbled backward. I found her first question easier to answer. "Kiss you," I said.

"Why?"

"I don't know. Just so…"

"Just so what?"

"Just so… so I could say I'd done it."

Allison squinted at me and slowly shook her head like I'd seen her do only once before, when one of her teammates had passed the basketball to a player on the opposite team.

"You know we're not friends like that," she said.

"I know…"

"And it's not fair to make me have to hit you."

I came for a first kiss, I ended up hearing myself say that I was sorry I'd forced someone to hit me.

"Let's just go," Allison said.

"Okay."

"And Tom?"

"Yeah?"

"Don't you dare tell anyone what happened."

I wanted to say, *Nothing happened*, but, "Okay," I said.

"Promise?"

"Promise."

"And don't ever mention this to Sarah."

"Why would I tell Sarah?" I said.

"Just don't."

"I already said. I won't tell anyone."

"Good."

"All right."

"Okay. Let's go."

"Okay."

I didn't tell anyone, and not just because Allison made me promise not to. Who goes around bragging about how a girl wouldn't kiss him? Not that it mattered much, though, because Allison had told Sarah, who of course told Dale, because they were talking again, and who wasn't ready to let my shameful present turn into my barely remembered past quite yet. Of course he wasn't.

"Was it like you actually kind of kissed and then she stopped you, or did she see it coming and shoot you down before you could even do it?"

Since he already knew more or less what happened, I told the only lie I thought I could get away with that would make me look slightly less like a loser than I actually was. "We kissed," I said. "She just freaked out. I just don't think she's ready for a boyfriend yet."

"No shit, Sherlock."

I was delivering Tuesday's newspaper and Dale was along for the walk. Sometimes he'd say how being a paperboy was easy, how he didn't understand why I complained sometimes, but he could stop and go home any time he wanted, he didn't have to deliver every last newspaper even if it was raining or snowing or boiling hot or you had a bad head cold or sometimes just didn't feel like it. It was easy to have an opinion about something if you didn't know anything about it.

"Believe me," I said, "if she wanted a boyfriend, it would probably be me. We're pretty good friends, actually. I'm just saying." I felt better because at least the friendship part was true.

"Man, you don't know, do you?"

"Know what?"

"You really, really don't know." No one had ever looked happier about someone else not understanding what they were saying.

"Whatever," I said. Most houses, I could toss the paper onto the porch or front step without leaving the sidewalk, but Dr. McKay's had a screened-in front porch like a fancy cottage so I put the newspaper in the mailbox. Dr. McKay was our family doctor and he was all right, but he'd delivered me fourteen years before, so I always felt funny about shaking his hand, his hands the hands that pulled me into the world. We started down the street toward the next house on my route and Dale looked left, looked right, looked like he was worried we were being followed.

"She's a dyke," he said.

"I told you, I don't care." I tossed another newspaper onto another porch. "What are you talking about?"

"You know: lez be friends, lez go homo."

"Homo? You mean, like…"

"I mean like she's a homo—you know, a homo. She likes girls."

"Girls?"

"*Girls.*"

I tossed another paper. "It's not true," I said.

"Oh, yeah? Why isn't it true?"

"Because it isn't."

"Are you a girl?"

"No, but she was my friend. She *is* my friend. I'd know."

"You think she'd tell you?"

"Yeah. Probably."

"Wrong. She doesn't want anybody to find out. Would you?"

I didn't have to, but I walked the paper to the next mailbox, lifted the lid and dropped it in; took my time doing it. We started walking again.

"Anyway," he said, "you can believe me or not, but I know. Sarah told me."

"If Allison doesn't want anyone to know, why would she tell Sarah then?"

Dale swivelled his head to make sure it was safe to talk. "Because that's who she likes. Sarah is the one she wants to kiss her."

There were only a few more houses to go before my bag would be empty and I could go home.

"Don't say anything to anybody though, okay?" Dale said. "Sarah told Allison she didn't feel that way, but they're still friends. Promise me you won't say anything, okay? Sarah would kill me if she found out I'd told you."

I tossed a newspaper that didn't make it to the porch. I walked across the frozen grass and picked it up and placed it on the cement step.

"Promise me, Tom."

"Okay."

"No, I want to hear you promise me. I'm serious, Sarah will kill me."

"Dale?" I said.

"Yeah?"

"Fuck off."

Long-Serving Physician Masters Human Anatomy, Struggles With Human Nature

"It's Bones and Guts and a Pump and, Maybe, Something Else"

FEET. JUST THE number of feet alone he'd looked at in his life. Fractures, sprains, foot fungus, plantar fasciitis, heel spurs, stone bruises, Metatarsalgia, Morton's Neuroma, Sesamoiditis, hammer toe, claw toe, ingrown toenails, turf toe, bunions, corns, calluses, tendonitis. And then the phantom pains, the I-can't-really-explain-it-but-it's-there twinges and aches, the no-less-sincere if entirely physiologically baseless complaints of the hypochondriac or the just plain lonely (a doctor's touch, after all, is still human contact). Start there and work your way up, from calf-muscle tears to quad strains to hernias to ulcers to bronchitis to throat nodes to sinus

267

infections and you've seen it all—*he'd* seen it all—acres of broken human bones, miles of infected organs, gallons of polluted blood. Thirty-three years a doctor, and an old man's bushy ear is a middle-aged woman's vagina is just another piece of meat with hair on it. And people wondered why he wasn't very good with names. He healed bodies, not people.

And sometimes he didn't do that. Inoperable. Terminal. Untreatable. Incurable. Irremediable. Buddy, you're SOL. And surprising how few people actually break down in the office when they hear the final, fatal verdict; don't wail in agony or spit and scream in anger or demand a different answer, this can't be happening, there has to have been a mistake. The shock, certainly, but habit probably played a part, too—don't make a scene, don't embarrass yourself or others, don't parade your emotions in public. Sometimes he even detected a whiff of shame, the embarrassment of the dying exposed before the living. And how often had he been thanked? "Thank you," they'd almost invariably say upon leaving. He tried to remember to not answer back, "You're welcome."

Only once had he been the stunned one. The Buzby boy, the one who'd disappeared down the sewer hole and was given up for dead but who came back and now delivered his *Chatham Daily News*: that one had made him… think. He knew the boy—knew the entire family, had been their GP since the mother was pregnant with the older sister—but that had never made any difference before; he'd watched other longtime patients die, not to mention more than one friend and even members of his own family. But that was the thing, that was the very thing: the boy *didn't* die. The boy was supposed to die—everyone said so—but he didn't. He didn't know all the facts, only what he'd read in the newspaper and heard on the radio, but the boy was given up for dead, that much he knew. The sun came up today, the sun came up yesterday, the sun came up the day before that and the day before that, and of course it was going to come up tomorrow—his entire professional career, his whole philosophy of doctoring, was based on the knowledge that things happened because they had to happen. He couldn't do his job—couldn't do it as well as he did it, anyway—believing that *maybe* or *possibly* or *if* or *perhaps* were words one could live by. Bones and organs and blood and here's how they work and this is why they don't anymore and I'm very sorry, Mrs. X, please see the receptionist on your way out about making your next appointment.

But the Buzby boy. He knew something. Paying him on Saturdays when he'd come to the house to collect, giving him a tetanus shot in the office when he'd stepped on a rusty pop top in his bare feet, he wanted to ask him… what, exactly? He didn't even know the answer to that. And even if he did, how would it look, a fifty-nine-year-old physician asking a teenage paperboy how, if there's no guarantee that the sun will rise tomorrow, everybody nonetheless acts as if it will? More: has to act as if it will.

He paid for his week's worth of newspapers, he gave him the shot and told him when he could take the bandage off, he didn't ask him anything.

———

I just delivered the news, I didn't pay attention to it— not on purpose, anyway. But if you wanted to listen to the University of Michigan Wolverines football game on Saturday afternoon on WJR, AM 760, you were stuck with the news updates that came on between quarters and during halftime. You could get up from your desk and turn the volume down until the game resumed, but if you were trying to get your geography homework done before it was time to start collecting for your paper route it was a pain having to get up and down, up and down. Some things you just had to put up with. The world was one of them.

Player personnel turned over so quickly in college football, you were really only cheering for the jersey and the team. In the case of the Wolverines, the team plus Bob Ufer, U of M's radio play-by-play voice and number one cheerleader, whose piercing cry of "Meee-chigan!" punctuated every Wolverines touchdown and pivotal defensive stop. His heart, he informed listeners at least once per game, was made of "cotton pickin' maize and blue" (the team's colours) and he blew a horn after every Michigan touchdown, the same horn that had once been a part of General George S. Patton's jeep. Football was war, and Bob Ufer had a military metaphor ready for every possible game situation. Today Michigan was way ahead late in the fourth quarter and Coach Bo Schembechler knew what to do: "General Bo's gonna stay on the ground now. There's no Luftwaffe. He's got the tanks in." Good. Saturday afternoons felt like Saturday afternoons were supposed to feel when the Wolverines won.

The game was over—Michigan 24, Purdue 7—before I was done identifying all the Baltic States and which ones bordered which and what the major sea routes were, and if I wanted to start collecting and be done in time for dinner I didn't have time to be messing around with the radio.

... the hostage-taking in Iran... the deposed Shah flew to a military hospital in Texas to recuperate from his operation in New York... claim that the Shah is a murderous dictator who needs to be brought to justice... the Shah is a sick old man being hounded by religious fanatics and political radicals... ultra-conservative Islamists seized the Grand Mosque in Mecca in an apparent attempt to overthrow the US-supported Saudi Arabian government... Muslim Pakistanis stormed the U.S Embassy in Istanbul and killed two US servicemen... sports, weather, and traffic right after these messages.

I snapped off the radio and shoved my homework in my gym bag and went downstairs to the kitchen for a C Plus. The phone rang and I answered. It was the owner of the building who said he needed to talk to Dad. Ordinarily, Dad would be downstairs in the shop, but he'd said he was going to close up early today to make sure he got to Colour Your World because he wanted to make sure he had what he needed for tomorrow, when they'd be closed. Sunday he was going to start painting our bedrooms. We'd gotten to choose our own room colours. I'd picked blue.

"Please make sure he gets this message and that he calls me back as soon as possible," the man said.

"Okay," I said, and hung up. I was going to write Dad a note, but I when I heard the downstairs door bang open I figured I'd just tell him instead. But it was only Julie and Angie.

"Hey," Julie said, heading straight for her bedroom without even taking off her coat. I knew she was going to get changed for her Saturday shift at Dairy Queen. Angie would probably walk with her to work. Angie didn't have a part-time job. She liked to tease Julie about hers, sometimes called her the "Ice Queen."

"What's going on, Tom?" Angie said, leaning against the kitchen counter, gloveless hands in the pockets of her baggy green army jacket. Unless it was freezing or storming, high-school kids tended to wear flimsy coats and running shoes and never wore gloves. Looking cool didn't seem worth freezing your ass off.

"Nothing," I said.

"Nothing," she said in a deep voice, her attempt to sound like me. "Nothing," she said, deeper still. "Nothing."

"Whatever," I said, getting my pop from the fridge.

"So what's the Miracle Boy up to today?" she said.

I stood there with my unopened C Plus in my hand. Angie smiled, having achieved the effect she'd obviously been aiming for.

"I saw the article in your sis's scrapbook. Not every-body makes the front page of their hometown paper. Congratulations."

I pushed the tab on my can, took a sip. I took another sip. "Julie never lets anybody look at her scrapbook," I said.

"I didn't say she did."

"You shouldn't look at other people's stuff without their permission."

"This coming from the guy who opens his neighbour's box of sex toys."

"I didn't know it was somebody else's until I opened it."

"Of course you didn't," she said.

She kept looking at me. I looked at the floor. I didn't have to stand there, I could have gone to my bedroom.

"That must have been a real drag for you," Angie said. "Dealing with all of that miracle bunk."

"It wasn't bunk," I said. What was it then? "It was…"

"It was what? Don't tell me you believed that stuff? Well, I guess you were just a kid. Still, it wasn't very fair of them to lay all of that on you. I mean, I get poetic licence and everything, and I know they've got to sell newspapers, but, c'mon: 'The boy who came back from the dead?' *Gawd.*'"

"Yeah, I know," I said, "but—"

"But what?"

"I mean, the fireman did say he thought it could've been fatal."

"Yeah, and he was obviously wrong. We're not talking about a Nobel Prize-winning scientist here, we're talking about a fireman. A *Chatham* fireman."

"What's being a Chatham fireman have to do with anything?"

"You're probably right. People everywhere need something to gossip about. And believe in."

It was my turn to say something. I looked at the kitchen floor again.

"Hey, Tom," Angie said.

I looked up.

"Do you want a Hertz Donut?"

"What?"

"I said, 'Do you want a Hertz Donut?'"

I didn't know what she was talking about. "Okay," was the only thing I could think of to say.

She punched me, hard, in the shoulder. "Hurts, don't it?" Angie laughed and laughed.

Julie came into the kitchen wearing her Dairy Queen uniform underneath her unzipped ski jacket. "What's so funny?" she said, already smiling even though she didn't know what she was smiling about.

"I just gave your brother a delicious 'Hurts, don't it'."

"Oh, man, you fell for that?" Julie said.

I walked past both of them as slowly, as casually as I could to the stairs, careful not to rub my arm. It itched more than it hurt.

Chapter Twelve

I listened from the other room when Dad called the owner back after getting home from the paint store. He sounded sunnier than I'd ever heard him on the telephone, never his favourite form of communication ("Hello, Frank, Bill Buzby here returning your call, how are you doing?"). He sounded angrier than I'd ever heard him sound anytime anywhere (every swear word I knew and a few that were out-and-out revelations). He sounded scared ("But I could go back to the bank and tell them I need more money… I didn't say it would be simple, I said… It's not too late, I just told you I can get it… I'll just tell them I need a bigger loan… It's not too late, Frank, I'm telling you it's not"). He sounded desperate ("I mean, the amount of work I've done over there, you have no idea. Look, we had—what do you call it?—a verbal contract, right? You can't just double the asking price just because you feel like it. Maybe I'll sue, then. Yeah, well, you let me worry about that").

My father had been right, things *were* picking up downtown now that the mall was under construction. Property values *were* increasing. Except that they were supposed to rise after we were property owners, not before. I went upstairs to my room and shut my door. I sat on the edge of my bed, didn't bother putting any music on. I felt bad, like I should have hung around the living room in case Dad needed to… I don't know, talk about what happened or just to have somebody around he could be mad at. I thought about all of the brand new cans of paint and brushes and rollers still in their Colour Your World shopping bags sitting in the kitchen. And that didn't make me feel too good either.

Julie was talking about going to Toronto again, but this time she wasn't bothering to talk about it with Dad, just Angie. And me, because they needed my help.

If Dad had been barely okay with the idea of her going before—and then only if acceptable accommodation and supervision were arranged in advance—now was definitely not the time to hope he'd seen the light and softened his attitude. After a lawyer he consulted advised him that, while he certainly could sue the owner of the building, number one it could end up being very expensive, number two he probably wouldn't win, Dad decided that no one was to ever mention our once-upon-a-time new home or the new mall. It was like when Mom left: it was all anyone could think about, it was something we didn't talk about. It was like the stale smoke that stayed in the air of the tattoo parlour long after a customer had put out his cigarette and left. And it was December, it was too cold to open a window to let any fresh air in.

This time the discussion wasn't about *if*, only *how*. *When* was already settled, was obvious: after Julie and Angie's final Christmas exam. There would still be nearly five more months of school left after the winter term began in January, but Angie explained that once the results of their Christmas exams were in and their overall grades tabulated, these were what the universities would use to evaluate the entry applications due in February. Ace the Christmas exams and don't stumble too badly on the way to June's finish line and that was that, bye bye Shat-ham and hello T.O. And because getting grades good enough for UofT apparently wasn't incentive enough, they'd also decided to treat themselves to a Toronto holiday if they got the job done to Julie's fussy satisfaction. Angie was in charge of the celebratory carrot (which bands they were going to see, what bars they had the best odds of sneaking into, whose couches they were going to crash on); Julie's job was to make sure they deserved it (endless flash cards, a semester's worth of notes mastered by rote, dirty hair tied back into ponytails because who had time to shower every day with all the studying they had to do?).

"Whatever," I said. "Just leave me out of it, okay?"

I meant it—it would be bad enough being the only one around when Dad hit the roof, I didn't need to add guilt or suspicion of complicity to the agenda—but I had to admit, it didn't feel terrible to be invited in on their scheme, kind of like the way I hadn't been happy that Dad had been considering suing the building owner even though it was undeniably neat to think that he might. Suing people was something people who were rich or who lived in big cities did.

"Don't be a total douche, Tom," Julie said.

Whatever a *douche* was, it wasn't good, you definitely didn't want to be one. But even douches have their dignity. "Why can't you just—"

"Because," Angie interrupted, "we already said. Without your saying that you saw her and talked to her, your dad isn't going to buy it for a minute."

Angie rarely took anything seriously. The trip to Toronto must have been important. Important enough for them to plead with me to assist them in maintaining the Dad-deceiving illusion that, while they were really in Toronto for three jam-packed days and two nights of post-exam jollies (whether or not Julie's virginity was still on the agenda, I tried not to think about), Julie was burrowed away at Angie's place studying because there were fewer distractions there; no meal times or housework to worry about, a study-space change of pace was as good as a scholarly rest. It wasn't as if Dad would have a clue that CCI's last exam was Friday, December fourteenth and not Monday, December seventeenth.

"What if he doesn't believe me?" I said. "Then I'll be dead too."

Although Dad was at work, we were in Julie's bedroom with the door shut and locked and The Ramones on the stereo. Ramones music made me nervous. I liked it, but it made me nervous. I wished we were listening to my Glenn Gould record instead. Bach was difficult to explain—even to yourself—but one thing about it was for sure: it made you feel the opposite of nervous.

"He'll believe you," Angie said.

"How do you know?"

"Because he won't have any reason not to. Plus, he'll want to believe. People lie to themselves all of the time. All they need is a good excuse." Angie winked at me.

Ramones records were loud and fast, but all the songs were short and now the side was done. While Angie flipped it over, Julie looked out the window like she was worried Dad's spying eyes might somehow appear at any second. *One-two-three-four* one of the Ramones counted off the first song on side two of the record.

"Okay," I said. "I'll do it."

They both screamed at once and suddenly The Ramones didn't seem so loud anymore. Julie jumped up from her desk chair and hugged me. Angie just smiled and said, "I knew you'd understand."

It wasn't the same, it wasn't as good as the week before summer vacation—classes weren't cancelled so that we could go outside and play softball (or organize a mass snowball fight instead), people didn't stare out the window and wonder why the minute hand on the wall clock was broken—but the countdown to Christmas break was better than there being just five more days of school. There was Secret Santa, for instance, everyone's name in a hat and keep it to yourself and nothing over three dollars, please. I drew James Dawkins, so doing my *Ho Ho Ho* duty was easy, anything food-based a guaranteed gut pleaser, a book of Life Savers picked up at the BiWay for less than the spending limit and the job was done. I'd been hoping for a three-pack of blank Maxell cassette tapes—luck of the draw made Dale my personal Santa, a secret he made no secret of—but now I would have settled for someone to talk to about having to play Secret Tom when Julie and Angie made their big city escape. At least I wasn't going to end up stuck with something stupid, like a book of Life Savers.

And at least the luck of the hat hadn't made Allison my gift giver or me hers. In the interval since the kiss that wasn't, we'd managed to avoid each other at school reasonably successfully, no enforced opportunities at water fountains or waiting to use the pencil sharpener to encourage us to talk about what had happened, or hadn't. And no chance for me to look at her and wonder if she knew that I knew that she'd never wanted me to kiss her because what she'd really wanted was Sarah to kiss her because she was… a what? A lez? A dyke? A homo? That's what people like that were called. I was standing at the bus stop just outside the school gates watching a stream of dirty water that only three days ago was freshly fallen white snow disappearing into the sewer grate.

"Take a picture, it'll last longer."

It was Allison, with a basketball under one arm and her gym bag hanging over her shoulder, just in time for the bus that took you downtown and home. I was startled but not surprised. You can only put off what's supposed to happen for so long.

"No practice tonight?" I said.

"Not until the new year."

"Right."

"How come you didn't get a ride from Mr. Brown?"

"Teacher meeting or something."

Allison nodded, made a dam with the side of her white running shoe. We watched the water momentarily pause then rush around it to get where it wanted to go.

"So are you guys moved into your building yet?"

Our building. As if what hadn't happened there between her and me wasn't embarrassing enough.

"No, that's not…" I used my own shoe as a water break like Allison had and the same thing happened to me. Water knew what it wanted. "We're not moving," I said. "We're staying where we are."

"Why? What happened?"

The bus slowed down and stopped. The door swung open with a loud mechanical sigh and we stepped up and dropped in our seventy-five cents and walked to the back. There was just us and a woman at the front reading a paperback.

"There were all these problems we didn't know about when we bought it," I said.

"What, like the plumbing? You should have talked to my dad. He can fix anything that's wrong with somebody's plumbing." We were sitting in the last row, the two seats between us occupied by our gym bags.

"It wasn't just the plumbing. It was also, I don't know, the roof and all sorts of stuff. Tons of stuff."

"That sucks."

"Yeah."

"But you got your money back and everything, right?"

"Oh, yeah. My dad made sure we got all our money back. And then some."

And then some? I'd officially gone beyond mere deception and was now fabricating entirely new untruths.

"That's cool," she said.

"Yeah."

The woman with the paperback rang the bell and the bus stopped and she got off and no one else got on. It was just the bus driver and me and Allison with her basketball in her lap.

"I just remembered something," I said. "On *Happy Days*, Ritchie and Joanie had a brother in the first season and then he disappeared and no one ever talked about him."

"What?"

"Yeah. He was always bouncing a basketball, even in the house."

"I think I kind of remember…"

"Chuck!" I shouted.

We were stopped at a red light and the bus driver looked back at us over his shoulder.

In a normal speaking voice this time, "Chuck," I said. "His name was Chuck."

"That's right," Allison said. "I remember now."

"Right? Chuck and his basketball."

The light turned green and we were moving again.

"What do you think happened to him do you think?" Allison said.

I shrugged. "I guess they figured three kids was too many so they just cut his part."

"But they didn't explain it or anything in the show. It was like he was there one minute and gone the next."

"Maybe they figured it was just easier that way, not having to explain it. What were they going to say? That he died or something?"

"I guess that would be sort of weird," she said.

"Like someone says he died fighting in Korea and then Ralph Mouth tells Potsie to sit on it."

"That would be weird. It wouldn't fit."

"Exactly."

Allison slapped her basketball and laughed and shook her head.

Lez. Dyke. Homo. Whoever she wanted to kiss and whatever else she was, Allison was Allison.

The bus pulled into the station. Every time you got off downtown now it was surprising how loud the cranes and jackhammers and pounding and drilling were, sounds that didn't seem so bad when you were used to hearing them all the time. There were walls missing and half of the roof wasn't built yet, but the mall had started to look like what it was going to be when it grew up.

Allison and I walked together without talking until we came to the Cenotaph, where I would go my way and she would go hers.

"Okay, see you," she said, slinging her bag over her shoulder.

"See you."

The machines and the banging and the drilling got quieter the closer I got to home. I opened the door to Dad's shop and the bell tinkled and I smelled the medical soap he used on his clients and I shut the door behind me and then there wasn't any more noise.

Woman Reads Paperback Book by Deceased Author

"I'd Never Heard of It Or Even the Author Before, But It Was Only $1.50"

SHE READ A book by a dead man and here's what didn't happen:

The dead man didn't make a dime—the dead man hadn't done anything but rot for more than a decade, and an eight percent royalty rate on a $2.95 paperback wasn't on eternity's agenda. Besides, she'd bought the book in the dark and damp back room of a Chatham junkshop, the popular books—the romances, the thrillers, the true crime—in the brighter and slightly less dank front, it and a handful of rarely disturbed others segregated in the rear of the shop under the slightly ominous sign **LITERATURE.**

The dead man didn't end up knowing that he hadn't wasted his life. Sure there were moments when he'd teemed with inspiration and exhilaration; brimmed with bruising purpose and inviolable faith; not just felt but *known* that what he was doing was good and mattered and would last. Sixty minutes in an hour, though, twenty-four hours in a day, seven days in a week, fifty-two weeks in a year: there are a lot of godamn moments. Plenty of time left over to not spend enough time with your children, to not try harder with your difficult mother, to not take the time to tell your wife how pretty she looks, to not be the brother you could be, to not bother to vote, to not help a friend, to not to not to not, a lifetime of brooding nots all because of THE BOOK, because I've got to get back to work on THE BOOK, because I need to be alone so I can concentrate on THE BOOK. A half-lived life littered with vacations never taken, minor-league hockey games not attended, promises not kept. A child waiting to play catch with his dad until he eventually realizes his father is never going to show up.

The dead man didn't act as the conscience of his age. He was neither the acknowledged nor the unacknowledged legislator of the world. The dead man's name was not commonly remembered. He didn't even make it out of his own country, a Canadian author writing a book set in Canada published by a Canadian publisher. And now his book was a Chatham Public Library discard picked up by a junk dealer for a quarter and resold at half the list price.

A woman read a book by a dead man, that was all. It was a good book, too—she had taste, could tell a dead phrase and a calcified cliché from the hard crunch of a crisp image and a sparkling insight—and after she'd finished it she decided, in spite of the limited shelf space she had in her small apartment, to keep it, to make it a part of her personal library. She even thought she might reread it one day. It deserved it. Good books, after all, are rare.

This time there wasn't any snowstorm to save us. It was cold but clear the night before Julie and Angie's train was scheduled to leave for Toronto, nothing in the sky but a bright white moon and even brighter stars. That night in bed I turned the dial on my transistor radio hoping for an encouragingly discouraging weather report—a gathering storm, an unexpected snow squall blowing in from somewhere, anywhere—but all I got was good reception and bad news: only a ten percent chance of precipitation, and even then merely—maybe—freezing rain. In the process I couldn't help but pick up snippets of the news as well, the lead story wherever the dial ended up being the International Court of Justice unanimously demanding the release of the American hostages in Iran and rejecting the Iranian position that the case could not be considered in isolation from the activities of the US in Iran over the last quarter-century.

I switched off the radio and put it on my nightstand, but couldn't fall asleep. I thought it might have been because of the light from the moon and the stars that managed to slip past the window blind, but even after I hung a blanket over top of it and the room was darker I still couldn't sleep. I thought about doubling up the blankets, but somehow I knew it wouldn't matter, the light would still get in. There was nothing to do but pretend it wasn't there.

Chapter Thirteen

"Let's go, Tom, you're going to be late, I'm not coming up here again" with a *rat-tat-tat* of knuckle applied to the bedroom door for an I'm-not-kidding-around emphasis. I knew I wasn't dreaming. Dreams were never this boring. Often confusing, sometimes scary, dreams—unlike wide-awake life—were rarely boring. Life was frequently all three at once. This morning, for instance.

Dad's continuing bad mood had worked to Julie's benefit: I'd hoped that the threat of him insisting on talking to Angie's parents before agreeing to let Julie spend the weekend at their house super-studying would have been enough of a bluff that Julie would have to fold her hand and be content to celebrate the end of exams in Chatham. But Dad didn't insist. Looked up from his sports page only long enough for Julie to explain every meticulously manufactured detail of why it was a good idea for her to hibernate at Angie's house for the greater academic good and how there was nothing to worry about since she'd only be across town and it was only for a couple nights, then said, "Okay, call if anything comes up, and no screwing around, you're there to study, good luck" and that was that. Dad wasn't angry anymore about the building being sold to someone else; Dad was sad. I liked it better when he was angry.

Breakfast wasn't my first truth test of the weekend that I needed to cheat my way through only because there wasn't any breakfast—not with Dad, anyway, who these days was given to taking a cup of coffee with him down to the shop even though it didn't open until eleven. I ate by myself and wrote down what I ate and was relieved to think that by the time school was done for the day and I was finished delivering the evening newspaper it would be dinnertime and Julie and Angie's train would have arrived in Toronto and night number one would be well underway, and if I managed to make it through supper I could stay in my room for the rest of the night and probably get by with nothing more than a *Goodnight* to Dad. Not telling the truth wasn't as bad as telling a lie.

It was the last day of school before Christmas vacation so it should have been easy to have fun. There was the Secret Santa gift exchange during the period before lunch. There was an assembly in the gym at the end of the day that would eat up two entire classes where all you had to do was sing Christmas carols and not talk too much to the people sitting next to you between songs. And it was Friday, the second best TV night (after Saturday) of the week and an excellent way to inaugurate two full weeks of no school. Before fourteen days of doing whatever I wanted, however, two nights and three days of doing what I promised Julie I would do.

I got the three-pack of blank cassette tapes I'd asked for from Dale; I gave James the book of Lifesavers which he immediately began to gobble; I sang "Rudolph the Red Nosed Reindeer" and "Silent Night" and "Jingle Bell Rock"—all of it while never not wondering how I was going to get away with living alone with Dad for the next 72 hours without making him suspicious. I went home and got my bag and delivered Friday's newspaper under a black-and-blue sky that was a bruise that was never going to heal. By 5:30 my bag was empty and there wasn't anything left to do but return home. Forget 72 hours, there was no way I was going to make it through supper. I began to work out my apology strategy on the slow retreat home: *I didn't know. I knew but I had nothing to do with it. I was part of it but only because Julie made me.* Every explanation sounded phonier than the last. How can you hope to get away with a lie when even you don't believe it?

Dad was straining spaghetti in the sink when I came into the kitchen. We didn't eat take-out food or get delivery anymore. Now we ate a lot of spaghetti.

"Get the salad dressing and the bread if you want it," he said. "It's almost ready."

I wasn't used to the absence of his ordinarily grumpy geniality or his new shorthand speech, but I knew it wasn't about me or anything I'd done. When Mom left he'd assured Julie and me that he loved us both just as much as he did before and that what had happened between Mom and him had nothing to do with us, that people could act and feel a certain way all by themselves and it didn't mean someone else had done anything to make them feel that way. Anyway, I knew things were going to get better once the mall was completed. Because of increased property values we might not have been taking possession of a new home and Dad wasn't going to have a new shop, but there was no stopping every downtown business from benefiting from the revamped and reenergized downtown. The mall might taketh, but the mall also giveth.

He served the pasta and Ragu onto our plates and placed the bowl of salad on the table and we sat down. Before he could pick up his fork, "Did you do that or me?" he said.

I put down my fork. "What? Did what?" Busted already, and I hadn't said five words.

Dad picked up Julie's bottle of red wine vinegar. "I must have. Habit, I guess." He set it back down and used the wooden tongs to put some salad on my plate, then his. He poured Thousand Island dressing on his salad and handed me the bottle.

"I guess we'll have to get used to this next year," he said.

I was already on my third forkful of spaghetti. I figured that the more often my mouth was full, the less likely it was I'd say something incriminating. Swallowing, "What?"

"What do you mean *What?* Your sister being away at university in Toronto and it being just the two of us eating dinner every night."

"Oh, right. Yeah, It'll just be us." I made up for lost eating time by shoveling down two successive forkfuls of salad.

Dad looked at me like he was about to ask me if I was all right, but twirled a clump of spaghetti on the end of his fork instead. If only we could keep eating for the next three days straight everything would be fine.

The phone rang and Dad said "They can't wait until you finally sit down, can they?" and I knew it wasn't one of those questions that the other person expected you to answer, and he got up and answered it and said hello like he was really saying *What the hell do you want?*

Pause. "Oh, hi, Mr. Hudson." His voice softened. Mr. Hudson was our landlord. "Good, good," he said.

"Right." Pause. "Okay." Longer pause. "Okay, but—" Pause. "Mr. Hudson, listen—" Pause. "Look," he said, sounding like he had when he'd answered the phone, "have you ever had to ask me for a rent cheque or have I ever asked you to do anything around here? You know I've always taken care of things myself." I put down my fork and watched my Dad with his back to me talking to the kitchen wallpaper, his nose a couple of inches from the wall. "That's right, and I—" Pause. "It *is* the point." Pause. "No, it is the point if—" Pause. "Well, that's unacceptable." Pause. "We'll see about that." Pause. "Yeah, well, we'll see about that too."

Dad hung up, but instead of sitting back down to dinner went to the cupboard and got a glass and turned on the tap and poured himself a glass of water which he drank standing up at the counter.

"What's going on, Dad?"

He poured himself another glass and drank it the same way. He put the glass in the sink and turned around, smiling like someone with a gun to their temple who's been instructed to look happy. "Nothing you need to worry about, pal."

"What did Mr. Hudson want?"

Dad grabbed his napkin and wiped the Ragu off his beard. "Do you think you can do your dad a big favour?"

"Sure."

"Do you think you can finish your dinner and do the dishes and dry them by yourself?

"Sure."

"Thanks, buddy," he said, mussing my hair as he left the room. "I have to go out for a few hours, so don't worry if I'm not back by the time you go to sleep, okay?"

"Okay."

"Thanks, pal," he said and grabbed his coat in the hallway and was out the front door, which I heard him lock behind him.

Of course I was worried. On the other hand, it didn't sound like he was going to be worrying about Julie tonight. And that couldn't be a bad thing.

Waitress at Local Tavern Despises Drunkards

"Men Are Awful Enough All By Themselves, They Don't Need Anything That Makes Them Even Worse"

SOMETIMES, IF SHE had had the means and knew for certain that no one would find out, she honestly felt as if she could poison them. Some of them, anyway. No, not all of them, but some of them.

Slinging beers backed with double shots of Canadian Club at the Merrill Tavern and waitressing the breakfast shift at Jeanie's Place was the difference between darkness and light, oblivion and renewal, forgetfulness and hope. The same number of hours on your feet perhaps, the same lousy wages and lousier long-term prospects, possibly even the very same customers sitting in the seats, but the one was death and other one was life. And it's not stale hyperbole when your father was an alcoholic sonofabitch whose idea of a fun Saturday night was beating the shit of your mother and coming to visit you and your sister when the lights went out.

She didn't drink, never had—how could she?—and she didn't like being around people who did, but six shifts a week at Jeanie's and five more at the Merrill and there was usually the same amount of money coming in every month as there needed to be going out. When she'd get back from the bar at one o'clock in the morning and send the sitter home and quietly open the bedroom door and see Rebecca asleep and safe and perfect in her bed, it was worth it, all of it was worth it. She'd take a long, hot shower and make herself a cup of orange pekoe and smoke a final cigarette and begin to feel okay. Then she'd check on Rebecca one last time and go to her own bedroom and make sure the alarm was set for quarter to six and fall immediately to sleep, too exhausted to dream.

The forever three *F*s of the ancient idiot art of weekend whoop-whoop: forgetting, flirting, fighting, and on a good night, all three at once, although hell to pay for someone if the result at the end of the evening is 0 for 3 come closing time. Might be the person they chose to come with (in ten years of waitressing, how many fights between friends did she have to break up?), maybe it's someone they're going home to (she wouldn't allow herself to think about that), it could be their waitress, who's only doing her job ("I'll tell you when I've had enough to drink, you don't tell me, bitch"), but someone has to suffer. That's what drunks do. Sometimes, if she had had the means and knew for certain that no one would find out, she honestly felt as if...

Like this clown, all tattoos and biker beard and black leather vest sitting and drinking by himself as far away from anybody else as he can get. Men who go to bars to get drunk alone are not, as a rule, happy people. And unhappy people live to make everyone around them unhappy too. She'd been doing this long enough to know to keep an eye on this one. 10:22 pm: she'd be home in less than three hours and tomorrow she had the whole day off and would take Rebecca to the movies and afterwards Dairy Queen. Just think about tomorrow.

Last call and the only ones left are her, him, and another him who thinks that, because he's here almost every night diligently wasting his liver and his life and knows her first name, they're friends, and then it's just the two of them. He hasn't spoken a word all evening except to order another Black Label and to tell her to keep the change, but it's the quiet ones you have to worry about. She lets him finish his beer while wiping down, washing off, and locking up until there's nothing left to wipe, wash, or lock, and then she says, "Hotel time, friend." This is the moment when it can all go wrong. Don't kid yourself that it can't. It has before and it can again.

The man stands up, slowly, like an awoken giant testing the air up there, and pulls something out of his back pocket. She watches him do it while wiping a glass that's already clean.

"Thanks," he says, putting his empty bottle on the bar and placing a ten-dollar bill beside it.

"You're all paid up," she says. So he's not violent—just stupid.

"It's yours," he says.

She looks at him, thinks she might recognize him, although not from here. She does: he's the tattoo guy, the guy from the place around the corner.

"I just found out tonight that my landlord has decided to raise the rent on my home and my business and that I might not be able to afford to pay it," he says. "I might have to move my kids and me and shut down my shop. And get a job working for somebody else. If I can remember how."

"That's… not good."

"It's good for anybody left standing when the mall is finished. It's good for them."

"Well…" Well what? What was she supposed to say? Knew what she could do, though. Pushing the bill back across the bar, "You're going to need this then," she says.

"I need more than ten dollars."

"Sure, but—"

"You got kids?"

She hesitates, but only briefly, before deciding to tell him. "A daughter."

"How old?"

"Eight."

The tattoo guy smiles. "That's a great age."

The waitress smiles too. "Yeah, it is."

"Buy your daughter something she needs," he says, walking away. "No—buy her something she wants. They're only that age once. Blink and it's over."

Hangovers on television were funny: the ice pack plopped on top of the head, the hilarious stories from the night before, the miracle of a life equipped with a laugh track and the familiar theme song after thirty minutes confirming that everything was all right in the end. Hangovers in real life weren't nearly as interesting. Dad emerged from his bedroom in just his underwear and T-shirt smelling like a case of empty beer bottles sitting by the front door too long, no bathrobe or socks, and started to prepare the coffee that Julie usually made before quickly giving up and deciding to begin the day with one of my C Pluses instead. At first I thought it was because it was just him and me at home, but when he took the can of pop with him back to bed, saying, before he left the kitchen, "Put up a sign in the shop door saying I won't be opening until two, will you?" I knew where he'd been the night before and what he'd been doing. Enough so, anyway, that I also knew it would be a good idea to get out of the house for awhile so it would be quiet and he could sleep.

It was too early in the day to deliver the newspaper or do the week's collections or catch the Saturday matinee at the Capitol, and because it was Christmas vacation there wasn't any homework to take to the library. Besides, it was the first official day of Christmas break—how lame would it be to be stuck inside a building full of nothing but books? There wasn't anyone I could call—I didn't have a girlfriend, I didn't have a best friend anymore, all I had was me—so I put on my coat and just started walking. I brought my football with me because I'd read that if you carried one around while doing ordinary, day-to-day things, it helped you become more sure-handed and less likely to fumble in an actual game. There were only five more months of public school plus two months of summer vacation and six months of high school until junior football tryouts.

The sound coming from the mall construction site of a powerful machine pounding something deep into the ground that didn't want to be there, *Boom Boom Boom*, over and over and over, sent me in the opposite direction, away from downtown and toward CCI. It was cold but not too cold, there wasn't any snow on the ground, so I decided to go to the football field behind the high school. In spite of what Dad had been led to believe, the semester was over and there'd be no one there to keep me from imagining I was returning an interception for a touchdown or blocking a potential game-winning field goal attempt. I checked my pocket and had lots of change and thought I'd get a chocolate bar first.

There were sun-bleached signs for products that didn't exist anymore (*Try Banana Breeze No-Bake Pie!* and *Pop a Charm's Pumpkin Pop*) hanging in the window of the old variety store near the school. Almost all of the variety stores were Mac's Milks now. The floors were shiny clean and the frozen-food section billowed with frozen air and the air inside the store was always cool and fresh and there was a slushi machine with five different flavours and hamburgers and hotdogs wrapped in clear plastic that you could heat up all by yourself in a microwave oven. The new stores had everything. The only thing wrong with them was that sometimes in the summer mayflies would cover an entire store front, the store's bright lights, we learned in science class, attracting them because whenever they're in doubt they'll instinctively head for light, the brighter the light the more powerful the sensation of safety. So many bugs would cling to the glass, you couldn't see in or out. But it never lasted long because we also learned that they only lived as flying adults for 24 hours. Yesterday there they were, the invasion of the mayflies, the next day they'd be dead on the ground, a graveyard of bugs in the parking lot an inch thick. When you stepped on them with your running shoe they'd crackle.

A handmade sign taped to the heavy wooden door of the variety store read DOOR STICKS, PUSH HARD so I did, and instead of an electronic burp, the dingle of a bell announced my entrance. The bell sounded old and stupid until I realized it sounded like the one in Dad's shop. I pushed the door shut behind me and walked past the shelves stacked with dusty cans of beans and cat food and stood before the rack of chocolate bars. An old woman drinking a cup of tea with the bag still in it perched on a stool behind the counter. Another woman, not young but not as old as the other one, was on her knees an aisle over pulling Twinkies out of a box and restocking the shelf.

"What would you rather have?" the one on her knees said. "Cancer and a million dollars or no cancer and not a million dollars?"

"How bad would the cancer be?" the old woman said.

"You'd have a year to live."

The old woman sipped her tea. *Slurped* her tea—she didn't have any teeth, it seemed. "Would I have all my hair?"

"No. But you could buy a wig."

"That's true. I never thought of that. That's a good point."

The old woman slurped her tea again; the other woman continued to slowly transfer the Twinkies from the cardboard box to the shelf. I grabbed a Snickers bar and dug a quarter out of my pocket. Candy bars were easy to pay for because they were always a quarter. Were always a quarter since the day, a few years back, when everyone offered up their usual dime and were informed that the price had increased to twenty-five cents. A fifteen cent increase might not sound like much, but for a kid on an allowance it was devastating to discover that his number-one junk food had gone up 150 percent in price overnight.

The old woman took my quarter without saying anything and rang up the sale on an ancient cash register with a clanging bang. I pulled hard on the metal door handle and heard her say, "Would the money be tax-free?" and shut it just as hard behind me. I tore open the Snickers bar and took a big bite. By the time I was finished I'd arrived at the football field behind the high school.

Wow. The CCI football team. Not all of it, maybe a dozen or so players, and without helmets or shoulder pads, but in their actual green-and-white game jerseys and occupying half the muddy field, not goofing around on their Christmas break with a friendly game of pickup but working out, several balls soaring though the air at the same time as receivers ran sharp routes, defensive backs backpedaled, linemen exploded out of their stances. There weren't any coaches and they were practicing because they wanted to stay in shape and stay in rhythm and to get better—not because someone said they had to. They were like I was with my Journal of Consumption, doing what they did just for the sake of doing it. Except that all I was doing was writing down what I ate and drank. I wished there was something I cared about enough that I did it when no one was watching. Something that mattered.

"Hey!"

I looked behind me.

"You!"

I pointed at myself.

"Yeah, you. Throw that football back."

I looked at the football cradled in my right arm. I'd done such a good job of instinctively holding on I'd forgotten it was there.

"Give it back, kid," another player yelled. Several others were now standing with their hands on their hips staring at me staring at them. I knew I should say something, should explain that the ball was mine, that I hadn't stolen theirs—I wanted to be one of them, why would I steal from them?—but all I could think was that, if I was seeing what they were, I'd think I'd stolen one of their footballs too and that anything I said would sound like a lie.

I turned around and ran.

The yelling, the cursing, the threats were the soundtrack to my sprint not towards a touchdown, but home. I'd been standing far enough away from the football field that they must have figured I was a lost cause, and my training with Allison paid off, I didn't stop running until I was standing on William Street cement in front of our door. I didn't feel safe until I was catching my breath going up the stairs.

The tattoo parlour was closed, so I tried to be quiet in case Dad was still sleeping. Before I took my coat off or even had a glass of water, though, I wanted to record the Snickers bar I'd eaten. I was hot and sweaty and thirsty and still a little scared, but I knew what would make me feel better the quickest. Dad was coming down the stairs as I was going up.

"Did you know your sister went to Toronto with her friend Angie?" He'd stopped halfway down.

"No."

He looked into my eyes, briefly, then walked past me down the stairs. I stayed where I was, wanting to go to my room and shut the door, but knowing I should follow him and find out what happened. I thought I'd be afraid if he found out what Julie had done, but instead I felt sorry for him. I walked back down the stairs and sat across from him at the kitchen table.

"Julie's in Toronto?" I said. I knew it was what I was expected to ask. "What's she doing there?"

His hands were folded on the table, like he wanted to pray but was too tired to raise them. "She was," he said. "And it doesn't matter. The important thing is that she shouldn't have been. And that she's on her way home."

Julie was coming home and I didn't get caught, only she did, and the worst that was going to happen was she'd get grounded. "What time is her train getting in?" I said. I didn't want to be around when she got home from the station. I hoped it was the afternoon train so I'd be out collecting when he let her have it.

Dad looked up from his hands. "Who said she was taking the train?"

"Nobody, but… How else would she get home?"

Dad lowered his eyes again. "Your mother is bringing her back. They should be home any time now."

Chapter Fourteen

I prayed. I prayed for the first time since I got lost in the sewer.

Dad didn't go into depth about what had happened, but *Julie Angie Godamn Toronto Toronto people underage drinking of course maybe drugs who knows alcohol poisoning hospital could have been really sick enough wasn't thank goodness next of kin Mom's phone number coming home Mom driving her home* told me enough to make me worried about my sister, about Mom being back in Chatham, about all of us.

I went upstairs to my bedroom and put on my Glenn Gould record because it was the closest thing to religious music I owned, and got down on my knees, elbows resting on the side of the bed. I asked God for help—for Julie to be okay, for everything to be all right—but when I finished and stood up, I felt ashamed. Not because I prayed, but because I hadn't spoken to God in seven years and the first thing out of my mouth was a request for a favour. Plus, my bedroom floor was carpeted and felt spongy on my knees and I knew that it should have hurt, at least a little bit, that talking to God shouldn't be so easy.

I turned off the record player and joined Dad at the kitchen table.

I hadn't seen Mom in a long time, so even though Julie was the one we were worried about, I couldn't help looking mostly at her when she and Julie came through the door. It took a few moments for her to look like herself, but once she did, she was Mom and it didn't feel uncomfortable or odd at all. She wordlessly winked at me like she used to do sometimes when there were other people around and she wanted me to know that she saw me, and I smiled. That was what I used to do.

Dad sprang from his chair and went to Julie and hugged her for a long time, like he was reminding her who her real family was, before he remembered he was also angry with her. Finally letting her escape his big arms, "This is entirely unacceptable behaviour," he said. "We need to talk. Right now."

Julie hadn't said anything, not even *Hi*, just stood there in her coat looking small and exhausted, like she'd just worked a double shift at the Dairy Queen after having been up late studying the night before. "Dad, I know. I know I screwed up. Believe me, I know. But right now, right now I just—" And then she started to cry, and then she buried her face in Mom's shoulder and wrapped her arms around her, and then Mom started to cry and put her arms around Julie and the two of them cried and held each other while Dad and I looked at each other like we didn't belong there.

"She's just tired, Bill, that's all," Mom said without letting go. "I tried to get her to sleep in the car, but she was too worked up. Just let her lay down for awhile and you can talk to her when she's rested." Julie's blubbering had shrunken to a soft sobbing, but she was still holding on tight to Mom. "Shhh, shhh, shhh," Mom said, gently running her fingers through Julie's hair. "You're home now, Dear, your father and brother are right here and everything's going to be fine."

Dad mumbled something that helped give the impression that he actually had a say in what was going on and Mom put her arm on Julie's back and eased her up the stairs to her bedroom.

Dad sat back down at the kitchen table. I looked at the small pool of water that had gathered on the floor from the snow that had melted off Mom and Julie's boots. He joined me in silent contemplation.

"I'll talk to her after she's gotten some sleep," he said.

I nodded.

"She must be worn out."

I nodded again.

"Anyway, the main thing is that she's home and safe."

"Yeah," I said.

We were both still staring at the water.

"Tom?'

"Yeah?"

"Get the mop out of the closet, will you?"

Mom still loved Jesus. Any question about whether or not she was once again PG (pre-God) Mom was answered around the dinner table when she took Julie's and my hand in hers before proceeding to say grace. Julie, up from her nap but still looking raggedy and pasty and dressed in pajamas although it was only seven o'clock, put her hand out for Dad's and he only hesitated a moment before taking it. Then Mom closed her eyes and lowered her head while she gave thanks (for Julie being home safe if not entirely sound, for the food we were about to eat, for all of us being together again) and Julie and Dad and I looked at each other like three actors who'd wandered into the wrong play. We didn't drop our hands or interrupt Mom's prayer, though, and eventually she finished and Dad removed the lid from the bucket of Kentucky Fried Chicken and we filled our plates and began to eat.

When we lived on Vanderpark Drive and had a backyard, sometimes, in summer, Dad would take Julie and me with him to Kentucky Fried Chicken to pick up coleslaw and potato salad and french fries and a loaf of warm Grecian bread to go with the steaks he was going to barbeque. If it was hot enough, Dad wouldn't wear a shirt or even running shoes or sandals when he was outside, and he'd drive to KFC the same way, with Julie in the front seat and me in the back, and he'd get her to go inside the store to order and pay. I'd carry the big white paper bag with the Colonel's picture on it into the kitchen and Dad would light the barbeque and Mom and Julie would set the picnic table in the backyard and I'd stand by with four plates ready to deliver our steaks as soon as they were done. If we ate late enough in the evening and it was the right time of summer, fireflies would come out just as we finished eating, and we'd sit there at the picnic table and see who could spot the next one to light up the dark.

I hadn't thought about any of that in a long time and didn't bring it up now. The coleslaw might have been the same—as kids, Julie showed me how if you put some of it in a strainer and ran the tap over it, its green colour washed away—but it was December and cold and we were sitting in our second-storey kitchen overlooking William Street and there weren't going to be any fireflies tonight. I was still hungry and Mom must have seen me eyeing the last few french fries in the box.

"First ask your sister and father if they want any more, Tom."

I looked from one to the other and they both laughed. "Go ahead," Julie said.

I poured what was left onto my plate and ripped the top off another packet of ketchup. Then it was quiet again, like it had been through most of dinner, but after Julie and Dad's laughter it didn't feel right anymore. Dad must have felt the same way.

"How's Bob?" he said.

Julie and I met each other's eyes. *How's Bob?*

"Bob is just fine," Mom said. "Busy. We're both busy. Too busy, it feels like sometimes. We've expanded our service to Etobicoke and Scarborough and Pickering and have two full-time employees now, if you can believe it. Of course we've been at it for, how long has it been now—six years? But as Bob always says, 'He that maketh haste to be rich shall not be innocent.'"

Dad nodded a couple of quick times in what seemed like obvious approval of Mom's growing courier empire then returned his attention to the last of the meat on his chicken leg. Mom smiled one last time before returning to her cup of tea. Unbelievable: Jesus was a wild dog who'd torn a bloody hole in our lives that would never heal; who, it turned out, grew up to be a puppy that—and this was the worst you could say about him—occasionally jumped up and got saliva on you when he tried to give you a kiss. I didn't believe it. I *couldn't* believe it. If this was what our life would have been like seven years later with God riding co-pilot, why weren't we still a family?

"So," I said. "Bob. He's not a Reverend anymore?"

Dad set down his drumstick. "Tom, let's—"

"It's fine, Bill, it's fine," Mom said, putting her hand, the one with her wedding ring on it, on Dad's hand. "He's just curious."

Dad gave me a long look that said *I'm watching you.* "He's just something, anyway."

"When I married Bob he was a practicing minister, yes, but for the last several years we've devoted our lives to the courier business, as you know. This is how God has decided we are to serve Him best."

"God wants you to deliver packages," I said. "This is what He decided your purpose in life is supposed to be."

"Knock it off, Tom," Julie said before Dad had a chance. For the first time since she'd been home she sounded like my big sister.

"I'm just surprised to find out she had to abandon her husband and children all because Jesus wanted to give UPS some competition."

"All right," Dad said, "that's enough."

"Why are you defending her?" I said. "She left you too, you know. She left all of us."

I got up from the table, the screech of my chair's thin metal legs shoved backward across the linoleum floor and the stomp of my feet up the stairs and the slam of my bedroom door letting everyone know exactly how I felt. I put on an album, but not Glenn Gould. I wanted something loud, and *The Ramones Leave Home*, which I'd borrowed from Julie when she was in Toronto, was perfect. It was loud all right. There was no way anyone was going to hear me cry.

Julie was grounded, but it could have been—should have been—worse. For deceiving Dad and going to Toronto and getting so drunk at the house of some friend of Angie her very first night there that Angie and her friends had to take her to the hospital emergency room because she wouldn't stop throwing up and had started to shake really bad and say crazy things no one could understand (and compelling the nurse to call Mom because she was the only adult Julie knew in Toronto), Julie wasn't allowed to go anywhere but school or work for a month. There were still a couple weeks left of Christmas vacation, so it wasn't even a full month. Even if it were, it wouldn't have been enough, and I knew why. Sort of. Somehow, Mom bringing her home and being there that first night softened Dad's anger, made him want to put the whole thing in the past as quickly and painlessly as possible. He and Julie had a talk in the kitchen to discuss what had happened and what her punishment was—I knew, because I was in the living room with the TV on trying to listen—but it didn't last very long and he never raised his voice.

It wasn't as if Mom and Dad had some big heart-to-heart and sorted out what had gone wrong between them. Mom wasn't even staying with us, had taken a room at The Wheels Inn. She was going back to Toronto the next day, Sunday, because she didn't want to leave Bob shorthanded come the Monday morning rush. She did say that, in spite of the circumstances, it was so good to see Julie and me again and it was ridiculous it had taken this long for it to happen and that she wasn't going to let it be this long until her next visit. Maybe, she said, some day we could even come and visit her in Toronto.

She also said she wanted to spend some time with Julie and me before she left, but when she came by Sunday and found out that Julie was at work—someone had called in sick and she was just glad to get out of the house—she asked me if I wanted to come along with her to the Dairy Queen so she could at least say goodbye in person. I was still mad at her, if a little less clear the next day as to exactly why, but I said yes. I was embarrassed that I'd cried after dinner the night before and I wanted to prove, if only to myself, that I was stronger than that, that whatever it was that had made me so upset wasn't going to get to me again.

Mom's car was an Oldsmobile Cutlass Supreme, big and long and new. I'd never been inside a brand new car before. It looked and smelled like we should have been looking at it in a car dealership instead of actually driving in it. I hoped my boots wouldn't get the new floor mats too wet.

The car stopped at a red light near the mall construction site, "Things are certainly changing around here," she said.

I didn't say anything. I was there not to cry, I wasn't there to make chit-chat.

"When is it supposed to be done, do you know?"

"Next year sometime, I think," I said. I couldn't ignore a direct question. The light turned green.

"It's hard to believe it's going to be 1980 soon," she said. "A new decade."

"Yeah."

"It sounds so strange, doesn't it? '1980.' Like the title of a science fiction movie."

"Maybe," I said. "A little."

Driving past Harrison Hall, there was a cheap temporary fence all the way around it like it had done something wrong. "What's going on with old city hall, I wonder," she said.

"They're going to tear it down too. I saw them use the wrecking ball a few times already. It was kind of cool. Man, was it loud."

Now it was Mom's turn not to say anything, and I felt stupid. I suppose I'd meant to sound like I'd seen something really special, like I was some kind of man of the world, but I just came off like a dumb kid excited to see something big get knocked over.

"My history teacher, Mr. Brown, him and a bunch of other people tried to stop the mall people from tearing it down," I said. "They wrote letters to the newspaper and got people to sign petitions and stuff."

"But it didn't matter," Mom said. She didn't say it in a way that was making fun of how useless it all had been, but how sad it was that it hadn't made any difference.

"Mr. Brown says it's important that people do their best to preserve all the old buildings," I said. "That they're kind of a part of who we are. He says that people need jobs, but that they need something else in their lives too or else they won't be very happy."

"Mr. Brown sounds like a smart teacher. Do you like him?"

"He's okay," I said. "He's a good teacher, I guess. I get rides to and from school from him sometimes."

"Really? He must like you too to do that."

I shrugged. "Dad knew him way back when he was at Ontario Steel and Mr. Brown was a university student working a summer shift there."

"Still, if he didn't think you were a nice boy and a good student he wouldn't bother driving you back and forth every day."

"It's not every day, but, yeah, I guess." I hadn't thought of it like that before. It made me feel good.

Mom pulled her car into the empty parking lot of the post office. "I just have to stop in here for a second, dear." She removed several envelopes from her purse.

"You use regular mail?"

Mom smiled. "These aren't for work, they're just some bills I got caught up on last night. Running a small business, they accumulate very fast. I'm afraid some of them should have been mailed off by now. Most of them are going to Toronto addresses, so I know it's silly, but I know if I don't drop them in the post before I leave town I'll be sure to forget by the time I get home."

"Give them to me, I'll do it."

"Would you, dear?"

"I'll be right back."

I peeked at the addresses on the envelopes, but none of them were interesting: Ontario Hydro, Dickey Office Supplies, the water company. I dropped them all through the big slot in the side of the building so that whoever was working first thing Monday morning would get them started right away on where they were supposed to go. I got back in the car and we were off again.

"Thank you, Tom."

"No problem." I flicked on the radio, but when I heard *Up to 15,000 more Soviet troops can be expected to enter Afghanistan should a potential coup take place in that country* I snapped it back off. "I deliver the newspaper to somebody who works at the post office," I said.

"Really, who?"

"Just an old man, Mr. Smith. He was in the war. He's got war stuff hanging everywhere in his house."

"You must see a lot of interesting things on your route."

"I don't know. I guess."

We were almost at the Dairy Queen when I realized I wanted to tell her something. Part of me said I should use the time left to ask a question like why Dad and she couldn't have worked out their problems like other people do, but that wasn't what I asked.

"Mom, remember when I was a kid and I got lost in the sewer?"

"Of course I do. I never prayed so much in my life."

"Right. Well, I don't remember much. I mean, I remember going down there looking for my ball and realizing I was lost, but that's about it."

"You were just a child, of course you wouldn't remember much."

"That's not what I mean. I mean, nothing happened to me. Not really. All that happened was I got lost. And then I got found."

We pulled into the Dairy Queen parking lot. "That was a long time ago, Tom," she said, smiling at me, "and the Good Lord was watching over you and everything turned out fine." That wasn't what I meant either, but I just smiled back. She turned off the ignition and pulled me to her for a hug.

Letting me go, "Now let's go surprise your sister," she said.

Decorated WW II Veteran Celebrates Thirty Years Service at Chatham Post Office

"Selling A Book of Ten Domestic Stamps Isn't the Same as the Voice of Destiny Softly Speaking Your Name"

NATURALLY, IT WAS nice not having someone trying to kill you. Nice, too, being able to sleep in your own warm bed with your wife and not in a cold, leaky tent with twenty smelly, farting, snoring men. And of course there were the silly rules and the sillier men who cared about them above everything else, and sometimes there was fear and nearly always there was tedium and which one was really worse? And it was true, you did sometimes—not as often as the movies led you to believe, but sometimes—see things that most people will never see because people shouldn't see them, so good for them but bad for you.

Selling insurance or used cars or working in the post office after you've helped save the free world is a different kind of war, however—not hell, certainly, but definitely not anyone's idea of heaven, either. Not much danger of being blown up by people in different-coloured uniforms or watching a new friend from Manitoba choke to death on his own blood, but, instead, the familiar feeling of *It has to be nearly noon, I swear, this fucking day has to be nearly half over, doesn't it?* This necktie a daily noose. This $39.95 (plus tax) suit a walking polyester coffin. He got it: he wasn't a kid with his comic books: you can't be a ninth-inning, two-out-one-on-down-one-run hero all of the time. But it would be nice to know what the score was. To understand all the rules. To know exactly what one was playing for. If anybody wins.

He joined up and chose the RCAF because at least he'd learn how to fly. He did—flew a Hawker Tempest that was good as a ground-attack fighter bomber, but also an excellent interceptor of V-1 flying bombs intended for England. He did what he did, what a Royal Canadian Air Force pilot was supposed to do. It wasn't so much that he was proud, he just did what he had to do. He did his job. And it's only 10:21 a.m.

Five hours and thirty-nine minutes more. *I'm going to drop dead from terminal boredom in this godamn post office, I swear.*

Once, somewhere way up there, returning from a successful mission over France, not lost but admittedly not as sure where he was as he should have been, out of the confusion of clouds: a German Messerschmitt 262 Schwalbe twin-engine fighter so all-of-a-sudden there he wondered if he wasn't imagining it for a moment, so close that he could see the face of its German pilot. If it weren't for the logos painted on the sides of their crafts they could have been teammates competing in the new Olympic sport of synchronized aviation.

The German pilot had a moustache and wore black leather gloves like he did. With his free hand he repeatedly gestured slowly but with purpose—pointed directly behind him. *What's this crazy Kraut up to*, he thought. Then he realized where he was and knew what the other man was trying to tell him: he was flying in the wrong direction. Not toward England and base, but Germany and death. The German pilot was directing him home. He waved and turned the plane around. He didn't tell anyone what happened for two entire days. Thirty-five years later, he could still remember the German pilot's moustache.

Julie *was* surprised to see us—you can tell when someone isn't faking and really is surprised—and managed to take her fifteen-minute break right away. Mom said she was buying, and everyone got whatever they wanted. I got a cheeseburger, fries, a root beer, and, for dessert, a Dilly Bar. There were no big goodbyes, everyone was too busy eating and drinking, and after Julie's break was over Mom drove me home and we hugged again. When I came inside, Dad was in the living room in his recliner watching football.

"Is your mother gone?" he said.

"Yeah, she left."

"She'll make it home before dark if she left now."

"We went and saw Julie at work and she bought us lunch."

"How was that?" A Dallas Cowboy receiver ran in for a touchdown and Dad leaned forward in his chair to watch the replay.

"It was okay," I said. "I'm going to my room."

"All right. Don't play your music too loud."

"I won't."

I put Glenn Gould on the turntable and was trying to decide what to read when I remembered that I had to write down what I'd eaten at Dairy Queen. I opened the middle drawer of my desk to get my Journal of Consumption, but spotted my collection book and took it out instead so I wouldn't forget to bring it with me on my route the next day. Because of everything that had happened yesterday, I'd missed collecting, would have to do it Monday.

I shut the drawer and picked up the book Angie had encouraged me to buy when I'd run into her at Coles, the one about the people who lived in the small town who talk about their secret lives, which I hadn't read even a word of yet. I'd actually forgotten about it. But that was one of the best things about books and movies and records. They were always there when you needed them. Unlike people who sometimes went away, unlike stars which blew up and disappeared.

Lying down, adjusting the pillows behind my head, I realized that because I had to both collect and deliver the newspaper, Monday was going to be a longer day than usual. I opened the book and flipped to page one. Before I started reading, though, *It's not anybody's fault*, I thought. *It's just the way it is*. And it was my job, after all. I was the paper boy.